BEYOND
THE
VEIL

BEYOND
THE
VEIL

LAWRENCE KELTER

LEVEL
BEST BOOKS

For Dawn

Praise for Beyond the Veil

"Lawrence Kelter is an exciting new novelist, who reminds me of an early Robert Ludlum."—Nelson DeMille, *New York Times* bestselling author

"Kelter is a master, pure and simple."—The Kindle Book Review

"Kelter knows how to craft a murder mystery."—NPR

Chapter One

Gwen Winter

Uber Dave eyed me in the rearview mirror with a sad hangdog expression that whimpered, *Why me?*

"Can't you drive any faster—any damn faster? I'll give you five stars. That's what you want, right, five *gold* stars? For the love of God, can you please just hit the gas?"

The engine growled, and the car sped up but not fast enough to send those all-important feel-good hormones coursing through my brain.

"…and a huge tip."

The speedometer needle rolled left to right—ten miles over the posted limit. The rear tires chirped quietly as he swung the wheel to avoid a cavernous, take-out-the-front-suspension-sized pothole.

Better, I thought. *Take a deep breath. Jana's not going anywhere. They hardly ever take the poor girl outside for fresh air.* I settled into the back seat, drew a deep breath, and felt my tension ease a smidge.

Uber Dave's car was one of those entry-level imports. The backseat was rigid and unforgiving. The seams on my Coutil bodice cut into my shoulder blades, and the front passenger seat was ratcheted most of the way back to accommodate a massive plastic cooler, leaving me minimal legroom. What's he carrying in there? Is someone in an upstate New York hospital being prepped for a lung transplant?

Listen to me making a stink like I was more important than anyone else.

I was supposed to be cured of that. My dad was ex-military. He didn't like complainers and often made it clear that whining was an unattractive trait in a man or a woman. But the way I see it, I had every right to bitch on the worst day of my life. Desperate times, desperate measures—isn't that what they say? That's why I'd hijacked Uber Dave for a seventy-five-mile drive up the New York State Thruway, frantic for an explanation as to why a red-hot poker had been rammed straight through my heart.

I'd only met Nas's younger sister, Jana, once. I wasn't sure if she'd remember me—if she'd even know who I was. Introducing us was something Nas felt he had to do because she had always been everything to him. She was his kid sister and had a kindred spirit before I came along. It was important to him that she sign off on our relationship, place her visa stamp on my passport—yes, Gwen Winter, your papers are in order. You can come across the border, but don't forget, I'll be watching.

Can I really? Though I sought her approval, I was snickering on the inside. I'll let you in on a secret, Jana. Your brother already penetrated my air space—not once, but often—as often as he damn well pleased.

Where are you, Nas?

Where the hell did you go?

Are you okay?

"Give him the benefit of the doubt," my mother said. "Maybe he—"

"Maybe he *what?*" *Was he kidnapped by aliens? Pistol-whipped, tossed into the trunk of a black limo, and buried in a shallow grave?* What could possibly justify what he did?

I couldn't stop worrying. *Is he alright?*

"I think the speed limit is higher on this portion of the road," I said.

"No, ma'am, it hasn't changed." Uber Dave tapped the gas pedal just enough to keep me quiet.

I pulled a folded hundred-dollar bill from the small sleeve of my iPhone case, crinkled it, and dropped it on the front passenger seat. "I. Don't. Care. Go faster."

He glanced at the Benjamin as it settled on the fabric-covered foam rubber seat cushion, then back in the rearview mirror. He looked wild, caged-beast wild, I-have-to-get the-hell-out-of-here wild. "I'm sorry, ma'am, I'm not allowed to accept cash tips, and I'm not losing my license just to get you to your destination a few minutes faster. There are patrol cars all over the thruway."

"Seriously? I can run faster than you're driving—in my heels."

"What?"

"Don't pretend you didn't hear me."

If I can't wring Nas's neck... Uber Dave's was so close. All I had to do was reach over the seatback. I could almost feel his neck in my hands, the white gooseflesh under his crisply manicured beard.

Uber Dave flipped the lid and reached into the oversized transplant cooler. *No human organs, thank God.* He handed me a bottle of icy cold Poland Spring water. Condensation instantly formed on the outside of the bottle. I didn't know whether to be appreciative or feel insulted. I accepted the water all the same. "Can't say I blame you. It's a safe bet I'll do less talking with a bottle in my mouth."

"No, ma'am, I'm just trying to make you as comfortable as possible. Please try to enjoy the ride. The trees are in full bloom."

Of course, they are. It's spring, and the pollen Geiger counter is in the red, nuclear. I had to knock down a double dose of Allegra just to make it out the front door. "Nothing stronger?"

"Excuse me? What?"

Hooch, you weirdo. It's a joke? "I've had a lousy day. A terrible, shitty day. On a scale of one to ten? About a billion."

"I'm really sorry to hear that. I kind of assumed—"

"Never mind." He knew exactly what had happened. Nothing could've been more obvious. Two in combination with any number in the world equaled four.

I pressed the cold cylinder against my forehead and watched the next road sign come into view. *Shoot! I thought we were closer than that.* Mile markers sped by. Being the lunatic I was, I counted them as we passed, "One, two..." Each subsequent too-long-to-arrive mile marker pissed me off all the more. "I'm going mad back here." *I'm stuck in this subcompact shit box trying to figure out what the hell happened to my life, and it feels like we're standing still.* "Wait until I get my hands on you, Nasir Zia. I'll tear your fucking heart out."

I saw Uber Dave's eyes flash warning in the rearview mirror—Mayday! Mayday! Uber Dave to the lifeboats. "Ma'am, why don't I pull over at the next rest area for a few minutes. Give you a chance to walk around and get some fresh air. Sound like a good idea?"

"Please, *just* drive." Uber Dave didn't deserve the me I was in the back of his car, the irrational lunatic, the girl who hated everyone and everything.

But I had to know what happened to Nas.

And God, despite it all, I hoped he was alright.

Condensation from the water bottle dripped onto my bag, and I remembered I had a small pill vial with Xanax inside. Seconds later, the water bottle was empty. I'd swallowed two of the peach-colored beauties, popped the little buggers like Tic Tacs.

Focusing on the passing mile markers became impossible as my vision became hazy. Stomach empty, the sedative hit me quickly. I floated away, out of my body and out of the car. I felt as if I was slipping into a warm bath. Eyelids heavy, the waterline rose, covering my face. The notion of drowning seemed as inviting as a loving caress.

* * *

I remember being awestruck by my sister's regal glow on her wedding day, by her jubilant smile. Alana's smile radiated through the temple, touching everyone, warming hearts like rays of the sun's aurora at daybreak. Adoration gleamed as she walked down the aisle—she was so deeply in love with her Jack, as she always had been.

And what girl wouldn't be?

He was that *guy, the one every girl wanted, gal pals, BFFs, and younger sisters alike, every horribly jealous one of us.*

He was absolutely that *guy for me, the one Alana had found first, the one she took off the market, leaving me for dead.*

I was three years behind my big sister through high school, again through college, and always would be throughout life—too young and too inconspicuous for Jack to take seriously, to notice. If he noticed me at all. Sure, Alana brought me out with them sometimes when she saw how desperate and lonely I was, but it was akin to taking a dog along for a run on the beach. Get in the car, Gwen. Good girl. Good girl. We'll toss a ball, scratch your belly, and take you home for a nice snuggly nap.

I was what my dad might've called an also-ran. He was always direct and never did the condescending walking-on-eggshells dance around me. Not like the others. There was this shuck-and-jive way of speaking that many used when around me, measuring each word with a micrometer so that I wouldn't take a nosedive from my precarious perch.

And crash.

It was predictable—the way most reacted to broken people. To me.

Poor little Gwen. Don't stress her out. You know what that will mean: an emergency session with Dr. Cooper and yet another change of medication, months of her barely clinging to life, and a drop of two dress sizes. Her poor parents, those nutritional supplements must cost an absolute fortune.

As if I wasn't gangly before, after a period of deep depression, my knobby knees looked like a pair of garden snakes had swallowed plump mice and were struggling to choke them down. It meant every one of my short skirts in the trash.

Was I ever going to fill out? Fully grown and still a stick. No ass. No chest. One particularly dickish high school guy used to call me Surfboard.

And all the while, I knew I was being an A-hole because big sis was a saint. More than a saint, she was an angel with spun silk for hair and dewy brown eyes that drank away my pain—always there when I needed her, tempting me with treats, stroking my hair, whispering words of encouragement. And the hugs. She gave the best hugs, bar none. It was as if she was inside me, permeating me with her strength, holding me up when I didn't have the will to stand on my own.

Is it wrong to be envious of someone you love, a sister who placed my well-being above her own? Yeah, of course it is. It's human nature, and to be human is to suffer. Check Nietzsche on that one. It was as if old Friedrich had been writing about me, as if we shared a flat back in 19th century Germany, and he observed my routine every agonizing day of my life.

If only there wasn't Jack, handsome, perfect Jack, charming Jack, helping-old-women-across-the-street Jack. If only Alana and I were on equal footing, without hunky Jack between us.

Not that I wasn't happy for her.

I was.

Of course, I was. Jealousy is one thing—sociopathy is something completely different.

Or so I told myself, over and over again to prove that my feelings were genuine.

The happiness they shared was so overwhelming it just wasn't right—wasn't fair. Or maybe I was the one who wasn't right.

Another weekend to endure, yet one more in an endless procession of weekends, approaching noon and still in bed. No place to go, awake for hours, starving, trying to pry myself off the mattress, and all the while Alana's picture-perfect wedding is stuck in my woodblock of a head. She's on the altar with Jack beside her. He can't take his eyes off her as their precious marriage vows are spoken, words meant to bind them, two as one. The crowd of witnesses is on its feet as the recessional plays. And now it's Alana who's torn between dividing her attention between the onlookers and her brand-spanking-new husband. That connection in their eyes—iron-forged, unbreakable, and meant to last a lifetime.

Can't she look away? Not even for a moment? You've already got the wedding band on your finger. Would it be so terrible to acknowledge Aunt Agnes and Uncle Morris? They drove all the way from Lima, Ohio, to the Big Wormy Apple just to be with you on your special day, hundreds of miles of driving in their sun-faded gold Buick just to see how in love the two of you are. Aren't they worth a fleeting glance? Can't you show them one damn smidgeon of appreciation?

You're holding his hand, his formidable hand. He's not going anywhere, not now, not ever. He's not going to vaporize if you turn your head. Still, you can't keep your eyes off him because he's just too good to be true. You'll be locked in his arms tonight—tonight and forever. Give Agnes and Morris two seconds of your time, would you? They're over eighty. What else do they have to live for?

How close do two people need to be?

Oh, I left out the best part, the kiss, the I-pronounce-you-man-and-wife kiss. There has never been a kiss more meaningful, as consequential. It said everything the vows couldn't possibly speak, what no words could possibly articulate. It was a Buttercup and Westley kiss, the purest, most beautiful, and magical, as if conjured by Merlin's wand.

More, as if God himself had ordained their union.

And here I am, following them as they exit the temple. Gliding past everyone, her feet never once touched the ground. And there I am in their wake, the also-ran, the skinny little engine that couldn't, destined to be the bridesmaid but never the bride. Freshly altered, my maid-of-honor dress hangs off my shoulders like heavy muslin drapes off a bowed curtain rod.

* * *

I felt tension tugging at my eyelids, prying them open against their will, the line between the here and then murky. One fluttered open—the other was slow to rise. *What else does Uber Dave have in the transplant container? Something useful? Red Bull? Iced quad-shot espresso? A fucking defibrillator?* "I need a beer."

Uber Dave practically jumped out of his seat, his hand clutching his heart as if an ax had come crashing through the door. Sucking air, he was silent for moments before proclaiming, "We're almost there, ma'am—less than five minutes away." There was an undeniable note of exhilaration in his voice as he made the announcement, as if he'd been locked aboard a transatlantic flight with a mad woman. He couldn't wait for the wheels to touch down and the hatch to open. "You seemed pretty out of it for a while," he said.

I absolutely heard him thinking, *Thank God. Too bad she woke up.*

My heart raced like a stallion's coming down the home stretch, pumping so hard it purged every last drop of tranquilizer from my system as we rolled up in front of Platt-Memminger Psychiatric Hospital, a sterile edifice constructed from massive slabs of fluted gray cement. It's rare that I feel the need to be critical of architecture, but seeing it for the first time was barely tolerable; twice was more than I could bear. The building was frigid-looking and impersonal, a blight on God's green earth, a state-funded Frank Lloyd Wrong.

Uber Dave unbuckled his seatbelt and bolted from the car, opening my door instantaneously. "We're here," he said. "We made great time too. I hope I did okay." Translation, "Get the hell out of my car, you raving psycho."

I couldn't fault him for wanting me gone, but he hadn't gotten pulled over by the police, and he did get a C-note to spend on caramel lattes, beard balm, or whatever else it was guys like Uber Dave indulge in these days.

I was already out the car door, running as fast as my heels could carry me through the revolving door and into the lobby, turning every head within the tomb's bland inner belly. The interior was even more drab than the exterior, with a hung ceiling and gray, fluorescent lights that hummed like a mind-numbing Space Invaders video game. The only thing missing was the intermittent blasting of virtual laser cannons. The metal-framed furnishings were made to last a thousand years—military-grade, bulletproof, tedious enough to lure Elon Musk's brilliant brain into a fog bank and wilt.

The female attendant behind the counter looked...sturdy, roughly a defensive tackle in girth. Thick skin covered meaty cheekbones, and she wore her dark hair in a ponytail. Her scrubs were neatly pressed and crisp. She was no doubt well-experienced and able to spot a loon like me coming from a mile off. I imagine she'd handled frantic visitors before, but none like this one, none like Gwen Winter. There was little doubt she was pondering my mental state as I rushed up to the reception counter. Visitor or patient, which was it? She appeared to be caught off guard, her mouth agape, her words coming in spurts. "C-can I help you?" she asked.

"Yes, thanks. I need to see Jana Zia. It's urgent."

Her eyes were wide and disbelieving. I knew what she wanted to ask but couldn't find the nerve. "D-does she expect you?"

"No."

"Are you family?"

"No. Well, yes. Sort of."

She looked me up and down; her eyes were billiard balls—strike that, they were ostrich eggs. "Sort of, huh?"

My eyes settled on her nametag. "Uh-huh. That's right, Rosemarie."

She looked lost, as if she'd never been in a similar position before. In her eyes I saw the uncertainty of a driver's education student, scared senseless with two left feet, and praying for a split-second break in traffic before merging onto the interstate. "Let's start with your name," she said.

"Gwen Winter."

She flipped around a clipboard. "Would you mind signing in, Ms. Winter?"

Sighing impatiently. "Is this necessary?"

"Yes, I'm afraid it is."

"Fine," I huffed. A pen was chained to the countertop as was once customary in banks when people still visited brick-and-mortar depositories in the flesh. The tether was barely long enough to permit holding the pen in a natural position as I wrote on the clipboard. "Are you really worried about someone stealing the pen?"

"Excuse me?"

"The pen. I mean *seriously*. It's worth ten cents." I wrote my full name next to the date, time of day, and the patient I was visiting. I had to massage my hand to work out a cramp.

"It's not the value of the pen we're worried about."

"Oh?" *OH! Snap out of it, Gwen. Mental hospital. Self-harm.*

"Thank you." She turned her focus to the computer screen and began tapping away with stubby pork sausage fingers. Her nails were like a man's, short and unpolished. "She's in therapy right now. If you'll have a seat, I'll—"

"I don't *want* to sit down," I snapped. *Was that rude? Too rude? Yeah, Gwen— that was over the top. Sure, you're going nuts, but what did poor Sausage Fingers do to deserve this? She's probably a good church-going woman, takes in stray animals, and bakes for the local elementary school fundraiser.* I should've taken it down a notch, but I didn't. I couldn't control myself. The rollercoaster was off the tracks. I continued barking like a rabid dog. "I want to see Jana Zia. Now!"

"Ma'am, if you'll just give me a few minutes, I'd be happy to—"

"Now. I said, now! What part of *now* don't you understand?"

A question (read outrage) came from a tea sandwich of a man, a bureaucratic type impressing no one in his brown closeout-rack suit and Cheap & Crappy Cuts franchise haircut. "What in God's name is going on here?"

Look at that cowlick, for God's sake, I thought. *It's sticking up straighter than the dorsal fin on a great white shark.* His voice belied his size, though. It was resonant and authoritative as he chugged forward like a Lionel model train. Face-to-face, I was overwhelmed by the odor of dry-cleaning fluid wafting off his suit.

"This is a hospital," he said. "I was at the far end of the building when I heard you yelling like you own the place. Well, you don't. New York State and the Office of Mental Health operate this facility. I'm the director, and I require decorum from patients, staff, and visitors alike." Choo-Choo Charlie pumped the brakes just long enough to take me in head-to-toe. His eyelids blinked like the louvers on a Morse code signal lamp, and his face contorted in bewilderment. He'd come at me with a full head of steam but suddenly stalled. With his forehead completely creased, he struggled for words. "Are you wearing a …*wedding* dress?"

Chapter Two

Gwen Winter

Rosemarie wadded up a handful of Kleenex and forced them into my hand, a huge wad, bigger than a bath sponge, enough tissues to soak up a commercial spill.

My eye makeup was waterproof, but the crocodile tears running over my foundation must've looked like camel tracks across the Sahara.

Turning to her boss for permission to assist me, Rosemarie simultaneously gestured to another scrub-clad woman to take her place behind the reception counter. "All right with you if I help this young woman?"

Pint-sized Mr. Magnanimous begrudgingly provided consent and an I'll-be-the-bigger-man nod of the head before pivoting on his size eight wingtips, crossing Lake Low Self-esteem, and returning to the land of the Lilliputians.

By now, Rosemarie had taken my hand and was leading me out of the reception area. Bless her heart—part of me was thankful she'd come to my rescue, and part of me wondered if she was bent on having me committed, leading me to the mental facility's inner sanctum, never again to know independence.

My head was filled with a lifetime of my shrink's warnings about psychiatric hospitals. Pushed to the brink of her pharmaceutical limits, Dr. Cooper always opted for tough love over a previously untried drug. "Trust me, Gwen, a psychiatric hospital is not what you want. It's not the panacea you're imagining."

But what if the looney bin was exactly what I needed and had needed most of my life? Maybe I'd be happier here. Safer. Protected. Maybe being institutionalized was the answer to all my problems.

The word sanctuary never sounded more comforting, as warm and fuzzy as it did at that moment. It seemed a hell of a lot less challenging than explaining to hundreds of friends and relatives why the man of my dreams left me standing at the altar. It's decided then, admit me—a rubber room for one with a view of the majestic Catskills. Send the bellhop for my luggage. Oh wait, I didn't bring any. My bags were packed and waiting for me back home, filled with swimsuits and lingerie for my honeymoon. *Burn them*, I thought. *They're of no use to me now.*

And maybe not ever.

"I didn't realize you were Nasir Zia's fiancée, Rosemarie said."

"You know Nas?" *What am I saying? Of course, she knows him. He visits Jana all the time.* "I was only here once, several months ago, when I met Jana for the first time. I didn't expect you to remember me." *Or notice me—no one's ever that observant.*

A picture may be worth a thousand words, but my expression, a tome, a data dump, terabytes of information instantly uploaded to her brain. That one powerful, all-expressive gesture, my sinking chin, and the downturned corners of my mouth told her everything she needed to know.

"You poor thing—I can't imagine that Nasir would do something like that. He seems like such a good guy." She took my hand, not to lead me somewhere, but to share compassion. "Tell me all about it, sweetie."

He is a good guy. Always has been. So, how could such a stand-up guy abandon me on our wedding day? It had to be the alien abduction. He was halfway across the galaxy on his way to God-knows-where. Or, as the wisecrack suggested, do all assholes go to Uranus?

Rosemarie felt like the answer to my prayers, a stranger I could unload on without judgment. My heart was filled with venom, and I was ready and willing to spew, to paint Nas a monster, a heartless fiend, who'd led me to the altar, then vanished into thin air. Rosemarie's smile was warm and sympathetic. With her chubby cheeks and round face, I wanted to invite her to a pajama party—a girls-only man-bashing sleepover. "I'm so sorry about the way I spoke to you out front. I'm such a mess; totally off my rocker."

"Forget it, honey. At least you didn't fling a fistful of crap at me. Every once in a while, a patient will go off the deep end and whip out a turd fastball faster than you can say Whitey Ford. You'd never guess it, but I've developed cat-like reflexes."

My God, she's great, my new BFF. I actually cracked a smile, a slight smile, more along the lines of a hairline chink in a bone china saucer. But the moment quickly passed, and I reverted to blubbering like a baby once again. "He-he-he—"

"The jerk didn't show. He left you high and dry on your special day. I guess Nasir isn't the great guy I thought he was. Doing that to you is beyond shitty."

God bless this gal—she's doing all the heavy lifting for me. I nodded. I sobbed. Wash. Rinse. Repeat. The rancor tank was empty. I was empty. No anger. No hate. No nothing. I had nothing left and didn't know how I managed to stay on my feet. Normally, it would be my sister Alana consoling me, but I'd shut her out. I pulled away from her and my parents at the temple because I couldn't bear the humiliation. After all the pettiness and jealousy, after all those years pining away for a husband… At long last, she and I were going to be on equal footing. Equality was so close I could taste it, but Nas let the air out of that balloon, didn't he? He set a fucking match to the Hindenburg.

A card swipe and the door to the staff break room opened, then closed and sealed us safely inside. I collapsed in a chair, not knowing if I'd ever stand again. I was completely devoid of the will to live—flesh and bones held together by buckram and lace, a carcass suspended on a meat hook.

She fished inside the fridge, found a bottle of water, twisted the cap, and handed it to me. "Hydrate, honey. You've lost a good five pounds in tears since you walked through the front door." She pulled up a chair, knee-to-knee.

"I'll get my head handed to me for offering this to you, but under the circumstances, would you like something to take the edge off?"

"I took Xanax."

"You *did*? Honey, if this is you *on* Xanax, I'd hate to see you when you're all wound up. How many did you take?"

"Two."

"How strong?"

"A half-milligram each."

"*She-it*, honey, you're wired with more voltage than the Christmas tree at Rockefeller Center." She tapped her temple with her index finger, a sure sign that she was pondering my dilemma and searching her lexicon of patient-soothing tactics. "Are you up to talking about it?"

My head shook, no, but the gesture was a lie. I ached to tell her, to tell anyone, about every excruciating detail of my day from the moment my eyes opened in the morning until now. But the thoughts wouldn't form. The words wouldn't come.

She gave me ample time to speak but was savvy enough to fill the silence. "My dear, you're not the only bride who's been left standing at the altar. You're not the first and you sure as hell won't be the last. A dickhead did it to me twelve years ago."

"Really?" *Oh my God, I want to hug this woman. She's the well from which all sisterhood springs.*

"Yeah, his name was Jeff, short for Jefferson, and to this day, I refer to him as Shit-for-brains. The SOB pulled the disappearing act on me just as I suspect Nasir did to you and caught me completely off guard. I was this goo-goo-eyed dummy, four months pregnant and totally in love with the loser." She gritted her teeth. "My life was going to be absolutely perfect. I was going to have a husband *and* a baby and live close enough to my parents so that they could help out babysitting when I had to work. Shear heaven, right?"

I hadn't touched the water. She picked it up and directed the opening toward my mouth. "Shit-for-brains sold cars and was damn good at it. Drove a cherry red Camaro, which is exactly where he caught me."

A small swig of water. "Caught you?" I pictured a large fish nibbling at the hook.

"At the peak of fertility, dollface. Impregnated me." She looked me over carefully. That bodice looks tighter than bejesus. It doesn't look like you're showing. Not in a family way, are you, sweetness?"

Oh, God, no. "No." We were going to wait a couple of years—learn each other inside out before complicating our relationship with children. *Nice and complicated now, though, isn't it?*

"Well, good. You're miles ahead of where I was when my betrothed hit the bricks."

"W-what happened?"

"Cold feet, I figure, same as most men—couldn't face the prospect of being tied to one woman and taking care of a crying brat. To this day, I believe his folks knew where he ran off to, but they wouldn't tell me. Honor amongst thieves—ain't that what they say?"

"That's horrible. And he knew you were expecting?"

"He sure as heck did—swore he was gonna provide for his child, but I guess that went out the window with his backbone. She motioned to my purse. "Have you checked your phone, honey? I'll bet it's been ringing off the hook."

"No. I had to turn it off. My sister and parents wouldn't stop calling me. They wouldn't give up, and I just didn't know what to say to them. My mom and my sister, they'll be understanding, but my dad, I know exactly what he'll say."

"Didn't give the young man his blessing, huh? I see. You know right about now might be a good time to turn on your phone—might answer some questions for you and your family. Besides, Mom and Dad must be worried clean out of their minds."

"I can't. Not yet."

"You've got *no* idea what happened to Nasir? Why he vanished? Not even an inkling?"

The most pitiful headshake anyone had ever seen.

"Just left you high and dry?"

As if it were possible, an even more pitiful nod.

"Well, that just plain sucks. I'm sorry, sweetheart. But lookit, I've done okay for myself, and I'm not half as pretty as you. I met another fella, and he turned out to be all right—twice the man Shit-for-brains Jefferson was with a heart big enough for me and my little one." She extended her hand and presented a modest (read paltry) engagement ring. "Been together ten years now. I bless my lucky stars every day."

"I'm really happy you found each other." I glanced down at my own engagement ring—four carats—might as well been glass. It was meaningless. The commitment it symbolized had been shattered.

"Some things just aren't meant to be. And that's what you have to tell yourself. They say everything happens for a reason. If you and this shitbird weren't meant to be, then you just weren't meant to be. I'm sure you're tired of heading out into the water and baiting the hook, but there are a hell of a lot of fish in the sea."

While I appreciated Rosemarie's encouragement, comparing me to a fisherman and a male prospect to a gill-breathing fish didn't make me feel any better.

Looking straight ahead through the glass-framed door, I saw a gray-haired woman in scrubs standing outside in the corridor. She wanted to enter the lounge, but Rosemarie tried to shoo her off. The woman seemed annoyed about being turned away. She glared at my BFF and held her ground.

"Honey, I wish we could stay in here as long as we needed to, but there'll be hell to pay if I don't let nasty old Alice Scruggs in here for her break PDQ." Rosemarie's eyes brightened. "Say, I've got an idea. Don't move a muscle. I'll be right back."

Rosemarie walked off. Through the door, I could hear her and Alice going at it. Rosemarie started off with a polite request but, failing to make her point, gave it to the old goat, both barrels blazing. Alice barked something I couldn't make out and looked to be positively outraged before storming off.

I didn't know what Rosemarie was doing or how long she'd be gone, but the few minutes I was left alone seemed to last forever. I was beginning to decompose all over again.

Of all places, I'm at a mental hospital instead of my wedding reception. The man of my dreams is a no-show and my only confidant is a state hospital worker

I've known a sum total of ten minutes.

The bodice of my ball gown wedding dress was lined with stiff buckram designed to hold in the waist. It must've been designed by the same Machiavellian devil who created the iron maiden. It felt as if it was made of thick leather that had been moistened and was now drying and tightening around me, squeezing my lungs like a vise. I was seconds away from tearing it off when Rosemarie returned, holding sweats and slippers in her outstretched arms. I tell you, the woman was an angel.

She smiled knowingly. "I thought these might come in handy. Can't be easy to breathe in that Victorian humping frock. Let's make you comfy and then we'll see about sitting down with Jana."

* * *

Rosemarie taped three wire hangers together, hung my dress on them, then covered it with a fifty-gallon lawn and leaf bag. "Are you feeling any better, sweetheart?"

The sweats had been laundered to death, the brushed fleecy insides of the shirt and pants were heavily pilled and lofty. The fabric smelled rich with fabric softener. They were warm and comfy. My feet sank into padded terry cloth slippers. The comfort was exquisite. "That's so much better, thanks."

"You looked beautiful in your dress, but I know you couldn't wait to tear it off. I'd wear my sweats all day long if they let me. But Doc Bellows, the Nazi you met at the reception counter, he's a stickler for formality. If he had his way, he'd have all the nurses in starched dresses and caps." She handed me the water bottle one more time. "Now swig this down, and we'll see if Jana is up for a visit."

It took a while, but I finally got the rest of the water to go down. I can't remember the simple act of drinking being more difficult. The water felt like sand going down my throat.

"I have to tell you, they keep her heavily medicated," Rosemarie said. "The poor thing—deep depression is a bitch."

"Is there no hope?"

"I pray there is, but Doc Bellows isn't exactly the share-and-share-alike type. He doesn't take the nursing staff into his confidence. He prescribes a course of treatment and expects the worker bees to adhere to it. I can't even tell you what made her the way she is, only how she's to be medicated and her daily schedule of activities."

"As I said, I only met her once before. Nas did most of the talking. I know this won't be easy, but…"

"I know—it's the not knowing that's killing you. Still, your first thought was to speak to the groom's sister? I mean, right from the church and all?"

The wedding ceremony would have taken place in a nonsectarian sanctuary, not a temple or mosque, and certainly not in a church. Still, her question begged a prompt answer.

"I didn't think anyone else would know what happened to Nas. He's so private and his parents seemed as shocked as I was, as we all were. His friends went running for cover, and I figured Jana was my only hope. I mean, Nas is so close with her. I thought if anyone knew what happened, it would be her."

She rolled her eyes. "I know Nasir and Jana shared a special connection, but I'm not sure she deserves all the faith you're about to place in her. Anyway, we'll find out." I could see in her expression she thought we were embarking on a fool's errand, but she lifted the receiver from the cradle of a wall phone, punched in a code, and waited. "Oh, hi, honey? It's Rosemarie Powell. Is Jana Zia back in her room? How's she doing today?" Rosemarie went back and forth with whoever was on the other end of the line for a few moments before she finally hung up. "Come on. The window of opportunity is about to slam shut. Jana's not having her best day."

"Can't be any worse than mine."

"No, I suppose not."

"Does she know I'm the one who wants to see her?"

"No. It's probably best we don't give her a reason to get revved up." She winked at me. "Know what I mean?"

"But she'll see me?"

"See you? Sure, she will. Talk to you? Understand you? *Communicate* with you? That's anyone's guess. You said you met her before, so you know what I'm talking about, right? At least you're not a total stranger. She doesn't do well with strangers."

I nodded. "Just once. She was. She was…quiet."

"She can be like that sometimes. Box of chocolates scenario, if you get my meaning. You must've gotten her on a good day. The poor thing—God only knows what she's been through. I sure as heck don't."

Nas had told me how his sister struggled, how her entire life had been one agonizing attempt to climb out of the pit. Seeing her for the first time and knowing what her life had been like was so damn hard.

How will I get through it now, knowing I'm only here to pump her for information? What happened to Nas? Where is he, and why the hell did he leave me at the altar?

Jana was barely capable of making it through the day, any day, and here I was, hoping she'd betray the trust of the one person she loved most in the world.

But she's all I have.

We paused outside Jana's room for a few moments. I watched her sitting in a chair facing the window, looking out at the crestline of the Catskill Mountains, lush with red oak and balsam fir trees, richly green from an abundantly snowy winter. I could see why she liked the view so much, why she spent long days at the window. The view was so serene and calming, and she needed tranquility as much as she needed air to breathe.

My father had stories about the Catskill Mountains, lots of them. He worked several summers at a small resort to help pay his college tuition. He'd entertained me with stories of guest gluttony, endless courses of food served to guests who couldn't possibly force down everything they'd ordered— triple appetizers, double main courses, and dessert, all followed with glasses of prune juice. He called them *chazzers* and said the hotel guests ate like pigs. He'd trot out a Borscht Belt tale whenever I wasn't eating, which was more often than I cared to admit. It was his cockeyed version of "There are kids starving in China," the guilt trip he laid on me so that I'd make all-gone with my dinner. He'd said he wished I had a healthier appetite and that I would eat too much instead of too little. He prayed I'd sprout chubby cheeks, but God never saw fit to grant his request.

"Are you sure you want to do this?" Rosemarie asked. "Maybe check your phone before we bother Ms. Jana? Maybe this is unnecessary." Her expression begged me to reconsider. "I can't believe I'm saying this, but maybe Nasir got into a traffic accident. God forbid." She made the sign of the cross. "Maybe that sixty-four-thousand-dollar question isn't a question anymore."

"No, I haven't checked my phone in a while, but I checked it a hundred times before that and—" I could feel my throat tightening. "I really think I should speak to her first. I think she might know something."

"All right. All right." She held up her hands. "I give up," she said, then knocked on the partially opened door before announcing us, her voice tiptoeing into the room like a kitten. "Jana, there's someone here to see you. Is it all right if we come in?"

Jana responded by turning her head in our direction, but there was no auditory response or visible change in her expression. It remained flat and lifeless, her bottom lip hanging like she was about to drool. It wasn't so long ago I felt the way she did, dead on the inside, struggling to make it from sunup to sundown. Despite the travesty of a day I was having, I had to bless my lucky stars. If I hadn't had the support of a loving family to help me find my way, I might very well be residing in the room next door to Jana.

"Get going," Rosemarie said, prodding me into the room. "The weather around these parts has been known to turn on a dime."

On the surface, Jana's expression was unassuming, but in her eyes, I saw the flashing red warning light. "Hi, Jana," I said, standing in front of her. "Do you remember me?"

She nodded, yes, but her movements were slow and indecisive, as if her thoughts had to cross an ocean before arriving on a distant shore.

"Thanks for letting me visit. I know you didn't expect me."

She seemed to study me intently. Even from the depths of the medicated soup her brain was bathed in, she sensed something was coming, something she didn't want to deal with. Her eyes flicked side-to-side, avoiding contact.

"Is it all right if I sit down?"

I hoped her silence would end with a yes or a nod, any gesture in the affirmative, but she didn't respond. Observing the exchange, Rosemarie gave me the okay to take a seat. There was only one chair in the room, and Jana was in it. I sat down on the edge of the bed.

"Do you remember that your brother and I were supposed to get married today?"

A telling glimmer of recognition—the slightest nod.

"I'm so sorry to tell you that didn't happen, Jana. Nas never made it to the ceremony."

I heard the circuit breaker trip, that quick, authoritative snapping sound that warns the house was about to go dark. She flashed from calm to anxious in the measure between heartbeats. Her pupils dilated. Her eyes widened. The breath seemed to catch in her lungs. A sudden but distinct hand tremor came and went.

Rosemarie was nearby, watching like a hawk. She took Jana's hand and rubbed it, comforting her.

"Where is he?" Jana asked. "Where is my brother?"

"That's why I'm here, Jana," I said. "I was hoping you might know."

"What happened to him?" she asked. Her feet shuffled nervously. "He's all right, isn't he?" Her breath escaped her lips in rapid puffs. I'd come all this way hoping to learn something, but she was having a meltdown before my eyes.

I shrugged. "I-I don't know."

SNAP!

"Who the hell are you?" she said. Her lips parted, and she gritted her teeth. "What have you done with my brother?"

Recoiling, I gasped. "Nothing. I'm Gwen. Remember? Nas and I, we were supposed to—"

"Who *are* you?"

"Gwen, I'm Gwen. Nas and I were engaged. Don't you remember? He brought me here to meet you, to tell you we'd fallen in love. He told you all about it."

"Liar." She flew out of the chair, her eyes flashing white-hot. She was taller than me, imposing.

"Easy now," Rosemarie said. "Calm down, Jana." Rosemarie was rattled, a knee-jerk reflex away from calling for help, restraints, sedation. "There's no reason to get so upset." She fired off a glance that told me, "Go! Run for your life."

Jana closed in on me before I could get to my feet. We were face-to-face, and I could smell her musty breath just before she pounced. "What have you done with Nas? Where's my brother?"

I toppled backwards onto her bed, and she fell on me with all of her weight, her hands going for my throat.

Rosemarie tried to pull her off, but Jana held fast. She locked on like a pit bull. She continued to pry us apart while at the same time hollering for help.

"Jana, please," I protested, grasping her hands to fend off a blow. "I love your brother, and I'm worried about him. We were supposed to get married today, but—"

"No. He can't marry you," Jana bellowed.

"What? What do you mean he can't marry me?"

It was as if we were Krazy Glued together. Rosemarie yanked and yanked, but the epoxy had cured. I somehow managed to roll to the side where Rosemarie's heft gave her a bit more leverage. She was able to lock Jana in her grip and slowly pulled her off me just as an orderly rushed into the room and jabbed Jana in the arm with a syringe. Whatever they injected in her arm must've been strong because her eyes glazed over instantly, and her arms and legs went limp. Rosemarie locked her arms around Jana's midsection to prevent her from crashing to the floor.

Jana's speech was slurred, yet somehow, three words were unmistakable. "You're not her."

I cried out, my voice hoarse, pleading, "Jana, you know me, I'm Gwen."

She was out on her feet but repeated the confusing message over and over again. "You're not her," she said. "You're not her."

Chapter Three

Gwen Winter

Tails tucked between our legs, we fled back to the solitude of the nurses' lounge to rethink strategy.

"Hon, are you thinking maybe it's time to check your phone?" Rosemarie said. "I have to tell you, I didn't have much faith in your plan, and Jana didn't tell you a blessed thing."

"No, she didn't. Worse—she wrung my neck and babbled some nonsense about me not being me. Well then, who the hell am I?" I felt a fresh lump forming in my throat. "It looks like I came a long way for nothing."

"You sure did, honey. I'm sorry, but it doesn't seem like she has the answer you're looking for. If you ask me, she's got no clue where her brother is or what in Creation happened to him. Kind of seemed as if she's worried about him now."

"I know. I didn't feel good about cornering her, and now…"

Rosemarie shrugged. "She doesn't have much to say in the best of times. Whatever pains her, she keeps it buried deep. Her therapist has been trying to root it out of her for years and hasn't gotten past first base." She peaked her eyebrows and pointed at my purse. "So, how about it?"

"The phone?"

"Uh-huh, the phone."

"Not sure."

"Well, *get* sure. You need a support system."

"You're a support system."

"No, darlin', I'm a Band-Aid. You need to be around people you love and who love you back. Ain't no one gonna judge you because your peckerhead fiancé hit the skids. Say, we've got some of that kava tea in the pantry—it's kind of soothing, and soothing is just what the doctor ordered." Her expression hung a question mark at the end of the sentence. She didn't wait for an answer, but instead opened an overhead cabinet and retrieved a box labeled Sleepy Time Tea. She filled a mug with instant hot water from the water cooler, and, *voila*, a cup of nerve-soothing tea in under a minute. "I'll give you ten minutes to quiet your nerves. After that, you suck it up and turn on your stupid old phone. Doc Bellows will have my ass if he finds out I'm still in here with you."

"So much for empathy."

"Honey, I'm just a well of compassion, but where my paycheck is at stake, well, empathy goes right out the window." I could see that it pained her to cut me loose. She came forward and wrapped me up in her arms. "It'll be okay, honey. Gonna hurt like the dickens for a long time, but you'll get over it. You're a fighter. I can tell." Retrieving a bottle of water from the fridge, she moved toward the door. "I'm gonna show my face at the reception counter before the commandant writes me up for insubordination or some shit. Hit the Power button on your phone, honey. It's not going to turn on by itself." She moseyed toward the door and left, but not without making a sisterly tough love face.

I turned on my phone and watched notifications flash on the screen while steam rose from the mug. There were literally dozens of messages from my sister, my parents, and friends. There were so many, and I feared the battery might die before they all listed on the Recent Calls screen. Listening to the messages, I stared at the new jewel-encrusted phone case I'd purchased for my special day, and my gaze was caught by the rhinestone facets, mesmerizing me while I listened to all the incoming messages, the crying and pleas of anyone who held me dear. I listened to each message carefully, hoping for news, good or bad, anything that might explain what happened to Nas.

But there wasn't any.

Not why.

Not where.

No one knew.

Or wasn't saying.

Listening to all the messages only added to my frustration. I hung on every spoken word, hoping to learn something about Nas, but in the end…I texted the hospital address to my big sister, Alana. **Waiting for you here.** Thinking about it in retrospect, announcing that I was held up at a mental hospital wasn't the most nerve-settling thing I could've done. *Better clear things up before Mom or Dad have a stroke*, I thought. I was about to add that one important tidbit when the phone rang. It was my sister, Alana. "I'm all right," I said. "Please come alone."

Chapter Four

Gwen Winter

I parked my dejected ass on a wooden bench in front of the mental health facility. The bench slats had been replaced with fresh redwood but the paint on the wrought iron end pieces had long ago peeled and rusted. My wedding dress rested over the back struts, wire-hung and garbage-bagged. My shoes and undergarments were contained in gray plastic Walmart grocery bags. Lovely. Exactly what every bride-to-be dreams of.

As Rosemarie was required to work in order to get paid, she couldn't hold my hand while I waited for big sis to collect me. A long wait turned into a longer wait, and still, there was no sign of Alana. True, the ride from Long Island was a lengthy one and getting off the island was never without complication. I pictured her stuck in traffic on the Long Island Expressway, then the Throgs Neck Bridge, knowing she wouldn't have a shot at making good time until she hit the thruway. A few people came and went while I waited but I was alone for most of the time. I couldn't complain about the solitude and found it somehow comforting. What was waiting for me anyway? Nothing great. Sympathy. Consolation. Encouragement to meet a new and better man.

It was a full seventy-five minutes later than anticipated when I saw her dashing blue convertible rolling toward me. "Brave face. Pick yourself up and show her a damn-brave face," I told myself. Then, muscle by muscle, inch at a time, I dragged myself to my feet.

"You made great time," I said, my hangdog expression worth every one of a thousand lashes I wanted to inflict upon myself for being so stupid, for being so ridiculously naïve about Nas. Facing my big sister, I was embarrassed beyond belief, mortified, once again buried beneath her shadow on what should've been my day of days.

"And you're a bitch, Gwen, a stark-raving bitch. How could you up and leave everyone, everyone who loves you? How?"

"How could I?" *Your betrothed didn't leave you standing at the altar, did he? You've got NO idea how I feel.* I didn't have to say any of it. Alana read it on my face, sighed, then looked away, hopeless. She unlocked the door for me to get into her Volvo convertible or, as she chicly referred to it, a cabriolet. It was Caspian blue (yes, Caspian as in the poetic majesty of the Caspian Sea) with a parchment leather interior so soft it made a newborn's bottom feel like alligator hide. Like everything else in her life, it was stunning, and I'm sure she turned heads everywhere she went today as well, even though she looked a mess when she removed her oversized Miu Miu shades, revealing a mascara-running, red-eyed mess. A wad of soiled Kleenex stuffed into the cup holder was testament to the tears she'd shed on her drive upstate.

She was always meticulous about the way she dressed, not matchy-matchy but matchy-elegant, sophisticated in a manner that couldn't be taught. Now, though, it looked as if she'd thrown on the first outfit she could put her hands on. By most people's standards, she was still well put together, but I could tell her ensemble didn't have that special flair, that classic Alana touch. Tears streamed down her cheeks. I tossed my wedding dress in the back seat as she pulled me into the open-top car.

"How could you take off like that? How could you? No one knew what you were doing or what you were thinking. I was so worried, worried to death. We all were."

"You know how I could, how after waiting all these years for Mr. Right, I got dumped on my wedding day. That's how I could. Yes, jumping into Uber Dave's back seat was impulsive, but I didn't know where else to turn."

And still don't.

"Uber Dave?" Her eyes opened wide enough for me to see all the red blood vessels winding through the whites of her eyes.

I was feeling emotionally detached, sad, and yes, of course, depressed and should've been crying, but the tear bottle was empty. Alana opened her arms, took me in for one of her ultra-nurturing hugs, and all that emotionally bereft detachment shit flew out the door. It was her superpower. Like Wonder Woman's Magic Lasso, her closeness and warmth surrounded me, filling me with her love. She'd always had strength enough for the two of us and was always willing to share.

God knows I borrowed heavily of her strength, selfishly, unendingly.

"Dad is *so* angry," she said. "When I left, he was halfway through a bottle of Chivas. And Mom, she's wandering around like a lost soul." She stroked my cheek. "My poor little sister. You deserve better. *So* much better."

"All is fair in love and war, right?" I said. "No one bats an eye when a bride is collateral damage." Her lips twisted as she clawed at the Kleenex box. I suppose she didn't know what to say. "What about Nas's parents? Did Mom and Dad call them? I can't believe they still haven't heard from him?"

"They were beyond mortified, Gwen. They must've slipped away at some point, although I never actually saw them leaving. I think they took it pretty hard. I mean—" Her head dropped. Tears dripped onto her perfectly imperfect outfit. "They love you too, Gwen. I don't think they had any idea this was going to happen."

"But they must know where he is."

"By now? Yeah, I guess they do but it doesn't seem as if they're willing to come forward. I suppose they'll read Nas the Riot Act. Call him a coward. Threaten to disown him or some shit. Nas is going to have to face the music at some point."

"He's the last guy I pegged to be a deserter. He always seemed so ready, on board with all of it, getting engaged, setting a wedding date. There was never that make-or-break moment, that when-can-I-meet-your-parents-moment? When a guy either puts up or shuts up. Does he man up or squirm like a spineless worm? 'It's a little too soon' or 'You kind of took me by surprise.' Or, or... 'Are we ready for this?' Nas never had to make that life-altering decision—do we go to the next step, or do I run from commitment like my hair is on fire? Nas didn't have to face that relationship-challenging come-to-Jesus moment. It seemed as if he'd long made up his mind. He was ready. Unswerving." My throat tightened. "What do you think, sis? Can I pick 'em, or what?"

"I like your après-wedding ensemble," Alana said, sniffling. She was good at changing the subject, had become an expert from years of talking me down off the ledge.

"Institutionally-washed fleece—packs well and goes with everything. I was planning to wear it to the beach in Maui." The quip jarred free a fresh hurt. "Shit, do you think I can cancel the honeymoon reservations—throw myself at the mercy of the Travelocity gnome and plead the Dumped Bride Excuse?"

Alana frowned as fresh tears welled up in her eyes. She didn't know what to tell me, so she hugged me again. This hug was longer and tighter than the first, a bearhug by any other name, a bone-crusher. Something buried deep down inside me longed for it, for her heart to beat as one with mine. It was the story of my life—fall down and run to big sis for support. I didn't have the strength to stand on my own two feet, so I'd stand on hers.

Even if it exhausted her.

Mom was a hugger, but her hugs didn't measure up to Alana's. Mom doled out her love in the kitchen, mending hurts with large helpings of rich, satisfying food. You came home with bad grades, mac 'n cheese. A boyfriend breakup, loaded baked potatoes. What in the world could she whip up of proportions epic enough to soothe a hurt like this one? Getting stood up at the altar had to be well beyond the range of her culinary skills. It was Emeril Lagasse in scope. It was lasagna layered on top of pizza, with a side of ravioli in scale—mountains of comfort food big.

If only I had an appetite.

She started the car, and we rolled slowly out of the parking lot. "Seriously…" my voice withered, the air escaping like from a pricked balloon. "What could've happened to him? We spoke this morning. There wasn't a hint of uncertainty in anything he said. He was showered and shaved, hanging out in his PJs until it was time to get dressed because he didn't want his slacks to get wrinkled while he waited in his apartment."

My grandfather was a big believer in hydrogen peroxide. Got a blister? Peroxide. Whiten grout—peroxide. Ant infestation. Bad breath. Sore gums—yup, peroxide is good for that too. Today, though, plain water was the elixir that mended all, from Uber Dave, Nurse Rosemarie, and now, big sis. "I've got a case of water in the trunk," she said. "Want me to pull over?"

"Nah, Grandpa always said efficacy drops off after the second dose."

She gave me a hard look. "There's a joke in there somewhere, but I'm not sure what it is."

"Everyone's been prescribing water as if it was penicillin."

"Baby girl, I think you need to lie down. Put the seat back and close your eyes."

"No, I couldn't sleep if I tried. Let's get home. Mom probably has a casserole going into the oven, and I need the whole damn thing." I needed the protection of my family and access to my meds: antipsychotics to control my rage, SSRIs to combat the battalion of depression Pac-Men that were chomping away at my gray matter, and a cocktail of hypnotics for sleep. I was a sleep meds master mixologist, using Ambien to knock me out and Trazadone to keep me flat on my back. If I didn't think that would work, I had a stash of old-school drugs squirreled away in the event a catastrophe like today's came to pass, a day when a razor blade and a warm tub seemed truly inviting. I'd codenamed it the Doomsday Cocktail, the one Marilyn Monroe was infamous for. It consisted of a choral hydrate tablet and the contents of a Nembutal capsule. Marilyn washed them down with a tumbler of champagne, but I was thinking along the lines of a Manhattan. Of course, there was always the chance that you wouldn't wake up, which was why I had the ingredients hidden well away. But knowing I had the nuclear launch codes gave me a weird sense of security.

"Are you sure you want to go to Mom and Dad's?" she asked. "The old man will be foaming at the mouth. Are you sure you're up for that? Why don't you come back to my place? You love Jack and the kids. That might be a better course of action."

I fantasized about how I might kill Nas, the where and the how. I visualized the back of his head bent over the dinner table with an icepick embedded in the base of his skull and a slow drizzle of blood running down the back of his neck, winding like a cat's curled tail. "What Nas did is unforgivable." I turned and looked off to the side, just off the road, where a fawn was nibbling on acorns in front of a thicket of garlic mustard. "I've got a lot to get off my chest, and I need to feed off Dad's anger to barrel it out. You and Mom, you'll be too worried about me to let the venom drip. Dad lives for moments like these to be vindicated for all the terrible things he'd ever said about Nas. Everything he's had bottled up will come pouring out in a tidal wave of hatred. I need his hatred. I need to feel it, *all* the poison, *all* the pain." Strike the ice pick slaying—puncturing the medulla is a relatively painless way to die. It was practically passive-aggressive in nature: kill him but don't hurt him. He didn't deserve my mercy. No one would believe I was capable, particularly the cops. I didn't want to be overlooked as a suspect. I wanted the world to know I killed him. He fucked with me, and I killed him. No sissy icepick, a blade dragged across the throat, his gaze imploring, disbelieving as the light in his eyes faded and went out. Hand me a dagger!

"You sure that's the healthiest thing for you to do? I don't want to see you sink into a funk, sis. Cuddling toddlers might not provide the catharsis you need, but in the long run, it'll be healthier than drinking Dad's poison."

"Or I could kill him."

"What? Don't even joke about something like that. Nas is an absolute-fucking-asshole, but he doesn't deserve to *die*."

"Really? You can't even indulge me this once? Right here. Right now. In this moment, you can't even give me the satisfaction of wishing him dead? Put yourself in my shoes. I didn't have a perfect wedding. I didn't get to throw the bouquet. I'm not going to get the chance to live my dream. Nas disappeared, vanished into thin air on our wedding day. No apology. No explanation. He just fucking flaked on the most important day of my life, and I don't have the right to wish him *dead*?"

Streams ran down Alana's cheeks. She turned to me, ashamed. "I'm sorry, Gwen. I'm just so sorry. I wish I could make it all go away. I can't imagine how you feel."

Of course, she can't. Ms. Perfect, living her perfect life. A fantastic husband, two beautiful kids, a house to die for, and a Caspian blue convertible. She doesn't have a clue how I feel—not a fucking clue.

"I'm dying. I'm dying right now. Can't you see what he's done to me? What he's doing? Why should he live out his years? Why does he deserve a chance at a full life? The *shit*. The heart wants what the heart wants, and right now, it wants to hate Nas's guts and plan his demise."

"Revenge, yes. Watching him eat his guts out when a better man falls in love with you. That's what you mean, right?"

"Yeah, right." *Whatever*. She just doesn't get it. I really do want him dead.

I hadn't eaten all day, not because I'm anorexic but because a bride sporting a paunch in a satin wedding dress is revolting. Suddenly, my generally contented stomach growled. "Say, did anyone think to take home the damn wedding cake?"

Chapter Five

Gwen Winter

Walking through the front door, Mom and Dad's place smelled like a bakery, the air heavy with wonderfully evocative aromas, the smell of love and fond memories. One day, I'd have a home steeped with that kind of charm, welcoming and warm. A home as comforting as a bed piled high with fluffy pillows.

I knew exactly what Mom was up to: rugelach, not just rugelach but chocolate rugelach, an enchanted confection made from chocolate and sugar, butter, flour, and sour cream. Washed down with a nice pinot noir, a girl would most definitely opt for a plateful of these bite-sized morsels over sex. Sometimes (as in my life before Nas), I didn't have a choice. They were what I settled for when I didn't have a man in my life. Cakes and blintzes and dumplings and soup—it was the craft my mom practiced to keep me going, one recipe at a time. "Sweets to sweeten your mood," she would say. The recipes had been handed down to her from her mother and grandmother and served much like a doctor's lexicon of prescription. She'd blend ingredients like an apothecary of yore, all the while singing a Yiddish lullaby her mother used to sing to her as a child. She told me the song was called "Raisins and Almonds," but she called it *Rozhinkes mit Mandlen.* The title was inconsequential. It was the spirituality of the melody that mattered. Presiding over the dough hook and mixing bowl, she'd add a pinch of this and a dash of that, measuring sugar in her cupped hands and seasoning until the mixture looked and smelled just right. She was conjuring the spirits of her ancestors' past, calling upon them for the strength to heal her daughter.

Mom must've paced the kitchen for hours before remembering what my life had been like before Nas and I met before her youngest daughter got her shit together and settled into a good place. She'd whip up her special concoctions when a megadose of Zoloft wouldn't cut the mustard, on the days when I'd look at a bottle of benzos and think, *Why the hell not?* I recalled how she would work her magic with her KitchenAid mixer and a rolling pin, flying around the kitchen like a whirling dervish, the air cloudy with blooms of flour and powdered sugar, her apron stained yellow from splattered egg yolks.

"Oh, thank God!" I saw her blast out of the kitchen like a rocket off the launch pad, far faster than I thought her legs could carry her. She'd traded her formal dress for jeans and a polo and had scrubbed the makeup from her face. She looked raw but focused, intent on working a fresh miracle. She engulfed me in her arms and lavished me with kisses while at the same time bathing me in tears. "You had us so worried. We didn't know where you were. I know what happened was terrible, but…" She clutched her heart. "*So* terrible, but honey, we're your family." I saw her attempt to choke back a fresh torrent of tears but was unable to control the swell. "We're here for you. Always. How could you just disappear on us like that?"

Her question was redundant. No answer was required. None was supplied. Not that I could think of anything to say. We held onto each other, afraid to let go, each preventing the other from falling into the abyss. When she stepped away, I was struck by how much weight she had lost for the wedding, every bit of twenty pounds and maybe more. Her face had thinned. Her eyes were tear-filled. Even so, enshrouded by her freshly dyed locks, she looked absolutely stunning. What a pity, all that effort, wasted.

We slowly migrated into the kitchen. It was mom's pride and joy, top-of-the-line appliances, quartz countertops, and enough workspace to prepare mess for an army battalion. The house was less than twenty years old and built in the contemporary era with a great room that encompassed the kitchen and family room. It was a living space the builder had called a super room, and it was a spacious area where the family had made memories—great meals, family gatherings, and life-changing moments. Standing in front of the fridge, I could see all the way to the patio doors at the back of the house.

Alana walked into the house a few minutes later and walked straight over to the fridge. My best guess was that she'd called Jack before coming inside and stole a minute or two to decompress, maybe even snuck a cigarette from the pack I knew she kept stashed in the Volvo. She cracked a beer, then sank into a chair and put up her feet. The long drive home from upstate was the cathartic equivalent of surviving a grenade blast. She was alive but wounded, in need of life support. I could see her skin blistering and disintegrating before my eyes. Looking as if she only had scant moments left to live, she gulped the beer like a longshoreman after a day of unloading barges. She couldn't have appeared more hopeless—my sister, the Chanel queen, let out a rafter-shaking belch.

"Manors, sweetheart," Mom said. "My goodness, is this how you were raised?" She turned to me, her eyes rolling like twin moons in orbit around Saturn.

Alana torched her with a scowl, her middle fingers twitching, dying to fire off a bird, *Don't fuck with me, Mom. You didn't spend the last two hours trapped in the car, having your guts torn out by that lunatic.*

Mom placed her hands on my shoulders, her face just inches from mine. "Honey, did you find out anything from Nas's sister? Did she tell you anything that might be helpful?"

A twelve-gauge might help. A garrote around Nas's neck might help. The piddling drivel I got from Jana didn't help; not an iota. The little she'd said provided more questions than answers. "No, Mommy, she didn't help. She's got no more idea what happened to Nas than any of us. It was a dead end. She said something ridiculous about me not being me."

Mom flinched. "What? What does that even mean? Of course, you're you. Who else are you?" She shook her head sadly. "I don't totally understand what happened to her, but..." The words were like sour milk in her mouth. "She's a sick girl, honey, a very sick girl. She obviously didn't know what she was saying."

"Yeah, but I was hoping—"

"I'm so sorry, sweetie. I understand. You want a reason—a compelling one. How could he do this to you? I just don't know." She sighed, long and slow, fresh tears emerging. "Come—I'm ready to take the rugelach out of the oven. I'll put on a pot of coffee, and we'll talk. Everything is better with sweets."

She was an intelligent woman. No way in hell did she believe pastry could heal such a raw and gaping wound. But what could she say? We were all at a loss. Loving, sweet, attentive Nas had done the unthinkable. No apology. No explanation. No nothing. "How are you fixed for wine?" I asked.

"Yes, please," Alana said with verve. "I'll take a double, a triple if you've got a giant-size glass."

"Yes, we have wine," Mom said. "Your father stocked up in case someone wanted to stop by after the reception. Are you sure alcohol is a good idea, sweetheart? Gwen, I don't want it to screw up your meds?"

"Are you kidding? I'll turn into a freakin' raving psycho if I don't get a glass of vino immediately." Worry was all my family knew how to do. It didn't take much to put their youngest daughter over the edge. The three of them were always on guard, listening for the snap of the twig.

I heard a chomp, then again, a moment later—another chomp, then another and yet more. I recognized the sound of the rapid-fire cracks—my dad was out back splitting logs, not just splitting them but annihilating them, turning them into toothpicks. *CRACK-CRACK-CRACK*. It sounded like mortars landing on Omaha Beach in those World War II movies he watched. "Is that Dad?"

Mom nodded, a sad nod that expressed her and my father's collective pain.

"He sounds pretty pent up," Alana said. "Look at the bright side—you'll be warm and toasty all winter long."

Mom shrugged apologetically. "He'll come in when he's tired."

"Hope he's got a big stack out there," I said. I'd split logs; attempted to is more like it. Unless I hit the log just right, the ax would bounce off the timber, leaving a shallow groove in the pulp. I was not what one might call hearty stock. My dad, on the other hand, was robust, a he-man Jew, a take-the-bull-by-the-horns kind of man. He was splitting wood instead of breaking heads, which is what I knew he'd prefer to be doing, Nas's, his parents, and their whole damn race.

"Better he stays outside for now," Mom said. Translation: better we stay out of his way. "He won't come in until he doesn't have the strength to stand up."

Alana followed us into the kitchen and immediately began opening and slamming cabinets in hot pursuit of the wine stash.

"This is so unlike you, Alana." Mom was right. Big sis was normally cool, calm, and collected, the embodiment of restraint, the everything-in-the-proper-time girl. Rattled Alana was diametrically different from Poised Alana. Mom didn't know how to react to her. Whatever was bubbling under the surface had thickened and burned on the bottom of the pan. "What's gotten into her?" Mom asked, whispering aside.

"Me," I volunteered. "I dumped all my angst on her on the ride home—I wore her down to a nub."

"Where the hell is the wine?" Alana barked. Wow, she was frazzled. "It's like you're safeguarding the family fortune."

Mom pointed to an overhead cabinet. "There, above the range—where we always keep the wine."

"Since when?"

"Since always."

"Not when I was living here."

"You moved out several years ago, Alana. We're allowed to change a few things," Mom said, allowing a bit of frayed nerves to come up for air. Good for her, how could anyone expect her to keep her cool at a time like this. She was the mother of the bride and should've been dancing the hora, glowing with pride, beaming happiness for marrying off her youngest daughter. Instead, she was slaving over a hot oven, perspiration dripping as she removed baked goods from the oven.

Alana tore open the cabinet with such force that a hinge snapped. "*Shit.*"

She moved aside bottles of sweet kosher wine until she found something potable that wouldn't send you into hyperglycemic shock. She rescued a bottle of red something but was unable to close the newly inoperative door. She gritted her teeth. "Dad's going to freak. Motherfucker."

Mom covered her ears. "Honestly, Alana, such language. Especially today." She slid her confections onto a cooling rack. "Just forget about it. It'll give your father something to do. Retirement is the worst thing that ever happened to him. He's always on the computer searching for things to get aggravated about, politics, discrimination, sexuality—he has zero tolerance for the modern world."

"Can you blame him?" I said. "After today? Everything he was worried about, everything he warned me about, came true in one fell swoop. But would I listen? No. I told myself that Nas was different. Nas was good. I said, 'You don't know him the way I do. He'd never hurt me.' Well, guess what?"

"Better Dad's outside taking his frustration out on that lumber than in here gloating about being right," Alana said. "He'd be insufferable."

"Your father would never do that, sweetheart," Mom said.

Mom was right. He wouldn't, not to my face, of course. He was a tough-fucking egg, but he wasn't one to gloat. A true soldier knows there's no true victory in tragedy. But Mom must've gotten an earful after Nas performed his vanishing act. He must've erupted with the force of a hydrogen bomb, decimating everyone within a ten-mile range. Not that he'd blame my mom in particular, but everyone was at fault at a time like this. The wood chopping had grown louder, sounding more like the strikes of a piledriver ramming steel beams into the earth. "I wouldn't be surprised if he's deforested the entire greenbelt."

Mom grabbed wine glasses from the cabinet, not the good gold-plated ones but the throwaways they give you with a bottle of overpriced swill at one of the local North Shore Long Island wineries. She never used the good ones. Those were meant to be handed down from generation to generation, untouched, unused, without so much as a fingerprint to mar the perfect finish. When and if *my* turn came around, I planned to put them in a hundred-year time capsule and save future generations the trouble of storing the family heirlooms.

Alana handed me a glass of wine. It was stenciled with the name of some pigswill-peddling vineyard. "Bottoms up," she said and immediately put the glass to her lips. "I'd better call Jack and see how he and the kids are doing."

There was no way she hadn't made that call before coming into the house. She was laying the foundation for her escape. Jack didn't need help. Jack was the best, a man of boundless patience and energy. He'd exhaust the kids by doing arts and crafts, playing hide and seek, then running around with them in the yard. He'd have them tucked in and fast asleep long before Alana got home, a sumptuous beef Wellington plated and steaming hot as she walked through the front door. Nonetheless, the I've-got-to-get-the-hell-out-of-here excuse was coming, something like little Madi got a bug bite or Sofia bumped her shin, tragedies only their mommy could fix. It was okay. Really, it was. Big sis was so good to me, not just now but always. She deserved a reprieve and the embrace of Jack's brawny arms. I'd allow her to flee without guilt. It was the least I could do. She didn't know why Nas bolted any more than I did. We could talk about it until the cows came home without getting anywhere. We could vent and fume and do whatever women need to do to deal with the biggest crisis imaginable. But after all the venom had been spewed, we'd be in the same exact place, spinning our wheels, wishing Nas dead, and still not knowing what the fuck happened.

Alana's wine glass was already empty. She wrangled the last trickle from the bottle. "I don't feel anything," she said. "Do we have any Jack in the house?"

I was sloshing wine on my tongue, hoping to absorb alcohol directly into my bloodstream, when Alana suggested a more efficient remedy. I was the offended party, and it made sense that I should have the honor of being the first one to get hammered. "Can we focus, people? Anyone interested in what happened to me today? Remember me, the bride that never was? The girl who waited a lifetime for Mr. Right and got dumped on her wedding day?"

Mom's hands trembled, and she squeezed her fingers into tight, white-knuckled fists, trying to make them stop shaking. "I'm so sorry, my sweet little girl. How selfish of us. Of course, let's talk."

"Thank you," I said gratuitously. We looked from one to the other, but no one knew how to broach the conversation. That's when the door flew open and smashed into the wall.

Dad was standing in the doorway, dirty, his shirt soaked with sweat, his chest heaving as he sucked in immense volumes of air. Ax in hand, he was the death dealer risen from the depths of hell to meter out punishment until his thirst for blood had been quenched.

He was exactly what I needed: someone to put an end to our ineffectual wheel spinning, capable of acting decisively. Gripping the ax, he raised it over his head and searched the room, looking as if he needed to impale it in the wall. "You're here," he said. "*Good*. Let's go find that no good slimy son of a bitch and give him what for!"

Chapter Six

Nasir Zia – The Night Of

Neither of them knew what to do.

Or how to act.

They were utter strangers.

Newlyweds—Nasir and his bride.

Nas had often envisioned his wedding night with Gwen, a dimly lit suite in a tropical resort, and clothes that had been cast across the floor in the heat of passion, one large swelling beneath the sheets, two bodies joined together, body and soul with no need for anything from the external world save air to breathe. He imagined a bedroom suite with a high, vaulted ceiling and a ceiling fan with woven bamboo blades making lazy circles above them. Never leaving the room, their suitcases would remain unpacked as they lusted and fucked, his hunger and her thirst equally unquenchable. Inexhaustible. Their fires burning. Incendiary.

It was such a pity—the simple thought of being alone with his love and what should've been aroused him.

Instead, he sat clothed on the edge of the bed, watching the news without looking at his new wife. He should've been burning but could scarcely find enough air to breathe, let alone ignite a fire. There'd be an overabundance of television watching in the newlyweds' future, far more than natural for a newly married couple. At least for now, it was as if each occupied a separate alternate universe, side by side but completely unaware of the other's mind, what they were thinking and feeling, their needs and wants. Of course, each suspected. Each knew but was too afraid to talk about it, to admit the vulgar contract they'd both signed, the bargain they'd entered into.

Room service was delivered. Polished steel covers over commercial china masked dinners neither of them had the appetite to consume. Embarrassed to be seen, she ran into the bathroom when the waiter knocked on the door. Nas avoided eye contact with the waiter as well as the serving cart was rolled into the room. He tipped generously before closing the door, sealing himself and his bride safely inside, safe from the outside world, prying eyes and ears, a practice they'd need to master, a practice that would, unfortunately, become routine.

"He's gone," Nas said, calling out to her. "Come. Have something to eat while it's hot."

She was still in the linen suit she wore when they stood before the officiant at the city clerk's office. Nas knew damn well it was not how she had imagined her wedding ceremony would be or had dreamed of. It certainly wasn't the wedding night she'd waited a lifetime to arrive, not a single moment of it.

"I...I don't think I can," she said, treading lightly. An Arab bride refusing her husband anything on the wedding night was unheard of, a sin against God.

He lifted the cover from one of the plates, allowing the aroma of the succulent dish to waft into the air. He imagined it was well prepared and tasty, but it was not what either of them would've ordered if given choices they were more accustomed to—the juices that should've begun to flow didn't. Couldn't. How could they? The woman in the room with him, his bride, was a stranger, a person he knew almost nothing about.

And she wasn't Gwen.

She wasn't the woman he loved. She wasn't Gwen. He closed his eyes and asked God why he'd been put in this position, this untenable situation he nor anyone else deserved. He wondered what had happened to his one and true fiancée, in the moment when she realized he wasn't going to show, that the wedding she'd dreamed of wasn't going to take place. He imagined the misery she must've felt, is feeling, and would long suffer. He sensed his guts shriveling, kinking, and knotting. How could he eat, now or ever? Was there any way he could ever make this right to the woman he'd promised his love and the woman he had taken for his wife?

"At least taste the food," he said. "You need a little nourishment, okay?"

"I'll try," she said, her expression flat as she pulled out a chair and sat down at the small table in their hotel suite.

The corners of his mouth rose halfheartedly as he sat down, facing her. It wasn't much, but he could see that she was trying. All things considered, it was as much as he had the right to ask. Neither wanted to be there, be together, married under such unnatural circumstances, but there they were, dealing with the travesty as best they could.

His appetite was less than hearty, but he tried to consume some of the food in front of him.

Studying her eyes, Nas attempted to read her mind and felt that she'd decided to match the effort she made. He took a step forward. *Do the best you can*, he told himself. *Be strong. Do what you've been asked to do. What's been ordained. Do what you must.* "It's not bad, right?" he said as he looked up and saw her picking up a vegetable with her fork. *Small talk. Better than no talk*, he thought, "It's not delicious maqlouba, but I've had less appetizing meals."

Her eyes rose to meet his, not commenting but acknowledging. Connecting, the mere suggestions seemed eons away.

Keep it going, he thought. *I destroyed the woman I love—don't make a mess of this too. Whatever it takes. Make it work. It has to work. It has to.*

He touched her hand lightly, and she flinched but didn't pull away, her eyes blazing into his, imploring, *What is this? What are we doing?* Contact lasted only a few seconds before he took his hand away, but he felt the brief gesture had done some good.

He spoke with his eyes, "We're together now. Neither of us wanted this, but we're here, husband and wife. With God's help, we'll make a life together."

It was the first moment of truth they shared. All that had come before was a lie, a deadly abyss they would stay clear of as if their lives depended on it. Because it did.

Chapter Seven

Gwen Winter

I watched grime and wood splinters mix with soap and water and run off my father's hands and arms into the kitchen sink.

"Not where we prepare food. There's a bathroom for that," my mother said. "You're filthy, Hank."

He shot her a scowl, a how-fucking-dare-you? scowl. How could his washing up in the kitchen sink hold any significance? How could anything? Soiling the kitchen sink with his sweat and filth was meaningless. Nothing mattered to him except wringing Nas's neck, squeezing it in his oversized hands until Nas's eyes bulged from the sockets and he told us something that mattered: the absolute-fucking-truth. This is the reason I made fools of you and your daughter—made fools of you and your entire Hebrew tribe. All the wood Dad chopped, the logs he pulverized, it was nothing. His ire was not nearly spent, not even close. With each swing of the ax, he was hobbling Nas, breaking bones and severing limbs. The flying wood chips was Nas's splattering blood.

He grabbed a dish towel and sandpapered his arms dry, removing equal parts of moisture and skin. Ripping open the pantry door, he twisted the top off a jar of cashews and shook a mound into his open palm, before rapidly firing them into his gaping mouth. "Call Muhammad and Amira. Let's sit down and find out what the hell happened to their son."

Mom seemed overwhelmed by the request, but then, overwhelmed was the order of the day. "Hank, they were as stunned as we were, taken completely by surprise. Did you see the look on Amira's face? She was looking for a hole to crawl into. She couldn't even look me in the eye."

"Actors, both of them," he said.

I shook my head in disbelief. *Sure, Dad, not an honest bone between them. Such cynicism.*

"There are no surprises with those people. That's the way Muslims operate—everything is cleared through the head of the family, through Muhammad. If you think otherwise, you're naïve. Nas would take his own life before he dishonored his father. Trust me, Muhammad is complicit. Amira, too."

"There he goes again," Alana said, her eyes rolling like a pair of golf balls circling cups side-by-side. "Do you think for two minutes you could separate my sister's wedding from the Middle East war? My God, Dad, you've been like this since the day Gwen first brought him home. Racist much?"

"I'm not a racist," he fired back. "I'm a realist." He snatched the wine bottle off the table just as Alana was reaching for it. "I think you've had enough."

"I'm thirty years old, married with two kids. Don't you dare tell me when I've had enough."

"Then drive home and drink yourself sick," he said. "That is, if you're sober enough to get behind the wheel."

"And there it is," Alana said. "It's all about you, isn't it, Dad? You've got to prove that you've been right all along, that a Jew and an Arab can't work. Well, I've got news for you. Gwen and Nas worked. They worked *great*, as well as any couple I know."

"Not today, they didn't," he said as he turned to my mother. "Please. Could you get them on the phone? Tell them we just want to talk—sit down at the table like civilized people. Believe me, I'd be delighted to have them prove me wrong."

"They'll never agree to it," Mom said. "They were mortified."

"I just want to talk," he said. "I'm not going in, guns hot. Maybe they've heard something. Maybe they suspected something was wrong. Or maybe, just maybe, I'm right, and they knew this was going to happen all along." He put his arms around me and kissed me on the head. "Look, I love you, kiddo. You and your ballbuster sister are the air I breathe. I'm the first to admit I can be like a bull in a china shop, but it's only because I want the best for the two of you. Nothing comes from nothing. If we don't put our heads together, the Winters and the Zias… All I'm saying is that talking together is the best thing we can do right now."

"Gwen, you want to weigh in here," Alana said, "or would you prefer Dad lay siege to their home and carry out a gratuitous waterboarding?" Alana had a name for Dad when he lost his temper, one she never said out loud, but I'd heard it time and time again, "Nuclear Winter."

"Hank, maybe Alana is right," Mom said. "Can't we sleep on it? Cooler heads, you know?"

Eyes closed, he shook his head, disappointment like sweat spraying in all directions. He looked like Vesuvius on the precipice of incinerating Pompeii. "Do you see us sleeping soundly tonight, do you? You see any of us sleeping at all? Should we bury our heads in the sand like cowards and wait for the answer to materialize out of thin air? Is that better, Carol? Is it? Is that what you honestly believe?"

He was right. We had to do something. Quarantined, we'd be at each other's throats, duking it out all night long. What happened? Why'd it happen? Jews and Arabs—they emerged from the womb holding daggers to each other's throats. Nas and I thought we were above it all, beyond it all. What place did a barbaric feud have in our lives, the lives of two people who were so much in love? We could overcome it. We could overcome anything. My head dropped. Who am I kidding? We couldn't even make it to the altar. "He's right," I said. "Call them. I need some answers, and I'm not getting any sitting in your kitchen wolfing down pastries."

Chapter Eight

Gwen Winter

Mom continued to stare at her phone moments after she'd disconnected. I suppose trepidation over delivering bad news kept her from making eye contact with Dad. "Hank, they're not home. They weren't home an hour ago, they weren't home thirty minutes ago, and they're not home now," Mom said as she put the phone down on the kitchen table.

"Try again," Dad said. "Leave another message."

"There's no point, Hank. I've been trying for hours. They'll call back after they've listened to their messages."

"And their cellphones?"

"Just like their home phone—straight to voicemail. They probably turned them off. I can't say I'm surprised. *My* mailbox is full, and I'm not planning to get back to anyone for at least six months. If ever."

I'd only been thinking of myself, but the embarrassment and abject humiliation must've been killing my mom as well. I couldn't imagine what everyone was saying. My parents had spent their lives sheltering me from the judgmental, from the prying gossip mongers. "How's Gwen feeling?" "Is she seeing anyone? Anything serious?" "She's home, right? She's not back in the hospital, is she?" Hank and Carol Winter were modest, private people. They had to be. My issues had made them guarded and forced them to shun the outside world to protect the family. Then, finally, when there was a glimmer of hope, a long-awaited chance for them to hold their heads up high, that son of a bitch, Nas—he destroyed the three of us. Mom and Dad were hemorrhaging as badly as I was, bleeding out.

"Do you believe this shit?" Dad abruptly clutched his stomach and gritted his teeth.

"Are you all right, Dad?" I asked.

"No, he's not all right." Mom lifted a cardboard container of cashews and shook it. "*Empty*. Hank, with all we've been through today, do you want to make a trip to the emergency room?" She shook her head. "He's got another kidney stone, Gwen. The doctor warned him, but did he listen? No, of course not."

"Oh no, not again."

"Yes, again. He's been hiding it because he didn't want anything to ruin your big day, but—"

"I guess that point is moot. *Anyway*, what's a kidney stone got to do with eating nuts?"

"The doctor specifically told him to avoid cashews, but he can't help himself. Now look at him—he looks like he's in the throes of childbirth. Can I bring you some Tylenol?"

His demeanor said, "I'm too tough to ask for help," but his response betrayed him. "Sure."

Mom was positive that he was suffering with a stone, but my money was on aggravation as the leading cause of his misery, or maybe a combination of the two. His face was beet red, his systolic blood pressure doubtlessly rocketing toward two hundred. "*Dad*, you need to calm the fuck down. I can't handle this on top of everything else."

"What would you like him to do, Gwen? You think he brought this on himself?"

Good thing we'd sent Alana packing. She and Dad shared a metaphysical connection, a virtual umbilicus that connected one with the other's pain. He got the flu—she ran a temperature. She stubbed her toe—he developed a limp. It was positively comical. Could you just imagine the two of them side-by-side, writhing and miserable? "Please, Dad, go lie down. Take a laxative or whatever you need to make yourself right."

He flopped down in a chair, clutching his gut. "Sorry, sweetheart, I'll be okay. It's been a lousy, rotten day."

"Ya think?" My relentlessly exasperating Apple Watch lit up and told me to breathe. The meddlesome timepiece was always sticking its two cents where it wasn't wanted. Stand—move—close a ring—you're usually further ahead by now—what asshole engineer designed provocation into the program? More to the point, why? All I need is the time of day and my dang messages. "Shit, it's almost eight-thirty. The Zias are in bed by ten most nights."

"This isn't most nights," Mom said.

Dad forced himself to rally. He didn't look robust, but it seemed he'd pulled that phrased one leg out of the grave. "That's my girl. I'll get my car keys. Those cowardly Zias aren't going to pull a bin Laden on us."

"What the hell are you talking about, Hank? Have you lost your mind?" Mom said.

"They're hiding, damn it," he said. "Like that piece of shit Osama bin Laden in the caves at Tora Bora. That's what they do."

"That's what, who does, Dad? Don't get started, painting everyone with your broad brush."

"Really, Gwen, you're defending them? After today? After what they did to you? To our entire family?"

"Not they, *him*. What Nas did has nothing to do with his family or any other observing Muslim on the planet."

"You believe what you want to believe. But me? No way. These people created the art of lying. It's in their DNA."

"*Ugh*." I raised an open hand, blocking any further assault. "Dad, I love you, but I can't take you right now."

"Let them prove me wrong. I'm not afraid to knock on their door." He stood and grabbed his car keys off the kitchen counter. "I'm not waiting around for an invitation. Anyone coming?"

Of course, I am. Complicit or not, they owed me a healthy dose of straight talk. Did they suspect? Did they know where he was? Why he did it? They owed me that much, at least. They'd always been nice, much nicer to me than Dad was to Nas. As angry as I was, I knew someone had to act as a buffer between Dad and the Zias if there was any hope of figuring things out. *Don't be stupid, Gwen. You and Nas, that's a pipe dream. The lava is out of the volcano, and there's no putting it back. The two of you are finished.* The explanation I wanted was about closure, not reconciliation. This was about confronting the man and clawing at his throat, tearing the truth from his diseased heart and stomping him to the ground. Accepting that sad truth made me feel a smidge better. I grabbed my bag and led the way out the front door.

Chapter Nine

Gwen Winter

Sitting behind the wheel of the SUV, Dad cocked and inclined his head every which way imaginable as if the correct angle would bring his Superman vision online. We were still a fair distance from the Zia's home—it was around a sweeping bend in the road. "The lights are on," he boomed. "I can see them from here."

I wanted to say that he was full of shit, that he couldn't possibly see anything from where we were, several houses away and around a curve. But as we drove closer, I could see that he was right. The Zias lights were on, not all of them, but the ones I knew they usually kept on. Their den and kitchen were located at the rear on the first level. From the front, it always looked as if no one was home, but the back of the house was usually illuminated at night, with light spilling through the patio doors into the backyard. Were they alone, or was Nas in there with them, squirreled away like a worm-ridden piece of fruit? Were they hiding their precious son, the one I loved? Still loved? Had loved? The one who came out of nowhere and T-boned me broadside while I was aloft on a cloud of ethereal ecstasy? I didn't have a clue, not a fucking clue. Nas had never shown a hint of reticence. Not a shred. Not an iota. It was as if I'd purposely been set up for the kill.

The exterior of their home was pristine, as if it was a shrine or something, immaculately groomed, freshly painted, and power washed, the windows crystal clear. Not so much as a long blade of grass protruding from the lawn. Not a weed. No chipped paint. Not even a damn spider web.

Dad hated having to take off his shoes when he entered the Zia mausoleum. But who can argue with the results? That oak floor was polished like glass, no dust or pet hair, nothing, not a smudge or a streak, not so much as an errant sesame seed lodged beneath the corner kitchen cabinet. It was as if Amira Zia spent her day hovering above the floor on a flying carpet, sucking up nanoparticles with her Dyson cordless. It was as if the entire house had been scoured, then hermetically sealed.

We parked a few houses away, then stole down the block like tiptoeing ninjas, masking any sounds of approach. There'd be no warning the Zias. No time for them to switch off the lights, hunker down, and remain silent until they felt certain we were gone.

Dad had never and would never forsake his military training. The lessons he'd learned were indelibly etched in his gray matter, *always cover the back of the house.* He stood off to the side, watching the backyard lights as he signaled for me to ring the bell. He didn't expect them to run, only to hide. It was a quiet evening, no one was out for a stroll or walking a dog, no teenagers blasting music on their car radios. In the absence of ambient noise, the sound of the door chime could be heard clearly, reverberating from inside their house. Dad was still waiting for the rear lights to go off when the foyer lights came on in the house. I heard the clack of the deadbolt, and the door opened—the air from within hit my nostrils. Like everything in that house, it was magnificent, cool and dry, sweet with an exotic essence I could never put my finger on, perhaps wild jasmine or bergamot. It tantalized the nose like a fine perfume.

Muhammad Zia's cheeks were wet with tears as he reached out and put his arms around me. I heard him struggling to clear his throat, but he remained silent for a long moment. He finally managed, *"Fadat besham."* I'd heard those words only once before, the day Nas proposed to me, a term of endearment that meant, "I am willing to sacrifice myself for you." He pressed me in his arms, squeezing me as if he were trying to drive out my pain. I'd believed Nas when he uttered those words. Even now, I wanted to believe Muhammad. I wanted to be able to forgive and move on. I wanted to rewind the clock to early this morning when the entire day and all it promised was still in front of me.

Now, there was only darkness except for the sconce lights bordering the front door and the impeccable aura projecting out into the evening. Amira appeared behind her husband; her head shrouded in a scarf, her eyes cast downward. The floor was not far away—she was petite, perhaps five-foot-two in her stocking feet. Was she embarrassed, or had she noticed a speck of soot lodged on the threshold? Impossible—it must've been a shadow or a floater drifting across her field of vision. "Please," she began meekly, "come inside." She scanned the street in all directions. Surely, the neighbors had heard that their son had disgraced the family. Quickly, come inside before we're forced to endure even greater shame.

Muhammad loosened his grip, allowing me to walk inside. Mom followed, as did Dad. He didn't take off his shoes.

Chapter Ten

Gwen Winter

The silence was devastating; the extended breaks in conversation ate at my heart, pauses instead of words, and silence in place of honest talk. The Zias had always been, for lack of a better word, chatty, especially Amira. She'd never been one to sit out a conversation, her lyrical voice and point of view ever-present. She always had something to say, whether or not it was relevant. And long-winded…? She brought a new dimension to the word interminable.

Dear God, I wish they would say something, anything. Actually, no I didn't. The hemming and hawing, the shrugging shoulders, and averted eyes, the shame they were trying to bear up against. It was more than I could handle. Did they know nothing? Nothing at all? How was it possible? They were so close with their son—their family was so tightly knit.

It was my wedding night. We should've been celebrating until we were unable to stand, laughing and dancing, giddy with happiness. Instead, we were sitting on our hands, the conversation strained, more than strained, retched, miserable. Guilt and contempt ebbed and flowed, drowning us mercilessly.

"I'm so sorry," Amira began, "that we didn't answer your calls, but we didn't know what to say to you."

"We wanted to," Muhammad said. "Please believe we wanted to—with all our hearts, we did. If only we had something to tell you, anything to lessen your burden, dear girl."

Dad was on his feet, pacing, too wound up to even think about sitting. He wrung his hands and scowled at Muhammad. "So, you're telling us he ran? He shit the bed and ran off like a coward?"

Muhammad raised his hands as if to cover his ears. "Please, Hank, the language, not in our home."

"Ah shit, Muhammad, aren't we past that? Your son abandoned our little girl on her wedding day. He made fools of all of us. You didn't have a clue?"

"Please, Mr. Winter," Amira said. "My husband already told you we don't like that kind of talk in our house. We're very devout people."

"You don't like what I'm saying?" Dad's eyes cut from one to the other. "You should only know what I'm thinking."

"Alright, Hank, calm yourself," Mom said. "You're not helping the situation."

"I'd like to know how I'm hurting anything?" Dad said, then swung his gaze at Amira. "Nothing, Amira? I could understand Muhammad not picking up on subtle clues—he's got a demanding job. But you? His mother? You had no idea that something was wrong? Nothing whatsoever?"

"Nothing. I swear," she said, tears streaming down her cheeks. "He was looking forward to his wedding day with every ounce of his heart. I can't tell you how much he wanted to marry your daughter." She sniffled, then turned toward me. "Gwen, you believe me, don't you? You must know how Nasir felt about you."

I thought I did. I thought I was sure. Of all the people I'd known, I never suspected that Nas would be the one to let me down. I turned my head, then stood and sidestepped past Amira. "I should've seen it coming." There was never going to be a Jack in my life, a perfect man like Jack with his big brown eyes and his perfectly imperfect finger-combed hair. I thought I'd found someone like him in Nas, but I was wrong. "Happiness is not in the cards for me. Never was. I guess I only saw what I wanted to."

"Oh, honey, please don't say that," Mom said, her voice quivering as she stood and put her arms around me, her eyes cutting into Amira, *Your son, how could he? Look what he's done to our daughter.*

"Let me put up a pot of tea." Amira hurried toward the kitchen, escaping.

Standing shoulder to shoulder, I was sandwiched in between my parents, the three of us cutting into Muhammad with our eyes.

"Jana didn't know anything either," I said. "Nas and Jana share their most intimate details, but I went to see her, and she acted as if she didn't know who I was."

Muhammad seemed to question what he'd heard. He spoke softly. "You did what? You spoke to our Jana?"

"That's right, the minute it was clear that Nas wasn't going to show. I hopped into an Uber and went to see her."

He seemed to question what he'd heard. "You-you went to see my daughter?" And then it sank in. "That's terrible. You're a terrible person," he said. "My daughter is not well. You went to see her in the psychiatric hospital?" He was now on his feet, running his hands along the sides of his head, aghast. "How could you drag my daughter into this? She's sick, very sick. She didn't have the strength to attend her beloved brother's wedding. Do you know how that killed her, that she couldn't be with her brother on his wedding day? How could you put this on her?"

"I wasn't with him on his wedding day either, Mohammad. I think the circumstances were a little worse for me. Wouldn't you say?"

"Now, just a minute," Dad said. "Don't get up on your high horse, Muhammad. My daughter is the injured party in this nightmare. Why don't you just calm the fuck down and appreciate this calamity from Gwen's perspective."

"I think you should leave." Turning toward the kitchen, he yelled, "Amira, they're going."

"Just who the hell do you think you are?" Dad said. The words "Sand monkey" slipping past his lips.

"I think it's time to go," Mom said as she pulled me by the arm.

"Fine, we're leaving," Dad said. "Your son and your whole damn family are dead to us."

"Oh no. Oh no," Amira said, racing into the room, agitated and frantic. "We're so sorry. So very sorry about all of this. Muhammad, please tell them how sorry you are."

I could see that Mohammad was seething and that his sentiment didn't mirror his wife's. Dad flung the door wide, and we went outside under the darkened sky. It was as silent as silence could be when a caustic word sliced through us, "*Sharmoota.*" It had come from Muhammad's mouth, not hitting our ears until it had ricocheted off every wall in the house.

"The hell did he say?" My dad was stunned and puzzled at the same time.

Sharmoota, I wondered what the word meant when Dad grabbed my arm and jerked me away.

Chapter Eleven

Nasir Zia

Nas was awake but not aroused. Nothing stirred in him save anxiety as the first splinters of morning light pried his eyelids apart. Through the narrow slits in the blinds, he could see the sky was just brightening—the clouds were stained fuchsia by the early rays of morning.

He was aware of his helter-skelter position on the pullout sofa in his hotel suite. His arms and legs were askew, his neck cocked at an angle, and the blanket mostly on the floor. He'd slept alone, not because his new bride had insisted on it but because he felt it was the right thing to do. He felt it was too soon for him to ask anything of her, least of all her body, though she would've been compelled to give it to him had he wanted it.

Getting in touch with his senses, he realized how quiet it was in the suite, dead silence except for the hum of the mini-bar refrigerator.

She's still sleeping, he reasoned. That's good.

Was she sleeping soundly? Was the quality of her rest what he was concerned with, or was it merely expedient that she wasn't yet about? The later they slept, the shorter the day, less time together, and less time for idle conversation. Fewer awkward moments. Less time wondering what the future held in store for them.

He dreaded seeing her for that first uncomfortable morning moment, shared fleeting eye contact before turning their heads. Who is this stranger in my room? *Will I always feel like this?*

"You know the drill. One day at a time, Nasir," he whispered. "Take a deep breath and put one foot in front of the other." He scrolled to the notes section on his phone and reviewed their itinerary for the day. They had a two-hour drive ahead of them. *Very good—with breakfast and lunch, that's half a day gone, half a day less to feel miserable.* He couldn't help but wonder how he'd feel if he were with Gwen on their first morning together as man and wife; how wonderful and joyous it would've been. Should've been.

He ordered breakfast for two, pancakes, eggs, toast, and tea. He didn't know what she liked but would eat whatever she left over.

The room was still silent as he tiptoed into the bathroom to shower. He lathered his hair with shampoo, then rinsed. Watching the suds run down his chest, then over his legs and into the drain, he realized this would become his new morning ritual. The roar of the water would mask his weeping and camouflage his tears until they swirled with water and ran down the drain. He wasn't allowed to show weakness or speak of his misery. He was now the head of a family and needed to act like it. Never had he thought of showering as a guilty pleasure, but he was sure that's what it would become: a hideaway where he could wash away his pain, a place where he could indulge his vulnerability.

He approached the bedroom door after their breakfast had arrived. Hoping to steal a few extra minutes, he was still tentative about seeing her and starting the day. Having decided he wouldn't disturb her if she was still asleep, he twisted the doorknob without making a sound. The curtains covering the western-facing windows were opaque, the room dark. He felt mildly optimistic as he edged closer to the bed, hoping to hear her breathing softly, still asleep. In the dark, the contours of the blanket over her body seemed odd, random in an unnatural way. He had to come within a few feet of the bed before he realized her head wasn't resting on the pillow. He turned and was able to see directly into the adjoining bathroom. Like the bed, it too was empty.

Chapter Twelve

Nasir Zia

onit, the front desk clerk, fired a look-dagger at Nas the moment the elevator doors parted, a heat-seeker that hit him right between the eyes. It was as if his sonar had been pinging the position of Nas's head all the way down from the eleventh floor.

Attempting to step out of the elevator, Nas was jostled by a gargantuan man, a cigar-chomping freight train, impatient to board the elevator before it was vacated. When Nas looked up, the clerk was gone.

Nas scanned the lobby for Ronit but didn't see him anywhere. Then, the office door opened, and a female clerk tripped from a shove that sent her through the doorway. She scowled in the direction of the door closing behind her, then smoothed her blazer before stepping up to the desk.

Nas made straight for her.

She saw him coming and fidgeted, then began straightening brochures on the countertop. Turning toward the computer screen, she began clattering away at the keyboard, speaking without making eye contact. "Can I help you, sir?" she said, but the subtext read, *I know who you are and what you want. Please, leave me the hell alone.*

Studying her name tag, Nas altered the query he'd been rehearsing from the moment he last encountered Ronit. "Excuse me, Ms. Emily, I've been speaking with Ronit. Maybe he mentioned me."

She glanced at him, then quickly back at the screen. "Is this about your wife?" she asked. What she'd meant to say was, "Stop nagging us. I'm sure she's all right."

"Yes. She was gone when I woke up this morning. We're newly married, and I'm very worried about her."

Emily had just returned to work following a full-day employee refresher class on guest protocols. The new material was in the forefront of her mind as she conjured and put forth a heartwarming smile. "You're a *newlywed*? Isn't that just wonderful? How are you enjoying your stay with us so far?"

"Oh, it's very nice, but my wife… as I said, I can't find her. It's been too long already."

"I wouldn't worry. She's probably out looking for the perfect newlywed gift for you. There's a mall less than a mile from here, two major department stores, and at least three jewelry stores that I know of." Her eyes twinkled with the promise of an idea. "Two can play at that game. Am I right?" She slid a map in front of him, then circled the mall location with her pen. "We've got a shuttle leaving for the mall in—" She checked the time. "Less than ten minutes. Wouldn't that be great fun, having a gift to surprise her with when she surprises you? The shuttle leaves from the front—"

He rattled his head. "*No*, I don't think she's shopping."

"Well, sir, did you try calling her?"

"Yes, of course, I tried calling her. The calls went straight to voicemail."

"Maybe her battery died."

"No, I don't think so."

"It's your honeymoon," she said, with a happy lilt in her voice. "I wouldn't worry too much."

He wanted to say that she would never run off without telling him that she wasn't like that, but he couldn't. He didn't know. This wasn't Gwen—this wasn't the woman he knew everything about. His heart told him something was wrong. He crossed his arms and looked down his nose at her. "You're very rude, miss. I'm clearly worried, and you're trying to blow me off with some bullshit about wedding gifts."

Her chest froze in mid-breath. "Now, sir—"

"Now, sir, nothing. Admittedly, this is my third trip to the front desk this morning, but you can see I'm worried sick. Am I really asking so much that Ronit ran off and dumped me in your lap? Who's in charge of security? I want to speak to someone *right now*. Get someone now, or I'll call the police and make a stink."

"All right, sir. Please try to remain calm. I'll get the manager, okay?"

"Yes, *please*," he said insistently. "And don't keep me waiting. If anything happens to my wife, I'll hold you personally responsible."

"Yes, sir," she said as alarm bells rang in her head, then did an abrupt about-face, flying through the door and into the office she'd just emerged from.

Nas drummed his fingers on the counter, stopping when he heard Emily yelling at someone behind the closed door. The low-octave voice of a man responded in kind. The heavy sound-deadening door transmuted the argument into insensible whale-like moaning noises that were impossible to interpret.

Nas had grown impatient when the door opened, and Ronit stepped forward. Nas could've been looking in a mirror. The two men were exactly eye-to-eye in height. Ronit sported a similar manicured beard—their facial structures were so alike, Ronit could've passed for a brother.

"Hello again, sir," Ronit began sheepishly, "you asked to see the manager?"

Chapter Thirteen

Nasir Zia

Nas dashed into the hotel lobby, still frantic, his shirt soaked through with sweat. Desperation was etched on his face, bold as war paint, new creases gouging deeper with every beat of his pounding heart. He scanned the lobby. There was no sign of Ronit or his assistant. If Emily was smart, she'd resigned or put in for a transfer, taken the rest of the day off at minimum. There was no trace of his bride, not in the building or outside on the grounds. The hotel approach was a dedicated road off a local highway. There was little chance she'd walked off on her own.

Which meant what?

She called for a car? She left?

Or worse?

There was the possibility that she'd bolted, that she'd rebelled against what was asked of her. Nas had hoped she wouldn't, that she'd give them time and let the relationship take its course, that she'd give their fragile connection a small chance to cure and grow strong. It was the only chance they had.

He thought the hotel lobby looked trendy, dark walls with white accents, LED track lights, and a dark marble floor. The furniture was accented in lime green. He didn't like it and was put off by the putrid color combination. He wondered how any professional decorator could recommend it. He wondered who was at fault, the decorator with terrible taste or the project manager who signed off on the travesty.

A large pitcher of cucumber water sat on the lobby table next to a stack of small paper cups. He filled the cup and quickly drank it down. Then again and once more. He was still dry as a bone, his tongue pasted against the roof of his mouth. Nervousness was sucking all the moisture from him.

Plummeting into a lobby chair, he covered his eyes so that passersby wouldn't see his distress, but his body language was a giveaway and spoke volumes to one and all. And with the complimentary breakfast buffet about to close its doors, the dining area was under siege.

A girl of about five or so wearing a dip-dyed T-shirt stopped in front of him and took a bite of a breakfast bar.

A moment passed before he sensed her presence. Lifting his hand, he managed a weak smile. "Why hello there," he said, forcing himself to be amiable. "Are you enjoying that?"

She nodded matter-of-factly. "Uh-huh. We almost missed breakfast. I really wanted some bacon, but…" She took another bite of the bar and chewed, her cheeks bulging as she ground the dense snack between her teeth. "It was all gone. But I had French toast sticks instead, and my daddy said he was going to take a few more chewy bars in case I got hungry later. We had to sit at one of those tall skinny tables on account all the regular tables were taken. I had to sit on a stool with a puke-green seat. My daddy told me to wait here while he refills his coffee. My daddy was angry because Mommy didn't want to get out of bed. That's why we were so late and had to come down without her. Is that what happened to you? Did you miss breakfast all together?" the chatty child asked.

"No, I ate much earlier."

Her eyes lit up. "Did they still have bacon? I told my daddy we're gonna have to wake up earlier tomorrow."

The child's precocious banter forced Nas's mouth to curl upward at the corners. "I don't eat bacon, but I think your plan for tomorrow is a good one."

"What, you don't eat bacon?"

"It's against my dietary laws."

"What, they got laws about what you can eat? I know they got laws about stealing and doing bad things, but telling people what they can eat is crazy."

"There are all kinds of laws, little one."

"Mister, that's just plain old *weird*. I'd pitch a fit if I couldn't eat bacon. There was this girl in my pre-K class, and she didn't eat bacon either. She had blonde hair like me." She twisted one of her curly ringlets. "I figured she didn't eat bacon because she was 'lergic to it like my best friend Anya is 'lergic to peanut butter, but maybe she was just following one of those laws like you got. You think that could've been it?"

Nas shrugged. "I don't know. Maybe." He did his best to bear up, to remain pleasant to the little girl while his insides shriveled. *Why am I here,* he wondered, *here instead of with Gwen. How did this happen?*

A man in a sweatshirt strolled over, coffee cup to his lips. He looked tired, ragged, his red eyes sat atop dark, swollen bags. "Come on, Maggie," he said without making eye contact with Nas. There was no warmth in the tone of his voice, only impatience.

"Daddy," Maggie began, "this man doesn't eat bacon. He says it's against the law."

"That so?" He cut his eyes at Nas, giving him a quick once over, then took hold of his daughter's hand. "You know you're not supposed to talk to strangers. Maybe if your mother got her lazy butt out of bed when she was supposed to, we'd have had breakfast together like a family ought to."

"Dad-dy?"

"*What?*"

"My hands are sticky."

"Let's go. You can wash up in the room." He scowled at Nas before guiding Maggie toward the elevator. He tossed his coffee cup at the trash receptacle and missed. Still glaring at Nas, he muttered as the doors slid shut, "No good pube face. The hotel is crawling with them."

Nas shook his head angrily as the coffee cup rolled across the floor, weeping lightened coffee onto the dark stone. It certainly wasn't the first time someone had judged him on his appearance. It wouldn't be the last. At least *pube face* was semi-original. Most of the time, it was *towel head* or *camel jockey*. He was adept at turning the other cheek, but the words, *ignorant mother fucker* screamed in his head.

"Mr. Zia?"

Nas jumped at the sound of his name. The voice seemed somewhat familiar, but he was nonetheless taken by surprise.

"I'm sorry I startled you," Ronit said.

"That's okay," he said as he let out a deep breath and jumped to his feet. "You heard something about my wife?"

Ronit nodded and gestured for Nas to follow him. "Come with me, please."

Nas followed Ronit across the lobby. They walked past the reception counter and down a narrow corridor. He was dying to ask what Ronit found, if they'd found his wife. His chest felt empty, as if his heart had been surgically removed. *Give him a moment*, he thought. *You'll know soon enough.* At the very end of the corridor was a smoked glass door with the word *Private* stenciled on it.

Ronit twisted the doorknob and pushed the door open. Standing to the side, he allowed Nas to enter. Ronit didn't look happy, but he didn't seem to be alarmed.

Emily sat at a desk, one eye on a large computer monitor, the other on Nas.

"She has something to show you," Ronit said. "Can you please step around to the other side of the desk?"

Nas couldn't hold it in any longer. "What did you find?" he blurted, his voice harsh with worry.

Emily tapped on the upper right corner of the screen with her painted blue fingernail, indicating where the digital time was displayed: 07:22. The image of the lobby vestibule was on the screen. She tapped a key on the console, and the video advanced.

Nas stared at the screen, fearful of what he was going to see. The time counter advanced, fifteen seconds, then twenty. "What am I looking at?" he said. "Where is my wife?"

"Please give us a moment," Ronit said, looking at the screen over Nas's shoulder. "Any second now."

A dark figure moved quickly through the vestibule and out the front doors, a slender form in black running gear with the hood of a sweatshirt covering the head. Nas gasped as the figure turned to the left, poised to break into a run. A woman's face was visible in profile for a split second.

Emily tapped a key, freezing the frame. "Is that your wife?" she asked. "I've been watching the video over and over. That woman is the only one that fits the description you gave us. You can't see her well, but—"

Nas shuddered, then ran his hands through his black hair.

"Is that her?" Ronit asked, pressing him for a reply.

Nas looked around the small office, uncertain of what to say, unsure of what to do. He turned to Ronit, then ran from the office, down the narrow passageway, across the lobby, and into the elevator. He was gasping for breath as he swiped the key card across the door lock and burst into his hotel room. Fully clothed, he stepped into the shower and turned it on full, allowing jets of water to pummel his face. He was mortified. The woman he'd seen in the video was there and gone in the blink of an eye, yet, he knew it was her. Tears ran down his face as he wailed. He had committed himself to this stranger, tied himself to her for life and throughout eternity, and didn't have the slightest clue that she started her day with an early morning run.

Chapter Fourteen

Gwen Winter

It was late morning when I trudged into the kitchen the next day, sometime between eleven and noon, probably closer to noon. I'd rolled around in bed for hours before falling asleep, only to have my eyes spring open on and off throughout the night. The time I'd spent in bed was no measure of the rest I'd gotten. My eyelids felt irritated as I shuffled into the kitchen.

Dad had already gone shopping and was unpacking brown paper grocery bags on the center island. The first items I noticed were three large canisters of nuts. I looked closer: cashews. Son of a bitch, that was Dad's shtick—he had to suffer more than anyone else and was leaving nothing to chance. Another option was that there was a buy-one-get-two-free sale. My father was a hopeless bargain hunter.

The coffee pot was mostly full. It was no doubt the second pot. My parents like their coffee and drank from barrel-sized mugs. Twelve six-ounce cups disappeared quickly, maybe two tankards a piece. Dad wasn't looking at me as he mechanically unpacked dry goods as if he were being paid piecework. He'd divided the counter into quadrants, placing like with like, canned goods with canned goods, dairy items for the fridge and so on. It looked as if he scored big. The way he exploited their sales, the supermarket would have to file for bankruptcy by close of business. Dad wasn't cheap but was incapable of passing up a bargain. And he'd put it all to use. If beans went on sale, he'd make chili. The five-pound bag of Spanish rice went on fire sale, paella. Chicken thighs and sausage on sale, call the relatives. It's time for the annual summer cookout.

He was muttering something under his breath, indecipherable yet unquestionably vile.

Head throbbing, I sat down in front of him with my coffee. The caffeine wouldn't help. It would only make it worse. *Guess I'm just like him, another martyr.* "I guess this is our life now." We were destined to ponder Nas's betrayal until we had an answer or all had strokes.

Muhammad had sent us on our way with a curse. I'd learned that sharmoota was the Arabic word for bitch or a whore. Normally, not such a big deal, except that it had come from soft-spoken Muhammad, the patriarch of the Zia tribe, a man who took offense at the word, bullshit. He'd always been reserved, the consummate gentleman.

"I don't get it," Dad said. "I don't get him calling you a bitch."

"I've been called worse."

"That's not what I'm saying." Dad appeared disoriented and placed a can of soup atop a can of store-brand creamed corn.

Must've been cheaper than dirt, I mused. He appeared to be absolutely flummoxed, a condition that was completely foreign to him.

"Ah, shit."

I tossed the creamed corn in the trash. "Problem solved," I scoffed. "No one eats this garbage anyway."

He scowled at me as he fished it out of the trash bin.

"Why didn't you buy a case of it? You max out your credit card or something?"

He flashed an eat-shit grin. Coming from me, he was happy to absorb a dig or two. "What I'm saying is, why would he swear at you, Gwen? I was the one who lashed out at him. I could see him tearing me an asshole, but why would he direct the insult at you?"

"You got him cranked up, and he blew. It was nothing compared to what his firstborn did to me yesterday. I got fucked in the worst possible way." I washed out my filthy mouth with coffee. "Does it matter?"

He gritted his teeth, then rinsed the can of corn, dried it, and added it to the correct stack of bunker provisions. "Of course not. Still, it doesn't sit right. There's no shortage of Arabic swear words. Why did he choose that one?" He shrugged. "I was up half the night thinking about it."

"That's the difference between you and me—you need things to make sense. Me, I disemboweled Nas in my dreams. I'm beyond trying to figure out what happened."

He frowned, then came around the island and smothered me in his arms. "Sorry, honey. I wish I could take it all away."

"I know, Daddy. I know you would. Do you think I'll ever find out what happened?"

"*Oh*, we'll find out all right," he said with a definitive nod. "I can damn sure promise you that."

Chapter Fifteen

Gwen Winter

I was more than expert at the fine art of brooding and could eat my heart out with the best of them. Now, expressing pure unadulterated misery, that was something else entirely. Locked in my bedroom, I strove to take the art form to a new level, one of soul-searing, grief-stricken misery. Lying motionless in bed that afternoon, eyes closed with my hands tucked at the sides, I could feel the will to live ebbing away.

I had laid lifelessly for hours, fidgeting and just feeling like crap. I thought about doubling down on my Zoloft even though weeks would pass before there'd be enough additional antidepressants in my bloodstream to make a difference. *What the fuck*, I thought. *Best idea in the room, right?*

When did the lies start? At the very beginning? Somewhere down the line? Or had Nas been dealing in good faith most of the way? Was his decision to betray me an audible? Had he, like Tom Brady, changed the play on the line of scrimmage because he didn't like the way the defense was lining up?

I remembered meeting Nas, our blind date. Not a true blind date but more along the lines of a vision-impaired encounter. There'd been a chance meeting in the city, prompting me to view his online profile, ephemeral though it had been. I knew what he looked like and what he did for a living, where he'd gone to school, and a summary of his favorite books and movies. Not a ton of information, mostly a blank page. A post here and there, maybe once every few months. He wasn't one of those I-downed-a-dozen-beersat-the-kegger guys, the ones who have to boast about every dumb-ass thing they did. In his eyes, I could see that he was quiet and reserved—maybe someone with the potential to be a good listener.

He was what my mother called, and what her mother before her would've called, "A good catch." He wasn't a lawyer fish or a doctor fish, which was the gold standard in days of yore. To my mother, the word *tech* was an elusive term. It took most of a holiday dinner to explain that a cloud developer was a real thing, that Nas made good money, take-good-care-of-your-precious-daughter money, and that he had a promising future in front of him.

He was sweet and compassionate, everything I hoped a man could be. A guy who asked what I liked to eat before making reservations. A guy who opened the car door for me and closed it after I got in.

Gallaghers, I love it there. It's the Winter gals après theater destination, our girl's day out, just me, Mom, and big sis. Everything on the menu is good, but to tell the truth, I'd eat asbestos if it came with a side of their Lyonnaise potatoes. Comfort Food and The Girl Who Couldn't Exist Without It. It should've been the title of a fable, like The Princess and The Pea. The vintage chairs in the restaurant are supportive and built to last ages. I somehow always manage to get the leg caught between floorboards. That's when I first saw Nas, looking over my shoulder as he got up from a nearby table and helped extricate my chair leg from where it was stuck and push my chair closer to the table. That's when I first saw him smile, the glint off his brilliantly white teeth as captivating as a hypnotist's gold watch.

Afterward, he went back to his table, rejoining his friends. We couldn't stop talking about him, the looks, the manners, the wisps of dark hair. Okay, so he wasn't drop-dead handsome but just shy of good-looking. Still, there was something about him I found captivating.

Had Mom only known he was an Arab, an anti-Jew, she wouldn't have pushed so hard for me to go over and talk to him. But every guy's got facial hair these days, am I right? How was she to know that he was an original member of the bearded clan and where that first meeting would lead us, to courtship, to love, and now…grunt. How could she know he was a Trojan horse? Beware charismatic men harboring treachery in their hearts.

And the first time we went to bed. Holy shit! It was pure tantric nirvana. We were woven together physically, emotionally, and in every other way. Unfortunately, we were connected with two completely different gods. And son of a bitch, if that lifetime-instilled guilt trip didn't keep me wide awake night at night.

Surrounded by the darkness of my thoughts, Dad often came to me and seeped into my head. "You little Arab-loving brat, you betrayed your parents, your kind, and every Jew who'd fought for the survival of the State of Israel. After all we've done for you." It became the elephant in the room, born the very first time he heard that Nas and I were dating. And it never went away. We simply ignored it, diverting our gazes, redirecting conversation, and side-stepping the most critical issues like seasoned politicians.

But Nas and I were good, and that elephant rarely followed me out of the house. Dad owned the problem. It was his issue to care for and nurture, to water and cultivate. There were no barriers when I was in Nas's arms, no Jews, no Arabs, and no discord. The only tension between us was sexual. We were a top-of-the-Ferris-wheel couple, clinging to each other while our car swung back and forth high above the world, teetering perilous and uncertain until the inertia of our love brought us safely back to earth, more connected than we had been climbing aboard.

Nas wasn't a wallflower, though. He had strong opinions and staunchly defended them. But he did so with dignity and accepted what I had to say. He was smart enough to know he didn't know everything.

No one did.

Least of all, me.

Duh!

I didn't sleep after our first date, wondering if he dug me, dug me deeply. Was our date the first of many or the disappointing last? Was I a one-and-done or a keeper? But I couldn't be anyone else but who I was. And I was a different person when I was around him: flirty, girlishly brazen, and somehow energy-charged in a way I was around no one else.

Around him, anyway.

I remember what it felt like when we were new, the raw energy, nerves sizzling all the time like the ends of live wires, torn apart, shooting sparks.

He was a blank page, a mystery.

A fucking mystery.

I never wanted to solve him completely because there's no magic in knowing everything. A relationship without surprises, without spontaneity, blah. Am I right?

And that last surprise was a killer, a mortal wound to the heart.

I thought I knew him and the demons that drove him well enough. More importantly, I thought I knew his heart, his true heart. What in the world changed in the span of a few hours that drove him from my side and plunged a dagger into my heart?

I reached for the amber prescription bottle as tears streamed down my cheeks.

Early in our relationship, I wondered if he would see who I really was, the train wreck hobbling on antidepressant crutches. Three weeks into our relationship, I broke down and told him everything, about a lifetime of depression, bouts of hopelessness, emergency room visits and extended hospitalizations. I thought he saw me and accepted me, not for how I had been but for who I'd become. I opened the bathroom vanity and showed him a shelf filled with prescription bottles, soldiers in the battle of my mental health war. "This is who I am, Nas. This is what it takes for me to be me: antidepressants, mood stabilizers, and hypnotics for sleep."

That was when he won my heart. "If these pills make you who you are," he said. "I'm happy to take them as well."

I spied the amber bottles on my bedside table. *Once more into the breach*, I thought. *Take up your lance and fight the good fight.*

It was late afternoon when I heard a soft rap on the door. Dad walked in waving the white flag, a tray loaded with take-out containers. The days of confrontation were over. There was no need for him to boast about being right that Nas and I would end in disaster. He came in offering a chow fun compromise. A comfort food settlement.

I recognized the containers at once, white cardboard imprinted with a red Fu lion. Golden Herb had yet to capitulate to the modern trend of packing take-out orders in flat plastic containers. The family-owned business had operated from its strip mall location for as long as I can remember and their broad noodles were nothing short of amazing.

He didn't have to ask how I was doing. Dad was not one to repeat the obvious. We ate in silence for a while, picking at scraps well after our hunger had been satisfied. A habitual bed eater, I couldn't tell you how many times Mom and Dad had performed emergency triage with delectable dishes on my food-stained blankets. I watched his eyes. He was waiting for his moment to speak. Something bold was coming. And something more, he had begun to clean up, snapping chopsticks in two and stuffing them into the cardboard containers along with soiled paper plates and napkins. It seemed as if he had someplace to go. "Out with it," I said.

He held out for a few ticks, then surrendered to my request.

"You always could read me." He was not a man to mince words, but he was more careful around me than he was with others, because I'd always been, you know, frail. Especially now. "I know a guy," he said, easing into something.

"What are you talking about?"

"Did you ever hear me mention the name Dan Ohana?"

"No." Of course not. He never talked about his army intelligence days. It was a closed book. "Sounds like the name of a spy." It wasn't much of a gamble. There was a gap in his history, a period he never discussed. He said so little about his past that one of our neighbors once asked if he was in witness protection. *Yes, of course—he testified against Gotti.* He was buddy-buddy with Sammy "The Bull" Gravano.

"Dan is a—"

A mercenary? An assassin? Dan's a what? "I know, it's classified." Like most of the details from his former military life, this too must be confidential, on a need-to-know basis. "I don't need specifics. Can he help me, yes or no?"

"I believe he can. It's what he does."

That's it? How vague can a person be? I always imagined, perhaps romantically so, that Dad was a spy in his earlier days, a Walther-wielding, SCUBA-diving covert instrument of death. He and this guy, Dan, likely staged military juntas and toppled governments? One thing was for sure, Dan was no rumpled gumshoe. Whatever Dan now called himself didn't matter. Intuitively, I knew the guy would be sharp. "When can we meet him?"

Dad wore a vintage Omega Speedmaster with a big black dial and white indicators. He glanced at it quickly.

I don't know why I was surprised by what came next. That was Dad; I never knew what he had up his sleeve. "We should leave now."

Chapter Sixteen

Gwen Winter

Dad drove a heavy-duty SUV. EPA mileage be damned—he drove what he liked and occasionally boasted that his Ford Expedition had enough towing capacity to pull a pair of Mustangs end-to-end. He enjoyed working with his hands and spent his free time building and fixing. No job was too big or too small—he'd attempt anything from brickwork and light construction to repairing a lamp. His rig practically drove itself to Home Depot.

I was a frequent passenger in the Expedition and liked riding high up. For some reason, the extra foot of ride height made me feel as if we were on an adventure, which I suppose we were, traveling east along the Northern State Parkway, then south on the Sagtikos. It was the same route we took to the Fire Island ferries for daylong outings at the beach. This, I knew, was to be no day at the beach. Digging into the great disappearance was going to be like pulling a giant bandage of a colossal-fucking-wound.

We pulled up in front of a block of low-rise buildings, retail shops on the street level with offices located above. Signs in windows offered professional services: attorneys, CPAs, real estate, and the like, low-rent advertising focused on street traffic.

"Want a slice?" Dad said, looking at the overhead sign for Gennaro's Pizza. "This place makes a thin-crust pizza to die for."

"You can't be serious. The chow fun is still trying to worm its way through my GI tract."

"Maybe on the way out, then." Dad shrugged and headed for the doorway next to the pizza place. "Dan's office is upstairs." The door opened with a crack as a thick chunk of paint chipped off the door frame. The stairs were well worn, and the walls had so many coats of what I imagined was lead-based paint that Superman wouldn't be able to see through it. The second-floor landing was made of those vintage hexagonal tiles, small white tiles set into black grout.

There were four doors on the landing. Dad made for the one on the far right. Unlike the other three there were no external markings on it, no information of any kind. Dad twisted the knob and walked in. Apparently, Dan Ohana trusted his neighbors, or so I thought. The door opened into a small waiting area, no bigger than the width of an early-era elevator. A few pieces of Home Goods art adorned the walls. The carpeting was stained, and a white noise machine emitted an annoying tone. Dad stood in front of the inner door and looked up at a ceiling-mounted video camera. I heard a metallic thunk, the release of a weighty electronic locking mechanism. Dad pushed on the door, and we went in.

Ohana sat behind a steel desk, holding a magnifying glass to his eye. He was reading printed matter and held a pencil in his left hand. "Hank, be right with you," he said before circling something on the paper in front of him.

"You lose your glasses again?" Dad asked.

Dan nodded and threw in a hand gesture, indicating the predicament was commonplace.

Dad smiled. "You know, you can get a three-pack at Costco for less than twenty bucks."

"As you've told me before," Ohana said. "I'm not a member. I don't need to buy canned tuna by the case."

I had this vague notion that with a surname like Ohana that Dan was a Pacific Islander, a-wide-across-the-chest, thug-intimidating, kinky-haired Samoan. Such was not the case. Ohana was a slight gent with a receding hairline and a demeanor that would make Truman Capote seem like a brute.

He wore a tan button-down shirt with the cuffs rolled up. A brown suit jacket hung over the back of his chair.

He stood and came around his desk to greet us, bypassing Dad; he extended his hand toward me. *"So, this is the lovely Gwen."* He took my hand in his. "Sweet girl, we'll find this *mamzer*. Don't think for a moment that we won't."

There was a hint of an accent in his voice. Mamzer was a dead giveaway, the Yiddish word for bastard. He could've used any number of vulgar expletives to describe an Arab who'd abandoned a Jewish girl on her wedding day. Calling Nas a bastard was being kind. What could I say? He didn't have to pull his punches. My fiancé sucks camel dick. "Thanks for meeting with us, Dan."

"Of course. Of course." He hopped back to his desk and sat down. He had a lot of spring in his step for a man who didn't look as if he had the strength to pick up his socks."

"Dan and I worked together back in the day," Dad said.

The day? When was that? Was that the day you took down a puppet government? Was it the day you put a bullet between an oligarch's eyes? If only he'd spoken openly about his days in army intelligence, I wouldn't be imagining the worst.

Dad slid into a chair and motioned for me to sit down next to him.

"I was horrified to hear about what happened to you, honey," Ohana said, leaning across his desk. "We've never met, but I can tell by looking at you that you're a fine person. And being Hank's daughter? This jerk should have his head examined." He lifted a file off his desk and let it fall. "This is what I do all day long. Credit card and cellphone records, all you have to do is say the word, and we'll be face-to-face with this maggot in no time."

"How do you...?"

"Questions like these you don't ask me, Gwen. You want this man—" He squinted at the name he'd scratched on a pad. "Nasir Zia to answer for his actions?"

"Yes."

"I wasn't really asking," he said. "I'm here to help you. Your wise father didn't want me to do anything until I had your blessing. Now, between you and me, I would've done it regardless because what was done to you, it's egregious. It's disgusting. *And* I owe your father many times over."

Dad put his hand on mine. "Gwen, this is up to you. It's your decision and yours alone. Your mother and your sister aren't part of this. They don't know I've brought you here, and for everyone's sake, it's better they don't. Take a little time and think about it. You don't need to rush."

I don't? How long do you think I can carry this burden? "I've made my decision." I made it before we arrived, before I knew of Ohana's existence.

I stood up and walked to the window. The sky was just as clear as it had been on my wedding day, the day I'd looked forward to since Nas and I first met. The window looks south on a parking field, one of the many the town of Bayshore used for those taking ferries to the various Fire Island ports. The lot was packed solid, not a spot to be had.

"So, honey," Ohana began, "Would you like me to get started?"

I was still looking out the window when a car pulled out of an end spot and a blue convertible pulled in. I knew that blue ragtop, loved it, and had always longed to have one of my own. With the top down, I could see that the driver had wavy brown hair and wore Ray-Bans. The passenger was a striking dark-skinned girl wearing a flame-red bikini top and denim shorts, not normally a cause for concern except that the ebony goddess sitting next to my brother-in-law Jack was not my big sister Alana.

Chapter Seventeen

Nasir Zia

Nas stood vigilant from the hotel balcony outside his room, watching the hotel entrance from eleven stories up so that he'd be able to spot his wife the moment she approached. His wet slacks and shirt hung on the balcony railing, flapping in the breeze. They were still damp from the shower, but any moisture that dripped off his clothes immediately evaporated on the sun-warmed balcony concrete slab.

Ronit had called Nas in his guest room and promised to ring him if anyone resembling his wife was spotted. Ronit sounded as if he'd become invested in Nas's matter and seemed to want to make amends for treating him indifferently earlier that morning. He offered Nas complimentary snacks from the galley shop and reminded Nas that he was there to help him in any way possible.

And so, Nas waited and hoped. The time was approaching noon, and he'd abandoned any notion that his wife was still out getting exercise. In his mind, the best possible scenario was that she'd stopped for something to eat, that she maybe found a quiet outdoor café where she could reflect and come to her senses. He didn't want to think about any other possibilities, but a litany of unspeakable atrocities filled his head and vied for his attention.

He walked inside and checked to make sure the room phone was firmly coupled to the base, then glanced at his prayer mat, which was still rolled out on the floor. His morning and noontime prayers had gone unanswered.

If his god turned his back on him over such an important matter, who else was there for him to turn to?

Feeling anxious, he went back out onto the balcony. No activity. No cars. There was no one walking in or out of the hotel—it was a barren, hopeless desert. The last he'd seen of his wife was a flash frame of her exiting the hotel on a surveillance monitor, to where, he had no idea.

Nas tried squeezing his brain for insight, but he knew so little about her, only what he'd learned from her at the one premarital meeting they'd had and the snippets of forced conversation they'd managed the day before. Small talk can only take you so far. Without shared history, flowing conversation had been difficult to maintain. Add to that the trying circumstances under which they'd been brought together and you have a Michelin Star recipe for failure. *Where the hell is she?* he wondered. Was their union as bad as all that? The answer was yes. Of course, it was. As bad a scenario for throwing two people together as he could imagine.

He heard a tapping noise, which he didn't immediately realize was a knocking on the door. He pulled his mind back from the great abyss into which it had sunk and walked through the hotel room to answer the door. "Hello?"

"It's Ronit, the hotel manager."

What does he want? Was the first thought that entered Nas's mind, but it quickly gave way to logic as positive energy pushed negativism aside, and he was reminded that Ronit had shown him compassion over the phone.

Struggling with his emotions, Nas sported a hangdog face as he opened the door.

Ronit stood in front of him, holding an airtight plastic container. Prying off the lid, he revealed a mound of cookies. The aroma wafting from the container was overpowering. "As-Salaam-Alaikum."

"Wa-Alaikum-Salaam."

"My wife supervises the kitchen downstairs," he said. "I told her what was going on, and she thought you might like some freshly baked googiyan." The aromatic treats were heavily encrusted with seeds and crushed nuts. "What would you like to wash them down? I can have the kitchen send up a nice pot of coffee or perhaps some chai."

"This is very thoughtful," Nas said, his throat parched as he spoke. He extended both hands to accept the offering.

"Have you heard from her?" Ronit asked hopefully.

Nas shook his head. "Would you like to come in?" He strained at the next comment. "I would appreciate the company."

Ronit nodded eagerly. "Yes, of course."

Nas pointed to the opened patio doors. "I've been on the lookout from the patio, hoping to see her." He closed his eyes momentarily, his expression bleak. "Anyway, it's beautiful out there."

"No problem. Cookies and fresh air, what could be better?" Ronit met Nas at the railing and took in the panorama, tall, budding trees stood like sentries, blocking what in reality was a too-close-for-comfort eight-lane highway. "I don't get a chance like this very often," Ronit said. "I spend most of my day at the front desk and on the phone." He filled his lungs with air, then turned to Nas. "We don't have to talk if you don't want to."

"I only wish I had words." He bit into a cookie and offered one to Ronit. "These are just what I needed. Please thank your wife for me."

"I will." Ronit snapped off a bite with his front teeth, then chewed slowly, savoring the flavors of the nuts and sweet pastry. "I love how the nuts crunch between my teeth."

Nas nodded without looking, his gaze sweeping left and right across the front entrance area.

"Most of our newlyweds are just passing through on their way somewhere else. They stop over for a night or two, then continue on their way."

"That was our plan as well," Nas said. He sighed deeply, disconsolately.

"You might not believe me but this is not as uncommon as you think, especially with arranged marriages. You can take one look at these couples and know that they don't know what they are doing or why they are where they are. The men, okay, the men are looking forward to the wedding night, but the ladies, they look like they're crossing a war zone, their eyes moving every which way, afraid the next step will set off a landmine." He turned to Nas, hoping to make eye contact. "Is this—"

Nas turned to him and nodded.

Ronit placed his hand on Nas's shoulder. "I know, it's the twenty-first century, and our people are still following these archaic traditions. Give it time, brother. Allah has a plan for all of us."

Nas's phone rang. He snatched it from his pocket and glanced at the caller ID.

"Is it her?" Ronit asked.

Lips pressed together tightly, Nas shook his head. "No," then indicated that he was going to take the call. "Excuse me." He turned away from the railing, walked through the suite into the bedroom, and closed the door. "Hello, sir," he said.

"Is she back?"

It took a moment for the word to come out. "No."

There was silence on the line, a silence that felt as if it would last forever. "Are you still there?" Nas asked when he heard a terrifying scream coming from the hotel room. He shuddered, and the phone dropped from his hand. Running into the suite, he saw that all was quiet. The drapes in front of the patio doors fluttered in the breeze, but as Nas stepped closer, he could see that Ronit was no longer standing at the railing.

Sounds came at him from two directions. The door was open, and it sounded as if there was some kind of disturbance in the outer corridor. He was about to step into the hallway to see what was going on when he heard a woman shriek outside the building. He ran to the balcony, looked over the railing, and gasped.

Chapter Eighteen

Gwen Winter

Back in Dad's SUV, I kicked off my sandals and tucked my feet under my butt. The sun was hitting the windshield at a weird angle, and I'd forgotten my sunglasses. I played with the visor, but it was like a T-Rex arm. I couldn't extend it far enough to do any good, so I was forced to push my head against the side pillar and shade my eyes with my hand.

Who the hell was the babe with Jack? Was she a client he was trying to woo? Was she an old friend? A long-lost cousin? Her long legs and unfathomable cleavage seemed to render those choices implausible. But Jack wasn't a stupid guy. If he *was* screwing around, he'd be smart enough to do it on the down low, at a dimly lit restaurant and an out-of-the-way motel. He wouldn't go wheeling around town with a half-naked Barbie in a flashy convertible, taking her to a popular beach where someone he knew might spot him.

As I had, "Train Wreck" Gwen, fresh from the disaster of a lifetime. First, the love of my life up and runs like a thief in the night, and now Jack, the man whose face should be on the Mount Rushmore of great husbands was spotted with his hands in the coochie jar.

I was devastated, not just because Jack's infidelity would devastate my sister, but because Jack, gorgeous, pure of heart, golden boy Jack, might be a lie. There were few things I'd bet my life on, but Jack was one of them. He was perfect, Jack, a man to be placed on a pedestal and exalted for being a loving husband and the perfect father. Jack, once glorious, now odious, an expertly camouflaged snake in the grass. And poor Alana, her life was falling apart almost as catastrophically as mine.

Thank God Dad didn't spot him. He would've jumped through the window and snapped Jack's neck. Shoot first, ask questions later. Alana Winter-Weinberg almost became a widow because Jack innocently gave a neighbor a lift to the ferry.

No, I don't believe it either. Even if the Nubian doll was his neighbor, rocking a body like hers meant trouble. Big trouble. Marriage-on-the-rocks trouble.

"So, what did you think of Dan Ohana?" Dad asked.

Dad's question extricated me from my coma. I was alone in my mind, content with bile coursing through my brain, my attention focused on a search and destroy all men mission. "I think he asked a lot of questions. Is he tracking down Nas or writing my biography?"

Dad took his eyes off the road momentarily and shrugged with upturned palms. "He's very thorough. What did you expect him to do, grit his teeth like Humphrey Bogart and mutter some bullshit written by a Hollywood screenwriter?"

"I don't know, but not the Spanish Inquisition. The background check they did on me at work was less intrusive than Ohana was." It was as if he was performing an oral colonoscopy. I tapped the dashboard clock. "We were there almost two hours. And he's *so* slow. Anyone who thought Colombo was irritating should spend one hundred and twenty agonizing minutes locked in a room with *that* clown. 'One more thing. Just one more thing. And what about? Could you clarify something?' *Dad,* I wanted to scream. 'When did you meet him? Where did you meet him? How often did you have sex?' And on and on. I mean, *really*? I'm surprised he didn't chart my menstrual cycle."

"I hear you. He went long and deep. It's not like TV, *give me a photo and the last known address.* This isn't scripted. I honestly couldn't tell why he felt all those questions were pertinent, but I'm sure Dan could, and he's the kind of guy who would've sat there all day and explained it to you if you asked him to."

The sun moved. I adjusted the T-Rex shade. Nada. It was as if the interior design engineer was having a good laugh at my expense. I could see this MIT geek huddling with his minions. "Okay, boys, let's design this thing so that it's only effective at blocking the blood supermoon eclipse that occurs roughly once every eighteen years."

I wanted to tear the damn thing off the hinges, but that would've ruined Dad's day, and I'd already ruined his life? And Mom's? Mine goes without saying. And now, dear Alana's Jack was parking his car at the bimbo garage. It was a perfect shitstorm with no end in sight. Thanks very much, Greta Thunburg. You warned us that life as we know it might come to a cataclysmic end. You told us to be proactive. I should've dragged Nas to the justice of the peace months ago and locked him down before there was any possibility of escape. But no, I had to have a big, fancy wedding, months of planning and preparation, fortunes spent, hope skyrocketing to the moon like Apollo 11. Plenty of time for a fish to wriggle off the hook.

Fool. You stupid fool. Someone in your position shouldn't take chances. Nas was your once-in-a-lifetime guy, and the chances of getting struck by lightning a second time...

One in nine million. I looked it up.

"Gee, I wonder if eHarmony will give me a credit. I think I had five months left on my Premium Plus membership when things with Nas got serious."

Dad scowled. I knew he would. It was as if I needed a fresh beating. Words were forming in his mind. I could see the wind up before the pitch. "Cut the crap, Gwen. Life dealt you a brutal-fucking hand. I get it, but there's no room in your life for any of this self-deprecating bullshit."

Tears. "You don't know how I feel."

"Of course not. How could I? But we'll track down this turd, get some closure, and you'll go about the business of living your life."

"Easy for..."

"...me to say? No, not easy for me to say," he shouted, cutting me off. "You and your sister are my life. Life's not easy. Never has been or will be." He reached out and lifted my tear-soaked chin. "But it's easier for me than it is for you at this moment, and that's what family is all about. Me, your mother, and Alana, we'd give our lives for you." He turned back to the road and sighed hard enough to dislodge the windshield. "Just breathe, kiddo. It's the only thing you can do right now."

And I'd have given my life for Nas, gladly. Willingly and without reservation. In my heart, we were already one, a sole entity, indivisible. I recalled a recent weekend in Manhattan, Nas and I strolling hand-in-hand through Central Park on a picture-perfect Sunday afternoon. We couldn't have been any more in love. That's how strong our bond was, our connection, rock solid. Or so I believed, led myself to believe. I never thought for a moment that he was capable of…relegating me to the role of detective. All that was left was finding out what had happened to Nas, following clues like a common gumshoe, a gumshoe with a broken heart, one that could never be mended.

Chapter Nineteen

Nasir Zia

Nas thought about putting their personal items away before the police arrived but didn't have the energy to lift a finger. Besides, most of their belongings were still packed in their suitcases. It wouldn't have been that way if he had been with Gwen. She would've worn one outfit to travel in, then slipped into something naughty the moment they were alone in their hotel suite. She'd have donned a swimsuit when they went out to relax at the pool before changing into something chic for the evening. Conjuring such thoughts emptied Nas of the will to live.

An EMT had sedated him, nothing strong, just enough to prevent him from becoming unglued. Sitting alone on the sofa, he rubbed his throbbing forehead and watched Detective Vito Scoldari ramble about, wondering what the investigator might be looking for. Nas had noticed the lushness and density of the detective's salt and pepper hair. His clothing carried the faint tang of tobacco. Scoldari was mute but conveyed suspicion with his eyes as he inspected the suite, going back to certain sections he'd checked before, avoiding others. Focused and self-absorbed during his reconnaissance, he almost never glanced at Nas.

There's nothing to see, Nas thought. *Nothing happened in the room.* Aside from the damp towels hanging in the shower and a few toiletries out on the counter, the bathrooms appeared unoccupied when Scoldari did his initial walk-through.

The detective had been out on the balcony more than once but lifted the yellow police tape and walked back out to look over the railing at the blood-stained pavers on the ground eleven stories below.

Scoldari didn't stay outside for long. He returned and sat next to Nas on the couch. The sealed container of cookies Nas had been given by Ronit sat on the coffee table in front of them. Scoldari stared at it for a moment before speaking. "Mr. Zia, walk me through it again, everything that happened from the time you heard the hotel manager knock on the door."

Nas was alert, but the medication was playing tricks with his mind. He knew what he wanted to say, but the words seemed inaccessible. His right eye twitched. His mental state had far less to do with the medication he'd been given and far more to do with his raw nerves, the fiancée he'd abandoned, and the bride who fled. And now, on top of everything else, a man was dead.

"I know you're upset, but do the best you can," Scoldari said.

"He…"

"By he, you mean the hotel manager, Ronit Latif?"

Nas nodded. "He brought me cookies. I think he felt guilty about blowing me off this morning."

"The assistant manager, Emily Roth, told me there was an argument. Apparently, you felt your wife had gone missing. Is that right?"

Nas nodded once more.

"And where is she now?" Scoldari asked.

Nas pressed his lips together. His shoulders rose and fell. "I-I don't know. She hasn't come back."

"When did you first notice that she was missing?"

"When I woke up, I think." I ordered breakfast and took a shower. She was gone when I went into her bedroom."

The detective's nostrils flared. "I'm not sure if I understand you—was she gone when you woke up, or was she still asleep? I mean, this is your honeymoon, right? That's what the assistant manager told me."

Nas was embarrassed. He knew that this was just the beginning of the detective's prying, Scoldari was going to peel back the onion, one layer at a time until the pungent truth was revealed. Speeding up dramatically, his heart knocked out beats in half-time. "We slept separately," Nas said sheepishly.

Scoldari's shrug left nothing to the imagination. "Is that a cultural thing? I'm asking because what you're telling me sounds strange. Your heritage is?"

"Pakistani."

"Right, but even so, isn't the wedding night supposed to be something special, a big deal, the unification of man and wife? Regardless of religious traditions, the basis of every wedding night is sex, right? Which brings us back to my original query, Mr. Zia. Why were two newlyweds sleeping in separate beds on their wedding night?"

Adrenaline destroyed what little tranquilizer was left in his bloodstream. "I'd rather not say."

Scoldari's eyes widened. "And I'd rather you did. You had an argument with the manager this morning, and now he's dead. Ever hear the expression *leave no stone unturned*? Well, this is one of those stones."

Panicked, alternatives ran through Nas's head, *Talk, talk, but be extremely vague. Lie if you need to. Call an attorney.*

Hesitation cost him dearly—the detective's gaze ratcheted up in intensity. Scoldari picked up the container of cookies, popped the lid, and used his hand to fan the aroma of the baked goods toward his nostrils. "These smell amazing." He cut his eyes at Nas. "These are the cookies the deceased brought you, I imagine—his peace offering?"

"Yes."

"Not exactly Chips Ahoy now, are they?"

"I'm not sure what you mean."

"Someone went to great trouble to bake these delicious whatever-you-call-thems just for you." He snapped his fingers, harkening a revelation. "Oh, that's right, the victim's wife baked these for you in the hotel kitchen. I met Mrs. Latif when I arrived. Lovely woman. So sad. She was crying her eyes out. Do you have any idea where she is right now?"

"No," Nas said, his expression saying, "How could I?"

"Try a little harder. Where do you *think* she is?" Scoldari said, turn-by-turn twisting the screw deeper into Nas's psyche. "She's at the *morgue*, Mr. Zia, puking up her guts and attempting to make a positive identification of her husband's remains, who, in case you missed it, hit the ground face-first. His head burst like a water balloon."

Nas gagged. Quickly placing a hand over his mouth, his eyes bulged, signaling alarm.

Scoldari pointed to the powder room. "Splash some water on your face, Mr. Zia. You look like hell."

Chapter Twenty

Gwen Winter

Alana's front door opened the second my wheels hit her driveway. She hurried out and was on top of me before I could climb down from Dad's massive SUV. Bringing out the big guns prophylactically, she swallowed me in one of her soul-nurturing hugs. I could swear I heard a bird tweeting in my ear and saw a rainbow wink at me from behind a fluffy cloud. "Are you hanging in there, girl?" she asked.

I non-answered, a benign expression that didn't say yes or no.

"Come on in," she said. "Let's get shit-faced."

"What about Jack and the kids?" I asked, clearing my throat as I followed her up the freshly paved walkway.

She turned to look at me. "Are you coming down with something?"

"No. Just a frog in my throat." It wasn't so much a frog as a snake, but I couldn't lead with that, now could I? I hadn't even made it past the front door. "Where's the fam?"

"Jack called out from work and went to the beach. Poor thing's been working like a dog."

You got the dog part right.

"He's such a good guy. He got home from the beach, showered, picked the girls up from nursery school, and took them to the playground, to be followed by dinner with the Burger King."

Or maybe he's got a guilty conscience? "Sounds very cool indeed," I said.

"Cool? It's fucking heroic. Do you have any idea what it's like taking the twins to the restroom at a fast-food restaurant? It's like a Steve Martin routine. First, you've got to sanitize the seat, cover it with tissue, then unsheathe their precious, tiny bits. Lift child number one ever so carefully onto the toilet only to have her jump off in a state of abject terror every time the automatic flusher thinks she's finished her business, which is like every ten seconds. Meanwhile, the other one is crying, 'Dad-*dy*, I gotta go pee-pee.'"

The picture was worthy of a drunken night at a comedy club. I clutched my stomach and doubled over, hysterical.

The cleaning service must've just left the house. There was a hint of pine scent in the air and the oak floors gleamed like the hood on a freshly detailed Bentley. Everything about the décor spoke to Alana's fabulous level of taste. I wouldn't be surprised if Martha Stewart had a drone hovering outside, sending back a spy video so that she could copy Alana's style.

"So it's just us?" I said, dropping my bag on one of the high-back kitchen stools. "What are we drinking?"

She opened the cabinet and retrieved two copper mugs. "I was thinking Moscow mules might be delish. Tempted?"

"It's not like I have to squeeze into a wedding dress or anything."

I saw her flinch, panic juice coursing through her brain.

"LOL," I said with air quotes. "Bring out your mules, your donkeys, and what have you—I'm good with anything that mixes with vodka."

"That's my girl." She smiled and pulled small bottles of ginger beer out of the fridge. The vodka and lime juice were already on the counter.

I was thinking about how to broach the subject of the dark-skinned beauty but chickened out when Alana handed me the icy copper vessel. *Easier after we drink than before.* I could feel the extreme cold radiating through my fingers as we toasted.

Me: "Over the lips."

"Past the gums."

In unison: "Look out stomach, here it comes!"

Alana took a sip, then giggled. "I say that to myself when Jack wants wifey to give him a BJ."

"Seriously?"

She nodded rapidly. "All except the stomach part. His family tree sprouted in Central Europe, not Nigeria. He's lucky if he can tap a wisdom tooth."

I flinched at the comment. Maybe Jack wasn't all I imagined he was. "What a drag." I gulped the mule. We laughed and toasted again. "Here's to dick," I said. "May I get some one day soon?"

"LOL?" Alana said, more apprehensive than hopeful.

I nodded. "LOL"

"I'm so glad you're able to laugh. I can always tell when you're a fucking mess. You get wicked funny. And your sarcasm is some next-level shit."

I swigged the rest of my drink. "It's how we play the coping game, sis. Psychotherapy 101."

"Here's to next-level shit." We toasted anew, and she topped off my mule with more vodka and a splash of ginger beer. "What did you do today? I called a couple of times, you know," she said, leveling her gaze at me. "What's up with the ghosting? I was worried about your bony ass."

"I know. Don't be angry. Extenuating circumstances, right?"

She popped an affirming thumbs-up.

"Anyway, nothing much. Dad kept me busy. Take out from Golden Herb. Spit-balling ideas about how to find and torture Nas. Run of the mill stuff." Not much of a lie, right? Yes, I left out the clandestine meeting with Hercule Poirot, the invasive little gumshoe Dad was entrusting with the manhunt for my ex-fiancé. But all in all, not enough to send me to hell.

Not by itself.

Of course, there were the other offenses that might buy me a one-way ticket to the netherworld, like attempted suicides, multiple counts of envy, and at least five more of the seven deadly sins. And let's not forget the showstopper, fornicating with a member of the enemy tribe. No question that Satan fist-pumped on that one.

Wow! Did that one ever come back to bite me.

Just like that, my brave face slid away. I felt my emotional tide changing direction. It hit me with a palpable thud, positive energy flowed away, and all my joy was sucked out of me. I put down the copper mug and stole into the family room, head down, tears breaching my armor like jagged rocks against an old wooden hull.

"Gwen?" I could hear Alana padding rapidly after me, coming to a stop and hovering over me as I fell onto the sofa. "What can I do?" she asked.

I shook my head and bawled like a colicky infant, at first screaming, then holding my breath.

"Sweetie, you're turning red." Alana slapped my cheek. "Come on, breathe, Gwen. Breathe."

I fought to get air into my lungs, but they were frozen, motionless, as if they'd turned to stone, not inflating nor collapsing.

Another slap. This one harder; hard enough to do the trick.

"Oh, thank God." She boosted me up and slipped her arm around me. "Walk. Let's walk. It'll pass." She'd been there before, talking me off the ledge when my life seemed hopeless when the only solution I could see was a razor blade and a warm bath.

"He's not worth it," she said. "The piece of shit."

Poor, poor Alana, once again carrying my dead weight. Jack had done God knows what with that buxom bunny. I should've been there for her, but I was glomming her compassion instead.

* * *

"Maybe alcohol wasn't the best idea—vodka and SSRIs, you know, not the best combination," I said. A couple of hours had passed, and we were out in the backyard, hiding while Jack put the girls to bed.

Alana had texted him, saying we needed space and to message her when the girls were down. She'd come in and kiss them goodnight.

She pressed her forehead to mine. "Mama said there'll be days like this."

Mom used to sing that song to us on rainy days when we were acting like brats, complaining that we were bored.

I sounded pathetic as I sang the next line. "There'll be days like this, my mama said." The verse ran in my head, *I went walking the other day, everything was going fine. I met a little boy named Billy Joe. And then I almost lost my mind.* "Jesus, men complicate the shit out of everything, the ever-loving shit. Don't you wish there weren't any?"

"The jerks…? Well, yeah. But Jack and Dad. There are a few worth keeping."

Dad, yeah, a real keeper, but the jury was still out on Jack. "So, Jack went to the beach alone?"

"*No*. Who goes to the beach alone? He's got a bunch of old friends."

"His home *boyz*?"

"And girls—friends from high school that still live in the area."

"Cool."

So, Jack had an alibi. Was Jack safe, or had the new information simply bought him time? There was something in Alana's voice that didn't check all the boxes. "Who goes to the beach alone?" she'd said. Well, actually, many. I don't know why I read something in her answer that may not have actually existed, but something told me to read between the lines.

And I would.

Until I was satisfied.

Completely.

There was no question that I was going to take top honors for being the flaming hot mess of the year, but personal consequences aside, no one fucks with my big sister. No one.

Chapter Twenty-One

Nasir Zia

It was after 9:00 p.m. when the door of the police station interview room opened, and Scoldari slipped in, chewing on a toothpick. He set a plastic takeout bag on the table in front of Nas. "Sorry I took so long," he said. "Not easy finding a falafel joint at this time of night." He looked at the tub of cookies Nas had insisted on bringing with him from the hotel. A few had disappeared. "Good thing you were smart enough to bring rations with you. You're not diabetic, are you?"

Nas shook his head. He had spent the last few hours alone in his mind, dreading that the detective might try to implicate him in Ronit's death. As if things weren't bad enough, he now had a stranger's homicide to agonize over. Ronit's wife was a widow, her life destroyed. He wondered if the couple had any children. He guessed Ronit was in his early thirties. If they had children, they'd be young and now fatherless. How many lives had been destroyed?

An avalanche of guilt was bearing down on him. *What Gwen must be thinking of me—what she has every right to think. That I'm a coward, a liar and a coward. If only I could tell her. If only I could explain.* He catastrophized about what Gwen had gone through, was going through. It ate at him like boiling acid.

Afraid that he was being monitored, he'd been afraid to use his phone to ask for help. To seek advice. Commiserate. *How many are waiting to hear from me?* he thought. He pictured his parents, waiting by the phone, wondering what had become of him and his bride, thinking the worst.

"You drink coffee?" Scoldari asked.

"I prefer tea if you have any."

"Yeah, I think we've got some of that. Probably store brand, though." He picked up the phone and begged a favor from one of the admins. He covered the receiver. "How do you take it, cream and sugar?"

"No, just plain."

Scoldari got back on the phone and conveyed the information. "…and a black coffee for me. Thanks, dear. Yeah, Interview 1." Grasping the chair by the seat, he pushed it in behind him and tented his fingers on the table. "Don't stand on ceremony, Mr. Zia. Eat your dinner. You must be starving."

"I'm not as hungry as you might think," Nas said as he looked into the bag and removed a cup of French fries. They were still warm and generously seasoned. He pushed one into his mouth and slowly let it decompose on his tongue until it had been reduced to salty pulp.

A woman brought in the beverages, coffee for the detective, a cup of hot water, and a packaged tea bag for Nas. Scoldari studied the markings on the tea bag before handing it over. "Trader Joe's," he said with peaked eyebrows. "Could be worse. Let's get back to your bride," he said as he tossed the teabag across the table to Nas. "Your wife have a name?" He slid a notepad out of his jacket pocket and readied a pen, doodling a circle to make sure the ink was flowing.

Nas was slow to reply but saw that he had no choice but to divulge his wife's identity. "Bahija Abidi."

"Can you spell that for me?"

Exhausted, he allowed the routine question to irritate him. "It's spelled just the way it sounds, detective."

"I've got no idea how it sounds."

"Try phonetics."

"This is a murder investigation—phonetics won't cut it. So, help out an old dimwitted detective, would you?"

Nas provided the spelling, making no effort to conceal his annoyance.

Scoldari squinted at what he had transcribed. "Wouldn't have guessed that in a million years. See, good thing I insisted. How about a photo?"

"I don't have one."

Scoldari sucked at something caught in his teeth. "I never met anyone your age who didn't have ten thousand pictures stored on their phone. Are you trying to tell me that you don't have one single photo of her?"

Nas pulled his iPhone out of his pocket and slid it across the table. "Be my guest."

Scoldari cut his eyes at Nas and glided it back.

"Address?"

Nas looked away, his eyes moving around the room, hoping for something to focus on, anything other than Scoldari's sour face.

"Was that a tough one?" Scoldari asked. He tapped his pen on the table, waiting. "Should I repeat the question?"

Nas pushed back in his chair, allowing room for his head to hang and his gaze to fall to the floor. "I-I don't know her address."

Scoldari huffed. "Well, fuck me. You married this woman, and you don't know where she lives. Even Russian mail-order brides have addresses."

"As I explained, it was an arranged marriage. We met just once before. At her uncle's house. I never—"

"Yeah, yeah, I get it," he said impatiently. "Uncle's address?"

Nas shrugged, his hands upturned, expressing the hopelessness of the situation.

Scoldari sipped his coffee. "Christ, this is bad." He stared at Nas disbelievingly, his head shaking slowly. "Let's try something else. You were only booked for one night. Where were you planning to go after you left the Marriott?"

"We rented a house in the Poconos. We were going to spend the time getting to know each other."

"One of those AirBnB things, I guess?"

"Probably."

"Probably? Is it possible for you to know any less about your honeymoon?"

"I didn't make the reservations."

"Of course not. Either way, I'll need the details so that I can check on your reservation."

Nas reached for another fry but dropped it back in the cup. "You don't believe me."

"Pardon my French, but no, not a *fucking* word. You've got a bride you don't know shit about and a honeymoon you didn't plan. The assistant manager told me you were shocked to learn that your wife went out for a run, like she was a total stranger to you and you knew nothing about her routines."

"Have you not been listening to me?"

"All right, that's the way you want to play it. Fine." Scoldari rose and began pacing back and forth in front of the table. "You and this Ronit Latif, you have any history together?"

"I never met him before."

"Of course not. Kind of like your wife. What about organizations—you belong to any?"

"The ACM, for my job."

"ACM, what's that?"

"Association for Computing Machinery, I think. I design and manage cloud servers."

"That sounds pretty high level. You know how to hack into servers?"

Nas felt his chest grow hollow. "You think I'm some kind of terrorist, don't you?"

"Honestly? More than I believe your cock and bull honeymoon story."

"It's because I'm Pakistani, isn't it?"

"No, it's because the guy who was pushed to his death was on an FBI watch list." He studied Nas's every movement intently.

"I have no idea about any of that."

"No idea of what? That he was being watched, or that I knew he was being watched?" Scoldari cut an eye at Nas, watching for a tell, but then seemed to ease off. "Okay, let's go in another direction. You said you were in the restroom when you heard a scream. What happened next?"

"I've answered that question several times already."

"Well, then, I guess once more won't hurt."

Nas's hand balled into a fist. "I'm not going to answer any more of your questions."

"Fine with me. I've got Homeland Security on speed dial."

Nas huffed out a pair of deep breaths before changing his tune. "I checked to see what was going on. I heard something going on in the corridor and figured that's where the noise had come from. Then, I heard all the commotion outside and went out onto the balcony to have a look."

"Where you and the victim had been standing before?"

"Yes."

"Eating cookies?"

There was a lot that Nas wanted to say but refused to stoop to the detective's level.

The door opened behind them. "Vito, got a minute?" a uniformed officer asked.

"Yeah, coming," Scoldari said. He pulled a French fry out of the cup and chomped on it. Wrinkling his nose, he spit it into his coffee cup. "Fucking thing is cold.

Nas watched him leave the room, then steeped the tea for a long while before taking the first sip. It was tepid, but he didn't mind. The tea was mild, not the kind he'd normally drink, but his throat was dry. The aroma of the food when it first arrived had been enticing, but now it turned his stomach. He stashed the uneaten fries in the bag along with his empty paper cup, knotted the bag, and dropped it in the trash pail.

The snap of the door latch startled him. Scoldari walked to the table and sat down. He placed a photo on the table, face-down.

Nas braced, expecting the worst, a crime scene photo of Bahija lying dead in a New Jersey swamp. Scoldari would accuse him of her death and the death of the hotel manager. He could almost see the conspiracy Scoldari was concocting, sedition, murder, and a Jihadi who claims to know nothing about the woman he had married.

Scoldari put his shoe on the chair. "The skirmish you heard in the hall— we've got that figured out now. A hotel guest walked out of her room and spotted a chambermaid lying on the floor, unconscious, her head bloody. She screamed like hell. Since coming to, the chambermaid realized her access pass was missing. Someone attacked her, took her pass, and used it to get into your room. Multiple security cameras throughout the hotel picked up a suspect, but the suspect wore a hoodie and kept his head down. He must've missed one of the cameras and posed long enough for us to extract this image off the video. Look long and hard, Mr. Zia. This may be the perp who pushed the manager off the balcony in your room."

Nas's eyes widened with a sense of hope he'd not felt in a long while.

"Disappointing, isn't it?" Scoldari asked as he flipped the photo. "They can take crystal clear pictures of Mars, but this is the best we could get off the security footage." The man in the picture must've been moving quickly. His image was blurred as he moved out of the darkness for a split second.

Nas stared at the grainy photograph, straining, trying to piece together the bits of shadow and light to make some sense of what he was seeing, his expression growing more dire with each passing second. And then it clicked. His mouth fell open.

"Do you recognize this man?" Scoldari asked.

Nas wrung his hands. His lower lip quivered.

"You *do* recognize him, don't you?"

Nas remained mute, his tremor growing more noticeable.

"Snap out of it, Mr. Zia, this is your get-out-of-jail card. Don't fuck this up."

Nas moved his head up and down. Unable to answer, determination building slowly, his lips trembled until a solitary word was spoken, "Y-yes."

Chapter Twenty-Two

Gwen Winter

Mom had mentioned on several occasions that in her youth, she used to doze off in front of the TV, evening after evening, only to wake in the middle of the night to a black-and-white broadcast test pattern. Apparently, each network had its own unique pattern, which meant the network was off the air. Nowadays, programming goes on twenty-four/seven. I'd never seen one of those test patterns in the flesh but the internet educates all. Those test patterns were long gone, but a morning talk show was playing on the TV in my room when I opened my eyes the next morning.

The only thing I could remember was crawling into bed after leaving Alana's house and driving to my folks' place.

It was so freaking amazing—I got a sound night's sleep without taking meds of any kind to herald the arrival of the sandman.

I felt overjoyed, a euphoric buzz that hung around for minutes. Sure, I still hated my life and the relationship with Nas, which was now nothing more than ashes and char. Horrible though it was, everything he and I could've been was now overshadowed by the manhunt to find him.

Why did I care where he was or what he was doing? I should've brushed him off, a pigeon dropping on the shoulder of life. But I couldn't. The psyche doesn't work that way—it doesn't allow it. Mine doesn't.

And harboring suspicion that magnificent Jack might be having an affair...

? What the hell is it? Does every man have a secret life, a scummy dirty side they hide from the loves of their life? How could Jack cheat on my perfectly perfect sister?

How could Nas flake on our wedding day?

Was it all men or just the turds the Winter girls fell for? What were we being punished for?

Wasn't there a single man that could be trusted? Were they all simply… shit?

I felt guilty for focusing on Alana's conceivable disaster instead of my own very real one, but the diversion made my life a little easier to deal with. Misery loves company, is what they say. Big sister shared everything with me: her love, her joy, and now her possible disaster. She gave me whatever I needed to get right with myself, intentionally as well as unwittingly. Her generosity knew no bounds—she would give her life for me if that's what it took.

I heard a light rap on the door, Mom's rap, a dainty I-don't-mean-to-intrude rap. I can't imagine how she'd managed to walk a tightrope all these years. Too much tough love, and I'd crumble. Too little, and she'd have spawned a feral witch. They were both inside me, the fragile child and the beast. Which one would triumph?

"Come in," I said in a welcoming voice because my mom, the mom of all moms who made Betty Crocker look like an apprentice baker, deserved at least a civil greeting. She deserved much more, but it was all I could offer.

"Hi, honey," she said, her smile warmer than the blood pumping through her heroic heart. "You look refreshed. Get a good night's sleep?"

I nodded enthusiastically. Having slept without the use of meds gave me renewed confidence. "Can't complain."

My comment didn't exactly bound with enthusiasm, but it was enough to light her up. Like an ornamental bulb, I could see the filament glow orange with warmth before building to radiate brilliant heart light.

Morning greetings had been worse. Much worse. Covers-pulled-up-over-the-head worse. I-want-to-die worse. I moved to the side, and she happily accepted the invitation to sit alongside me, paying the toll with a loving kiss on the head.

"I'm proud of you, honey. You're handling this *mess* like a real trooper."

A trooper? Maybe one that had smothered a grenade and gotten blown in half. But yes, I was still on the battlefield, the war ongoing. "Thanks, Mommy."

"Are you hungry? Would you like some eggs?"

I shook my head. "I'm not feeling eggs this morning." It was the politest refusal I could put forward. Eggs reminded me of Nas. He asked for the same thing whenever he stayed over, two over easy, black coffee. How he could eat the same thing morning-after-morning was beyond me. Or maybe, he thought it was the only thing I could manage. Guess I'll never know.

In either case, eggs were permanently banned from my morning routine.

"Do we have any yogurt?" I asked.

"Oh God, yes. Your father's been stockpiling like Armageddon is coming. He came home from Costco with a 20-pack. He knows you like your yogurt."

"That's sweet, but I think I'll head back to my apartment today."

"But you're not due back at work for over a week."

"I know. It just feels like what I need to do."

Mom scooched up close and put her arm around me. "You *could* hang around here a little longer. Dad and I love having you around."

"I need my routine. Something to keep me distracted. I was thinking of going back to work a week early."

She didn't have to say a word. I could read the message in her eyes, "Oh no. Everyone will know."

"It's going to come out eventually, Mom. 'Tell me about your honeymoon. Was it fabulous?' I might as well meet it head-on."

Another kiss on the head. "See how strong you are?" She put her arms around me, her head resting on mine in an embrace that said everything would be all right. "Does your father know you want to go home?"

"Not yet, but how long can I lie around waiting to hear about Nas?" My throat became dry. "I might never."

"Don't think like that. You know your father is working on it."

I thought about Dan Ohana, Dad's mousey little PI, sitting behind a desk in his hermetically sealed office, firing off questions like a Gestapo interrogation officer. Would he be worth his salt? The only thing Mom had been told was that Dad knew a guy, a guy who might be able to tell us what became of Nas. "I'm not sure Dad's elite task force is as capable as he hopes."

"Let's keep our fingers crossed."

"You know, Dad's always been so secretive about his past. All I ever get out of him is, 'Army Intelligence.' His stories are so generic. You can't tell if he was in Berlin or Bayonne, Mumbai, or Michigan. I'm not a little girl anymore. Doesn't he trust me enough to tell me the truth?"

"He doesn't even trust me, his wife of almost forty years. It's not that he doesn't trust us. He feels that nothing good can come from it. I know he was overseas quite a bit because I know where he kept his passport and visas in between trips."

"How were you able to live like that?"

"Believe me, I cried every time he walked out the door and again when he returned home. He had his mission, and you and Alana were mine." I saw that she was deep in thought, a laptop pinwheel turning while the CPU worked on a solution. "Did you and your sister have fun last night?"

Very smooth, Mom. Segue, well done. "Of course. She's the best big sister ever."

"She's always been your best friend." Mom wiggled her toes. "I need a pedi. Should we get our nails done? It'll be fun."

My feet were still under the covers. I slid them out from under. "They don't need it."

"Then just change the color." She rubbed my foot with hers. "We can go to lunch afterward. You can take the railroad into the city later in the day if you still want to." An elbow in the side accompanied by a sassy wink. "Or tomorrow. Too bad Alana's working. We could've made a girl's day out of it."

"I'm pretty sure she's taking the day."

"She *is*? I'm always the last one to know."

"Last minute thing; we kind of overdid it on the Moscow Mules last night. She said Jack played hooky yesterday, and what's good for the goose…"

"Oh, that's right—Alana told me that Jack went to the beach with his friends. Honestly, this new generation is way smarter than we ever were. They take care of themselves, personal days, family days, and vacations up the wazoo. When I worked, I got two weeks of vacation each year, and that was it, maybe, if I even took all the time I was entitled to. Snowstorm, I went to work. Walking pneumonia, I still got my butt into the office. Our generation thought the company couldn't survive without us. Kids today take every day they're entitled to and then some. All they care about is the paycheck."

"That's right, Mom, barbarism in the workplace is dead and buried. It's good that Jack still stays in touch with his old friends."

"Imani, Jeff, and Jack are as thick as thieves—they always were."

My jaw dropped. "Imani? Roly-poly Imani Davis?"

"Why do you look so surprised? She and Jack were always close, science projects, term papers, study partners. Besides," Mom continued, "she's anything but roly-poly these days. You should see her. She lost all her baby fat, and she straightened her hair. You wouldn't recognize her today, a real knockout. And she's still the same sweet girl she always was, teaches special needs children at the elementary school."

"I'm stunned." But not for the reason Mom was thinking. The Imani Davis I knew before the make-over to end all make-overs was always that kid walking around with her head down, sad all the time. She never dated and was never invited to parties. I was thrilled to learn that she'd emerged from the cocoon, that she'd fought her way out of the doldrums. I hoped she was happy, that the monarch butterfly was enjoying her time in the sun.

Hunger forced me out of my room and down to the kitchen. Opening the refrigerator, I saw the yogurt containers Dad had arranged in stick-straight lines. Once a soldier, always a soldier, I suppose. The man's name was listed in the thesaurus alongside the word orderly. *Oh good, peach.*

I wanted to say that I thought I saw her in Jack's car but decided to play my hunch close to the vest. "Is she involved with anyone?" I asked, revisiting the conversation as I put a spoonful of yogurt in my mouth. *Good one, Gwen. Very smooth. Mom will never suspect you're prying.*

"I'm surprised you'd even ask," Mom said. "I don't think I've ever heard you mention her name before."

I shrugged. "Just making conversation."

She pulled a wilted hydrangea from a vase of mixed flowers. "I don't know, Gwen. Between you and me, I think she might be partial to women. Now, don't gossip about it. I could be completely wrong. It's just the impression I got."

I smiled on the inside. "Women, huh? That's cool."

But if it was Imani in the car with Jack, her body language didn't speak elementary school teacher, and it most certainly didn't speak longtime school chum. Despite Mom's gut feeling that Imani was gay, I was worried that it was Jack's special needs that interested her most.

Chapter Twenty-Three

Nasir Zia

A day's beard growth on a man with facial hair isn't noticeable to most, but to the trained eye…barbed ends sprang out here and there, and the neatly shaven hairline on his neck was no longer sharp. His eyes were glassy. They spoke to his weariness, but the real story was the worry that lay behind them, the dread that chugged through his brain like an industrial tractor tilling soil, snapping roots, and dredging stones.

Nas had somehow managed to identify the man who'd been caught on camera lurking around the hotel. He knew him only as Uncle Huzi, the pet name Bahija had used when she greeted him on the evening she and Nas met for the first time, the only time Nas had met Bahija before they were wed. Uncle Huzi was clearly the eldest, older than either of Nas's parents and older than Bahija's mother and father. He'd said almost nothing throughout the evening, but it was clear that he was the one whose opinion mattered, the one who had to be convinced. He and only he would decide if Nas and Bahija would wed.

Throughout the evening, Scoldari had pushed Nas to drill deeper into the recesses of his memory to find the details Scoldari needed to pursue Ronit's possible assailant and recover Bahija.

What Nas remembered of the night he and Bahija first met was unending misery, being stuck in traffic on his way to meet a woman he didn't know and didn't love, a woman he'd never met before. He remembered the thoughts that were going through his head that night, his hatred of Islamic laws and traditions, of a culture that dictated who he was going to marry in spite of everything he felt and wanted. In spite of what he knew was right. Above all, despite the love he felt for Gwen Winter.

Bit by bit, from the pit of his agony, details surfaced—he remembered a small apartment in Forest Hills not far from Queens Boulevard. He recalled that they'd gotten stuck at a red light at the corner of Queens Boulevard and Yellowstone Boulevard and how his skin crawled while they waited for the light to turn green. He didn't want to be there, in an untenable situation from which he couldn't be extricated, pulled into a vortex that would drown him and suck away his life.

Nas had become the center of attention at the police station, the well from which all information sprang. He was amazed at the speed with which the police were operating, their professionalism, and efficiency. It spoke volumes as to how important the case was.

An assortment of police personnel had come and gone throughout the evening and into the morning, asking questions and refining details. He'd been visited by investigators, a facial recognition specialist, and others. He was too tired to remember the individuals' roles or who had asked what. Their faces had become a blur, an amorphous composite of features.

He heard the doorknob twist. Whose turn was it now? Was it someone he'd already seen or someone new? He was actually relieved to see Scoldari's familiar brooding face at the door. He had a fresh plastic bag in hand. If nothing else, the enigmatic detective was making sure he didn't go hungry. Nas had seen both sides of the detective since being dragged into the police station, the root canal specialist picking at his last nerve and the infantry soldier spearheading justice. He greatly preferred the latter.

"This is the good stuff," Scoldari said as he unpacked containers of cream cheese. "Best place around, all primo." He tore open a second bag, and steam rose from the pile of fresh bagels. "Look, still hot."

"Thanks."

"You've earned it."

"You seem chipper this morning." Nas stretched while sitting in the chair he'd occupied on and off for most of a day in the dingy police station interrogation room with fluorescent lights that hummed like dentist drills. The shirt that had been crisp when he dressed the previous day was now rumpled and pungent from nervous sweat. Too tired to stand on ceremony, he helped himself to a plastic knife and paper plate. He selected a bagel and began cutting it in two. "What did I do to earn such special treatment?"

Scoldari beamed with approval. "I think we've got a solid lead on this Huzi guy. The details you gave us were enough to feed the beast."

"I don't understand."

Scoldari ruffled. "*Hey*, computer guy, snap out of it. Even a relic like me has heard the expression *garbage in-garbage out*. You gave us the good stuff, enough solid information to interface with the FBI database and get back a solid lead." He ripped a bagel in half, placed a splotch of cream cheese on a paper plate, and dipped into it with the torn edge of the bagel. "Man," he began as he chewed, "nothing like warm bread. When I was a kid, my dad would go to the bakery for fresh Italian bread every Sunday morning." He sat back in his chair, savoring the flavors. "I can still taste it."

Nas was methodical. He spread cream cheese evenly on both halves of the bagel before taking the first bite. "Is my clearance level high enough for you to tell me what you found out?"

"A cooperating witness like you?" He toyed with Nas, his head weighing one side to the other. "Yeah, I think I can do that."

"Fantastic. While you're doing *that*, can you also do a cup of tea?"

"Feeling your oats, huh? Sure. As witnesses who spend the night go, you're top five percent." He used the phone to call for beverages.

"Honestly, I'm just too tired and worn out to give a damn," Nas said half-honestly.

Scoldari nodded.

Nas felt relieved that Scoldari had not continued to push him on his fledgling relationship with Bahija, details too damning to admit. He was hoping the detective wouldn't revisit that angle as he had already decided that he wouldn't be able to cooperate with the police if that happened. It was the line he couldn't cross.

"So, tell me," Scoldari began, "was it this 'Uncle Huzi' who made the honeymoon reservations for you and the missus?"

Nas searched his mind. "No way for me to know. I don't think so, but there's no question he was involved."

"Part of the process? Is that more of that arranged marriage mumbo jumbo?"

Mumbo Jumbo? Suppressing a smile, Nas mulled over the term in his mind. Mumbo jumbo was an apt description, a tradition dating back hundreds of years that was far more a financial transaction than a commitment of love. And his marriage to Bahija was so much worse than that. It was a contract rooted in the most archaic of Islamic soil. But Scoldari didn't need to know all that when a simple yes would suffice. "That's right, Detective, more of the same religious gobbledygook."

"So, Huzi had intimate knowledge of your plans."

"Yes, I'm sure he did."

"Then showing up at your hotel…I mean, that wouldn't be difficult for him to do, right? All he had to do was plug the address into the GPS and drive."

"Yes, I suppose."

Scoldari heaped a fresh mound of cream cheese onto his plate. He scooped a clump with his bagel and leaned forward across the table. "I'll tell you what I'm thinking—your wife, she's not missing at all, and she certainly isn't lost. She's exactly where she wants to be. Smart money says she had second thoughts about this arranged marriage thing. And she and this Huzi guy, they're in the wind."

"No," Nas said, scoffing at the suggestion. "She would—" The word *never* stopped before it escaped his lips. He thought about Gwen, what he had done to her, and how wrong it was. His abandoning Gwen. His sham marriage to Bahija. Nas hadn't had the guts to say no, to put a stop to this travesty. *But maybe*, he wondered, feeling oddly proud of his new wife, *maybe she had.*

Chapter Twenty-Four

Gwen Winter

Going home to my apartment was not as depressing as I thought it would be. It was late afternoon by the time I got into the city after indulging and lunching with Mom. True to form, the Long Island Railroad had been late or, as they spin it, "On or close to schedule."

The sun was eye-level in the sky and dropping as I walked into my Chelsea apartment; the rays flowing through my windows cast accurate silhouettes of my tabletop knickknacks on the opposite wall.

I closed the door and swallowed a deep breath. It felt good to be alone, quiet inside and out. Home felt like home.

Somehow, the near-fatal wound I was dealt on my wedding day was beginning to close, not all at once but little by little, perhaps a micron at a time, just enough that I could tell progress was being made. There'd be a scar, of course, a jagged, ugly, gaping mother of a scar that I'd carry to the grave, a dense lesion the carrion squigglies would really have to work on to gnaw through. But the injury hurt slightly less each day. With each new morning, I convinced myself that I was stronger than I believed I was, that I could overcome the hurt, that somehow there'd be a future. My dad was a warrior, a once-more-into-the-breach motherfucking warrior with the heart of a lion. I'd learned from him, perhaps inherited some of his fire. Channeling his strength and determination came more naturally than I'd anticipated. The connection I'd never felt was now stronger than ever.

I wasn't supposed to be here by myself. We weren't supposed to be divided, Nas and me. We were supposed to move into his place. It was bigger than mine and closer to both of our jobs.

And it was his.

And should've been mine.

That feeling of belonging, him to me and me to…

Our home.

An ache built in the pit of my stomach. *I shouldn't be here*, I thought. *But here is where I am.*

I shouldn't be alone. But I'd learn to live with it, to exist alone. Just me, Gwen Winter, standing on her own two little feet.

Again.

Into the bedroom, standing in front of my closet—shoes *off*, jeans *off*, jammies on. Heaven.

Standing in front of my wardrobe, the collection seemed inadequate, as if all of my outfits had met while I was away and decided they were no longer up to the task. "Bring us sisters," they cried. "We want to grow bigger, stronger, fresher." Of course, my darlings, straight away. I'll check my credit card availability and make straight for Bloomingdale's.

Crap! Out of the blue, it dawned on me that some of my best shit was still over at Nas's place, some of my most fabulous shoes and my sexiest lingerie. Such vanity. What a hollow, superficial thought to entertain at a time like this, or ever. But, if I couldn't have Nas on my arm. In my bed. In my heart. I'd have Blahniks on my feet.

How the hell was I going to get all of my stuff back?

Did it really matter?

I could do without the satin skivvies. Who was I going to wear them for anyway?

But the shoes. My shoes. Fuck.

Show me a woman who doesn't love great shoes, and I'll show you a girl with bunions, massive bulbous bunions, feet like cloven hooves. Even then, most would walk over flaming coals, endure excruciating pain for a righteous pair of Jimmy Choos. I glanced at my freshly painted toes and pictured them in a new pair of peep-toe stilettos. No question, new shoes would help ease the pain, and I was in a hell of a lot of pain.

Night fell over Manhattan. Lights were coming on all over the city, skyscrapers twinkling like a forest of decorated California redwood Christmas trees. Chatter grew louder outside and rose to my windows as the cafes and restaurants filled and the streets swelled with the living.

Lying on the couch wasn't cutting it.

Wouldn't.

Couldn't.

Not for long.

With the coming of night, loneliness and isolation descended on me. And because the gift of one good night's sleep had never promised another…

I'd lived through many of those maddening never-ending nights, Alaskan polar nights that felt months long, lying awake in agony. Tossing and turning, wondering if I'd go mad before my friend the sun welcomed me with a pat on the back that said, "You made it, kid. One night down, only about twenty thousand to go. Put another notch on your belt."

Without Nas.

Without the love of my life.

The man I couldn't live without was now one of the many I couldn't live *with* and I wondered just how much I'd hate him come morning.

And the day after.

And the day after that.

Would I hate him just as much, decades down the road, when my wardrobe consisted of stretch pants and sensible shoes? When my ankles were as wide as my knees, and polite children referred to me as ma'am?

Would I still hate him then?

Would I die carrying that burden?

I woke my phone, hoping one of those life-emboldening suggestions would pop up and save the day, the ones that always arrived at the most inconvenient time, *Five ways to live a healthier life* or *How to get the most bang for your buck on social media.* They hit while you were in the shower when you'd been waiting all day for an important phone call, or in the middle of a big presentation at work, and all eyes were on you.

After losing my shit at Alana's from downing copious amounts of Moscow Mules, going for cocktails seemed a seriously bad idea. But somewhere in this sleaze-overridden, grossly over-commercialized city, there had to be a place I could sit quietly and sip a glass of chardonnay without getting hit on by an absolute-fucking-neanderthal.

I had scrolled through Yelp for a low-stress bar when a call from a 518-area code flashed on the screen with the name Rosemarie Powell.

Who was this? I wondered, *An extended warranty on the car I don't own? Long-term care insurance?*

Rosemarie Powell? Who the hell is—? *"Ahh,"* I gasped. I didn't remember giving her my phone number, but there was so much of that day that I couldn't recall, didn't want to recall, or had pushed from my mind.

"Hello?"

"Hi, sweetie," she said. "I hope you don't mind me calling. How are you doing?"

"Rosemarie? Rosemarie from the hospital? Is that really you?"

"It's ain't Lady Gaga. How are you? Are you holding your own, honey?"

"Oh my God, it's so nice of you to call. I honestly don't remember us exchanging numbers."

"Nah, I kind of took the liberty while you were changing out your wedding dress. I hope that was okay. You're not gonna block my phone number, are you?"

"Never."

"It's good to hear your voice. Tell me what's been going on. Did you ever hear from that louse?"

I pulled the phone from my ear, sighed, then put it back. "Not a fucking word. He hasn't reached out, and no one claims to know where he is."

"No one?" Rosemarie said disbelievingly. "That's *such* bullshit. You can't tell me his mom and dad don't know where he is."

"We don't believe them either."

"I'm so sorry, hon. I was hoping he'd have given you some closure, at least."

Rosemarie was probably home from work by now. I could practically see her sitting at her kitchen table with a tall can of beer in her hand, her head hung in despair.

There was a pregnant silence on the line. "Are you still there?" I asked.

"Listen, dollface, there's something I thought you should know.

What now? I could feel stitches popping, the wound tearing open, Nas eviscerating me once again. "*Oh?*"

"Yeah, sweetie—I don't know what it means, but…" I heard a heavy sigh. "When I got to work today, I'll just say it—Jana's not here anymore. She was released."

"*What?* Released to where? Why?" Nas told me she'd been a patient there for years, that it was the best place they could find for her, that she thought of it as her home.

Another pregnant pause. This one grew to term.

"Rosemarie?"

"I don't know. I don't know, and I don't know. I asked around, and all I could find out was that her parents came and got her. Her file is with Dr. Bellows, who, as you've seen, is not exactly forthcoming. I'll try nosing around again tomorrow."

"Can they just do that? I mean, doesn't she need the help?"

"They can do anything they want. And from what I've seen of her when her dad's around—I'm sure she'd give consent if he demanded it."

What do you mean, 'When her dad's around?'"

"I mean, he rules the roost. His wife has no say in anything. She's essentially mute when he's around. And Jana, she kind of cowers before him. She's like a puppy afraid of getting swatted on the snout. That's not the man you know?"

No. No. No. No. "What?" The Mohammad Zia I knew had always been reserved and gentle, a man who deliberated over everything he said, a man of compassion. Was Rosemarie right? Was this the man I knew?

If not, who was he?

Chapter Twenty-Five

Nasir Zia

"Over there," Scoldari said, pointing to the big Crown Vic parked in the corner space of the police station lot. "The white one, sticking out past the squad cars."

Nas approached the hefty sedan and looked it over, stem to stern. "You inherit this boat from Kojak?"

"Get in," Scoldari said, "and don't bump your head on the door frame getting in, wiseass." He got behind the wheel and fired up the engine. "Hear that? That's a Ford-built V-8. What do you drive, one of those imports with a Tonka Toy engine?"

"I drive a Prius."

"Saving the planet, are you? How very environmentally minded of you. Does your car have a forward gear?"

Nas turned to him, rolling his eyes as he buckled the seatbelt. "Gets me where I need to go."

"Not like this beast, it doesn't." Scoldari clicked the column-mounted gear selector into Drive and peeled rubber out of the lot. "Feel that? That's what a car is supposed to feel like when you hit the gas." He tapped the odometer. "A hundred and eight thousand miles, and it's barely broken in. Bought it at an auction last year."

"I seriously can't believe they still permit gas guzzlers like this on the road. Ever hear of global warming?"

"More like global bullshit." Stopping at a red light, Scoldari angled his head toward Nas. "Let me ask you something, did you ever hear of the ice age?"

"Of course."

"It took place thirteen thousand years ago and wiped out the mammoths and mastodons, all the giant creatures, far tougher mother fuckers than you and me. And it wasn't triggered by giant sloths or saber-toothed tigers burning too much fossil fuel. To this day, no one's figured out what caused it. Global change has been going on since the planet formed. They think it has something to do with orbital variation, not because I'm not driving an Asian-built four-banger."

As the light changed to green and Scoldari pushed on the gas, he stroked the armrest as if it were a pet tabby. "That's real American velour, my friend. And elbow room, try stretching out in one of the department's Chargers. There's no comparison. I've been on stakeouts sixteen, eighteen hours long in this car. It was like taking my living room on the road. This is one of the most reliable cars ever built, interceptor package, oversized alternator, and gobs of ground clearance—it's overbuilt from bumper-to-bumper. And you should see how cars move out of the way when they see this Chris-Craft blazing down the express lane. I don't even bother putting the fireball on the roof. This car clears a lane like Moses parting the Red Sea."

Nas lacked the energy to embrace Scoldari's bravado. Succumbing to weariness, he yawned and leaned back against the headrest. "Wake me when we get back to the hotel." He closed his eyes, but they didn't stay shut for long. Cigarette smoke sailed up his nostrils. He coughed, and his eyes shot open. "You smoke?"

Scoldari held a smoldering cigarette. "You don't mind, right? I've been dying for a ciggie all day." He cracked the window. "Perfect evening, right?"

"I can't breathe. I've got—" He hacked and gasped. "Bronchitis."

"Oh, for the love of God." Scoldari lowered the window and flicked out the cigarette. "Why didn't you say something?"

"When was I supposed to do that?" he asked in a raspy voice.

Scoldari shrugged. "Sorry. Anyway, we've got more to discuss."

Shaking his head, Nas sighed, then coughed again. "This is a nightmare."

"Don't look at me," Scoldari said. "I'm just trying to puzzle this mess together."

"Can't we talk about it tomorrow?"

"What's the point? You gonna know any more in the morning than you do now?"

"I'm exhausted." All Nas wanted to do was lie down, close his eyes, and pretend the last few days had never happened. He'd be with Gwen, if only in his dreams.

"You'll be back in your hotel room in twenty minutes. In the meantime, your stuff has been moved to a new room with an officer posted at the door."

"Is that really necessary?"

"No, I just like to squander department resources."

Nas stared at him in disbelief.

"Relax. I've got my reasons."

"Are you going to fill me in?"

Scoldari smacked his lips. "Yup. You see, it's like this. My guess is that this Uncle Huzi, whoever he is, seems to feel responsible for your wife. From what I've been able to decipher, it was Uncle Huzi who blessed your marriage, and I'm thinking he's had a change of heart. I think he's been in touch with your short-term wife and told her he was going to make the marriage contract null and void, Capish? He decided to undo what was done, and he told her he was coming to get her."

Nas summoned his strength. "That doesn't happen. Such an action would have grave consequences."

"Oh yeah, like what? He's a man. He won't be murdered or sexually castrated like women subjected to Sharia law. What's the worst that could happen to him?"

"He'd be ostracized by the community. He'd be cast out."

Scoldari chortled. "Well, I'll see you an ostracized and raise you a homicide."

The comment hung in the air for moments before Nas replied. "I don't follow. What does the hotel manager's death have to do with my marriage?"

CHAPTER TWENTY-FIVE

Scoldari shrugged. "Maybe nothing and maybe everything."

"Please, Detective, I'm too tired to play your games. Whatever you're trying to say, just say it."

"Think about it, computer guy—if all had gone to plan, Uncle Huzi wouldn't have had to explain nothing to nobody. What if it wasn't the hotel manager Uncle Huzi intended to push off the balcony? What if..."

The crushing weight of Scoldari's theory cut through Nas's fatigue like a hot knife through butter. He gasped. His eyes filled with dread.

Scoldari raised his open window. "And that, my friend, is why I'm posting a cop outside your door."

Chapter Twenty-Six

Gwen Winter

It was early the next morning, but not that early. The driver who picked me up at the Long Island train station was no Uber Dave. The ride upstate to see Jana continued to cycle through my mind. I'd been crazed and had given poor Dave such a hard time. In retrospect, he'd handled it like a champ, and I'd come to regard him as the gold standard of Uber drivers, the bar by which all others would henceforth be measured. How I wished he was here with me now.

The current guy confirmed my destination, and that was it—he barely said another word until he dropped me off. I'd tried to broker polite conversation, but he was immune to any invitation to engage. His social skills hovered somewhere between a rock and garden moss.

"Here we are," he said, his expression indicating that he was present in body only and thrilled to dump me at the curb.

I wanted to say, "Hey, Chatty Cathy, you know Tesla has just about perfected driverless cars. You'll be an anachronism before you're thirty." But that was Gwen before the disaster. New Gwen had started sleeping on her own, no sleeping pills, no nothing. Not even a cup of sleepy-time tea. And that's because I wasn't the guilty one. I wasn't the one who'd disappeared into thin air. I harbored no guilt and took no responsibility for what took place on our wedding day. That dubious honor belonged to scummy Nas alone.

It's odd how the psyche works, but there it was. Maybe I was meant to live alone, unbridled by a partner and sleeping like a log. There'd still be plenty of ups and downs, but marriage had never provided an exemption from life's roller coaster ride. And never would. If anything, it made the peaks higher and the dips exponentially deeper.

I was back on that street again, the same one we'd stolen upon the night Nas fled, ever vigilant for the presence of Mohammad and Amira Zia, parents of the worm who'd slithered away, the man who'd shown the world he wasn't a man at all.

We'd come to his parents for answers and received none.

This time would be different.

The house looked completely different in daylight, sun-bleached, almost regal, as if royalty resided within. The doorbell chimed with such authority I half-expected a formally dressed manservant to greet me at the door.

No one greeted me at the door. I rang the bell over and over, becoming more irritated with each touch of the buzzer. I wasn't kidding myself—hounding the Zias was a half-baked idea, but resolve marched me to Penn Station, and determination sat my ass down on the train. These people owed me an explanation.

I knew Mohammad kept long hours and was usually on his way to work at the crack of dawn. He owned a business, importing spices from the Middle East. Nas often commented that his father worked like a dog. I was hoping that this was one of Mohammad's sun-up to sun-down days.

I wanted Amira alone.

Around the far side of the house, past the garage, I went to the fence and peered over the top. There she was, Mohammad's obedient wife, tending the garden while the master toiled for coin. The yard was surrounded by lush trees and arborvitae. She was completely hidden from the neighboring homes but nonetheless honored the required dress code and was wearing a long-sleeved shirt and ankle-length skirt, her head covered with a kerchief. As thoroughly adorned as Amira, a vampire could frolic in the sunshine without compromising any of its undead flesh.

She was so absorbed with her chores that she didn't hear me unlatch the gate and steal up behind her. I figured she'd jump when she realized I was behind her, and she did, clutching her heart, breath freezing in her lungs.

I remained silent while she got to her feet. *You go first*, I thought. *This should be awkward, for you.*

"Gwen," she began, guilt-ridden crocodile tears spilled from her eyes. "I didn't know if I would see you again." She stepped forward and put her arms around me, but she must've been stricken by the frigid cold I radiated and stepped back. "I've been so worried about you, dear. My heart—"

"Where's your son? Don't tell me you don't know where he is because I know you do. You and Mohammad have been lying to me all along."

"Gwen, we would never. I swear to Allah. If we knew anything, you'd be the first we told." She pulled off her gardening gloves and wiped her tears. "How could you think such a thing? My son has disappeared and brought shame upon our family. Do you think for one moment we'd keep something like that a secret?"

How could they not know? Worse, how could they pretend not to know?

"You're lying to my face, Amira. Could you please stop thinking about yourself for a moment and think of me? Remember me? I was supposed to get married to your son. How many times did you tell me you loved me? How many times did you say I was like a second daughter?"

"Many times. Many, many times. I do love you. Do you think I don't understand how badly you were hurt? I would do anything to fix this. Anything."

"Anything?"

"Yes, anything."

"Good. Then start by telling me where Jana has been taken."

Desperation screamed from her eyes, then her head slowly sank. "You gave us no choice."

"*I* gave you no choice? What is that supposed to mean?"

I saw her eyes darting back and forth, averting contact. She tried to step past me, but I moved between her and the house. "What—do—you—mean?" I asked. She tried to slip past me again, but I was too quick. "Amira, talk to me."

CHAPTER TWENTY-SIX

"I beg you, please leave us alone."

"Where's Jana? Why did you move her? Nas said she's been in that hospital for years. Why all of a sudden did you take her out?"

"My husband told you, she's not a well girl. And now, since you visited her, she's much worse." Wiping tears, she pushed me aside. "Now go! You've done so much damage already." I watched her trudge toward the kitchen door. "Go away," she bawled. "May your God forgive you."

My God? Did she actually say, *My God?*

"*My* God has nothing to forgive."

My cell phone rang. I glanced at the display and saw that it was Dad. I put the phone to my ear, thinking his timing couldn't have been worse.

I couldn't have been more wrong.

Chapter Twenty-Seven

Nasir Zia

Nas awoke in his new hotel room, fully dressed with his face wedged between two pillows, his lips pasted to the sheet, nauseous with a hideous nightmare still raw in his mind. The reverie embodied everything he rejected about his religion: the veneration of eternal life over actual life on earth, the belief that this life is nothing more than a rehearsal for the afterlife, a preamble before the manuscript, proof of worthiness.

In his dark dream, he saw himself preparing for death and the assurance of an everlasting existence. There was no mystery behind his dream, nothing to decipher. He understood its meaning as clearly as if he'd scripted it.

Although he'd attended public school, his parents had insisted that he study the Qur'an and subscribe to its teachings. And he seemingly did just that. He prayed as required, fasted when expected to, and went through all the motions exactly as he was required. But in his heart, he was a Westerner who lived for the promise of a long and happy life, a life together with Gwen, a life he had been denied. He wasn't preparing for death because he embraced it. It was his existence, his current life, that terrified him. Losing Gwen, followed by a charade marriage and the travesty of an innocent man's murder, his struggles should've been proof of worthiness enough for Allah or any other god.

By all counts, he was worthy of immortality.

But not love.

If only I could tell Gwen what happened. If I could only explain. He felt acid burning his throat. Nausea, like a sea swell washed over him. *She has to know I still love her. I must find a way to tell her.*

Nas's last memory of the previous night was switching off the lights and falling face-first into bed. His feet had swollen during the night and were now imprisoned within his shoes. He pried them off one at a time and peeled sweat-saturated socks off his feet, but jumped up when he felt acid rising up his esophagus and hurried to the bathroom. The nausea was nothing compared to everything else he was feeling. Swigging a hospitality bottle of mouthwash, he peeled off his gamey clothes and stepped into the shower. Lifting his head, he gargled to kill the vile taste in his mouth.

The water, like frigid daggers, pummeled his skin. He shivered but stood unyielding, hoping the deluge would either drive the nightmare out of him or drown him. He didn't relish the prospect of death but prayed he'd find the courage to accept it if it came.

If it brought the nightmare to an end.

Bare-chested, with a towel wrapped around his waist, he fell into a chair and checked his phone. He'd gone over a day without checking it, but there had been no new messages or calls. The battery was practically dead. He retrieved the charger from his backpack and plugged it in. Connected to the AC umbilicus, his phone lived. He scrolled the long list of missed calls and texts that had begun to pour in when he didn't arrive on time for the wedding ceremony. Dozens of texts: Gwen, Gwen, Gwen, Gwen, Gwen, Gwen, from his parents and hers, from friends and colleagues. He'd stunned them all. He imagined them saying, "I can't believe it. I just can't. Nas has always been such a good guy."

Until he wasn't.

Until he'd done the unspeakable, destroyed the woman he loved, dishonored himself and his family.

If only they'd give him the opportunity to state his case, to explain. They'd see him differently, even if they didn't understand. Didn't accept.

His phone quickly charged to fifteen percent. *If only I had such insights,* he thought. *If only I could envision my life's battery icon. How much juice was left? Seventy-five percent? Fifty? Or was the indicator in the red? How much longer will I need to endure this pain?*

Swiping to the Favorites Screen, his finger hovered above his father's name. He wasn't supposed to call, not for days, not his father and not anyone. He was supposed to be alone with Bahija, man and wife, on their own without interference from family.

He'll be furious, he thought and moved his finger away from the phone. *But he demands so much, so damn much.* It felt as if hands were around his throat, choking him. He could feel his face grow flush and his temples pound. His heart thudded like a kettledrum.

Call him. Show some balls.

His finger shot out like a firing piston so hard he thought the screen might crack. One ring. Two. Three.

"Marhaba. Nasir, is that you?" Mohammad said, unable to conceal his shock.

"Yes, father. I'm—"

"We agreed you weren't going to call."

"Yes, Baba, I'm sorry, but…" Shame caught in his throat. How could he be responsible for such a disaster? How could he speak of such incompetence to his father?

"Nasir, you've caught me at a very bad time. I'm installing your sister at a new facility."

Nas gasped. It had been years since he'd seen his younger sister truly smile or could hold her head up proudly, but he knew she felt safe where she was, in the care of people she trusted. "What? Why would you do that, Baba? Jana liked it there. She—"

"*Nasir*, I told you, this is not a good time. I've got my hands full. Can't this wait?"

Can't this wait? No, it can't. He never verbalized what he was thinking. He'd been taught to respect his father, respect him without conditions. He heard a commotion on his father's end. "What's going on? Is something wrong with Jana? Is she okay?" She was so fragile and had undergone years of treatment without improvement.

"Nasir, I have to go. I'll call you back."

"But, Baba—"

The line went dead.

Chapter Twenty-Eight

Gwen Winter

Dad was waiting for me in the SUV when I got out of the Uber in Bay Shore. I could see his gaze following me as I approached. I could see that he wasn't happy.

He lowered the window and called out to me, "Why did you go to see Amira on your own? If only you had stayed with us instead of running back to the city, we could have confronted her together."

He was peeved but not angry, which was his disposition a great majority of the time. I could've come back at him with any number of caustic barbs about how shitty my life was, and couldn't he show a little sympathy, but that didn't work on a man like Hank Winter, a man with a backbone as substantial as a double-wide trailer. Ignoring him did the job. Or perhaps it was the overnight bag I had slung over my shoulder that appeased him. It was probably hidden from his view when he hurtled his initial unpleasantry. He already seemed ten degrees cooler by the time I walked around the SUV and got in. No doubt my testosterone-charged father saw the overnight bag and took it as a win, even if it wasn't. It meant I had planned to stay under his roof again, under his protective custody.

"Why are you waiting for me out here?" I asked. "I figured you'd be upstairs with Magnum, P.I. coordinating the offensive."

"Funny, very funny." He smiled in spite of himself and opened his arms. "Come here, you." His compass only pointed in two directions: raging hostility or heartfelt love. There was no middle ground. He either loved you or hated you, and I was fortunate enough to fall into the first category.

Dad's embrace made me feel safe, Fort Knox safe, as if no harm could come to me while my head rested on his shoulder.

"Listen, kiddo," he began, "what Dan is going to tell you might be a little tough to hear." He gritted his teeth. "More than a little, actually."

The breath caught in my lungs. What was I going to hear? That Nas had fled the country? Been mauled by a bear? All the uncertainty. The weight of not knowing. I loved and hated Nas all at the same time. But if something had happened to him, I'd never forgive myself. *"Oh my God, Dad. Tell me already."* I put my hand on my chest. "I can't breathe."

He pressed his lips tightly together, and for a moment, I actually believed that Hank Winter, the toughest son of a bitch I'd ever known, was going to cry. This was the real reason he was angry and not because I'd gone back to the city. This is why he wanted me under his roof. "B-baby girl," he stammered, "he was with someone else."

Chapter Twenty-Nine

Gwen Winter

Pity radiated from Ohana's eyes from the moment I entered the room. He could see that I'd been told about Nas, that Nas had been cheating on me, and how the news tore me apart. I felt like my guts had burst, as if the contents of my internal organs were intermingling like swirling gobs of goo.

No doubt Ohana was thrilled he'd dodged the bullet, that he hadn't been charged with the responsibility for dropping the bomb. Super soldier Hank Winter had already taken that heat, absorbed all the radiation from the blast, and was still standing, skin-charred, flesh disintegrating, and hanging by a thread but still standing at my side offering whatever he had left.

Get it over with, screamed in my head. *Unload the misery so that I can go home and die. Or maybe I'll just die here, here and now. Why wait? What's the use?* Why couldn't Nas just fuck me over like any normal asshole? Did he have to vanish into nothingness to be with someone else? Did the news have to come bit by bit, gouging away at my self-esteem like a sculptor with a razor-edged chisel?

How could I have been such a fool? To think, the man I loved led me to the altar knowing there was someone else.

And hiding that someone else.

I wanted to cry again like I did in the SUV when my dad broke the news, wads of tears, a box of Kleenex worth.

Hold it together, at least in front of the snoop. He's not family. He doesn't get to see you peeled raw. "You've got something to tell me?" I asked.

The look on his face, as if I'd asked him to embark on a suicide mission. General Washington had just signaled the attack, "Charge the blue coats and die on the field of battle."

Ohana sat down at his desk where a finger of scotch rested in a squatty glass. A second glass on the far end of his desk was empty, no bottle in sight. They likely killed a fifth, rehashing what Ohana had learned about Nas and his secret ho.

Spill it, for God's sake. I'm in agony.

"I started by checking Nasir's credit card records," Ohana said. "Oddly, there'd been no recent activity in days. It led me to believe he was holed up somewhere, perhaps in a friend's place, or with a family member. But the more I thought about it—" He looked at my dad, his gaze asking, *Does she need to know it all?*

Dad nodded, instructing him to tear off the bandage. He then put his arm around me and rested his head against mine.

"The more I thought about it, the more suspicious I became. You rarely see this kind of activity when an ordinary citizen just wants to get lost for a while. It's usually fugitives from justice who are, on the run, wanted criminals. I didn't think Nasir would be that hard to track down, that he'd be that savvy, but—"

"But *what*? What does this even mean? Are you saying he's a felon, that he's involved in something terrible?" How much more slowly and painfully could he make this? It was as if he'd inserted a thin port into my heart and was watching me bleed to death one drop at a time. *Just come to the fucking point!*

"No paper trail," Ohana said. "I believe he's using cash wherever he goes so that he can't be traced via his credit card charges. That shows a level of sophistication I didn't expect to find."

"Or at least that his flight was preplanned," Dad said. "I'm sorry, Gwen, but it doesn't seem like he woke up on his wedding day with a case of cold feet and an abrupt need to run. I can't explain why or when he made the decision, but it's clear he was not planning to come to the ceremony."

Screw dignity—I covered my face and wailed tears of fury, of agony, and shame. I felt as if I were drowning, as if my lungs were filling with fluid. "How could he?"

Ohana pushed a box of tissues across the desk and angled his chair until he was looking out the window, away from me.

Dad kneeled in front of me. "Gwen, look at me. It's going to be all right. We're going to find this asshole, get the truth out of him, and then you're going to move on."

My gaze said, *Do you actually believe anything you're saying? How can you possibly…?* The dad I knew was incapable of demeaning me. *I know how much he loves me, but hell, don't lie. Treat me like an adult.* "Please don't patronize me, Dad. You can candy-coat it as much as you like, but this is a pure shit sandwich."

"All right, then just suck it up," Dad said. It seemed as if he was reaching for something else to say, like, *You've been up against worse* but stopped before putting his foot in his mouth, which is what I preferred. It was the dad I knew. Somehow the truth stung less unadulterated, with all the bullshit stripped away. Dad straightened up, and I turned my gaze to Ohana. "That's not all of it, right? I assume you've got more to say than *he pays with cash.*"

Ohana sighed. "Sounds like you want your money's worth."

First law of the Hebrews: never pay retail. Where there's a bargain to be had…? I nodded.

"Going back several months, there weren't any credit card charges that stood out. I was looking for hotel bookings, air, rail, rental car reservations, that sort of thing. There was nothing there that indicated he was planning a trip."

"You mean planning to flee, don't you, to run off like a coward? How could I have misjudged him so badly?"

Ohana clammed up.

"Don't do that to yourself, Gwen," Dad said. "You were in love. You were planning a wedding, not conducting a background investigation. *No one would've seen this coming. No one.*"

"Sure, Dad, whatever you say." Why was I God's punching bag? Had I murdered children in a former life? Did I run a Nazi death camp? I didn't believe any of that Buddhist reincarnation crap but wasn't I entitled to some sort of an explanation? Didn't I deserve to know the truth? "Are we finished here?"

Dad's face told me there was more, much more, acid cocktails more. I snatched Ohana's glass and swigged his scotch. The look on their faces, priceless. "Please, just make it quick."

Ohana once again turned to my dad for the okay to proceed and received another affirmation. "I monitor police activity in the tri-state area. I don't pay attention to the small stuff, but the felonies… I'm on top of all of those: assault, grand larceny, shootings." One more check-in with Dad before continuing. "Murders."

My blood turned cold. Saying I wanted Nas dead and meaning it were two very different things. "Oh God *no*. Tell me Nas is okay." I searched Ohana's eyes, pleading for relief. What else could they throw at me?

"Not Nas," Dad said. "*He's* okay, but…"

"Oh, come on, the two of you are killing me. *What?*"

"I'm sorry to tell you this, but Nasir is a person of interest in the murder of a hotel manager in New Jersey," Ohana said. "He's being questioned by the police."

Chapter Thirty

Nasir Zia

Nas walked holes in the carpet, his mind a muddled pot of emotions. There are only so many balls you can keep up in the air, and less when you're carrying the weight of the world on your shoulders. So many tragedies had befallen him in the days since he'd left New York. Too many for the juggler to keep aloft and each heavy beyond reason. He'd never used drugs, not even pot. But now, he wondered if he could survive without their help. He wanted to be sedated, put out of his misery until the mess had been cleared up. At least some part of it. Perhaps then he could deal with the remaining issues. As it now stood, he was collapsing under the weight of his troubles, and the agony of having lost Gwen forever was as if a plastic bag had been pulled over his head, suffocating him.

The room they'd moved him to was not a suite like the one he'd occupied with Bahija. It was a spartan bunker, just big enough to accommodate a bed, end table, and a dresser. It was strictly bargain-basement, the room the architect had sandwiched into his plans to meet the requirements of his contract. What could he expect? The police department was now picking up the tab. He'd been asked to stay put until the authorities had a better handle on identifying and locating the alleged perpetrator. "More for your safety than anything else," Scoldari had told him. "It shouldn't take long."

He ran to the hotel room door when he heard a knock. He couldn't stand being alone and didn't care who was on the other side of the door as long as it was someone to talk to, about anything, the murder, his missing bride, his poor sick sister, or changing the linens. Any distraction would do.

Scoldari stood in the threshold holding a Starbucks paper cup. "This is some kind of chai bullshit. I don't know what it is but the last time I went to Key Food a box of Lipton went for about four bucks a hundred. How Starbucks has the nerve to charge what they do for hot water is beyond me." He looked past Nas into the room and rolled his eyes. "Low rent district, huh? Tell you what, grab your shoes. Let's go for a walk."

"You have news?" Nas asked, his eyes wide but standing statue-stiff in front of Scoldari.

He nodded. "I have news." Three finger snaps later, "Your shoes? Or do you prefer to go barefoot?"

"Oh." Nas turned and grabbed his shoes. He closed the door and followed Scoldari into the corridor without putting them on.

A fresh pair of clerks stood behind the reception counter, faces Nas had not seen before. He couldn't imagine what Ronit's family was going through and the grief that lay before them. A family had been fractured, splintered into bits so small they could not be reassembled. He didn't understand his role in the tragedy, but somehow he had played a part. Feeling ashamed, he hid his face as he walked past the counter and out the lobby doors.

Scouting the area, Scoldari spied a bench situated near the valet station, sat down, and signaled to Nas. "You going to try the expensive tea?" he asked.

Nas sipped the brew and nodded favorably. "Very good. Very good."

"Yeah, right? For that money? It ought to be. He sat quietly for a moment, then his eyes flashed, and his mouth gaped. "Holy shit, can you imagine if you were sitting here when what's-his-name hit the ground? My God, the shock alone is enough to throw your average Joe into cardiac arrest. I mean, fucking boom, splat, blood and guts everywhere."

The cup of tea tumbled from Nas's hands. He closed his eyes and trembled.

"Well shit," Scoldari said with a grimace. "There goes four bucks and change down the effing drain." He patted Nas's shoulder. "Sorry. I don't know what I was thinking. We've spent so much time together I thought I was talking to one of the boys. Deep breaths, Nasir. Take in the fresh air." He watched Nas inhale and exhale over and over until he settled down. "You going to be okay?"

Nas nodded unconvincingly.

"Good. So, listen, Nasir, I think we know who this Uncle Huzi is. We matched up DMV shit, rent rolls, and IRS records." He pulled a folded piece of paper from his jacket pocket, an enlargement of a New York State driver's license. "The photo is so old the son of a bitch actually had hair. But if you look closely…" The name on the license copy read Arshad Huzaifa. "Forest Hills, NY. Look good to you?"

Nas stared blankly at the license. The man depicted had a full head of hair—his complexion was smooth and without wrinkles.

"You seem a little bit out of it, Nasir. Concentrate. What do you think?"

He nodded slowly. "Yes, I believe that's him, Bahija's uncle. Much younger, of course, but the eyes are the same."

"I think so, too." He placed the photo in Nas's hands. "But you look like you've lost your grip, so take one more long, hard look for me, okay?"

Nas studied the photo and handed it back. "That's him. Do you believe he actually pushed Ronit from the balcony?"

"Well, Nasir, it was either him or you. So, yeah, I'm leaning that way. Plus, we've got him on a traffic cam driving west over the GW in a late model Toyota Camry, gray with a black interior. He doesn't own a car, and it's not a rental."

"Can you find Bahija?"

Scoldari peaked his eyebrows. "That's not the question, is it? We'll find the car, but will she and this Uncle Huzi still be in it? Days have passed. They could be anywhere by now, right here under our noses or on a garbage scow to Nova Scotia. It all depends on how well-connected this joker is. Sorry, I wish I could be more positive, but I'm not one to blow smoke up the ass. We've been trying to reach Bahija's parents to see if they have any idea where he may have taken her, but we haven't had any luck so far." He picked up the empty paper cup and walked it over to the refuse container. "Nasir, any chance a member of your family knows this Uncle Huzi? I mean, where did he come from? They didn't just pick him out of a hat. They trusted him to approve your marriage. I doubt they did that sight unseen."

"I believe Bahija's family suggested him. I was told that he's a mullah with the local mosque."

"A mullah, what's that?"

"A mullah is a well-respected member of the mosque, someone highly learned. Mullahs teach and sometimes act as judges of Muslim law."

"That's good to know. So, if we visit the right mosque, they should know all about this Uncle Huzi, right?"

Nas rubbed his beard. "Yes, in theory, but…"

"Yeah?"

"They are very closed-mouthed. I doubt they'll talk openly with you."

Scoldari lifted his leg and rotated his ankle. "Size twelve, double E. Oh, they'll talk." He dusted his pants leg and set his foot back on the ground. "Give your parents a call. It might prove helpful."

Nas turned away. "I-I've been having trouble reaching them. They're busy people."

Scoldari's eyes were two jumbo eggs. "Seriously? With all you're going through, you haven't checked in with your family?" He sucked in a chest full of air and blew it out through his nostrils. "I call bullshit."

Chapter Thirty-One

Gwen Winter

Dr. Cooper's "green room" was not a place where celebrities waited before appearing on a late-night TV talk show but a waiting room painted green, not an obvious green but a beige-green she'd specifically selected to quiet the mind, to slow the heart rate, and still breathing. Green is calming. Green is natural. Light-reflecting knockout drops.

I sat on my hands on her Hampton's-chic sofa while the wall color soaked in, the short wavelengths as relaxing as a scalp massage. I needed a few noiseless minutes to get my thoughts straight before seeing the exalted Dr. Cooper. All the world's a stage, right? And I was about to perform. Dr. Cooper was my tough love guru, my brain doctor, longtime shrink, and comrade-in-arms. Together, we fought the depression wars with medication and talk, patience and persistence.

Opening the door, she was every bit the Cruella de Vil I'd known since childhood. She pulled me close for a hug. It wasn't an Alana hug or even a Mom hug, but a light professional-to-patient squeeze offering support with no chance that her embrace could be misconstrued as anything else. She wore a taupe hip-length cardigan that covered a black tee and leggings. The medical professional appeared nowhere close to her age, though a shock of gray had sprouted in her jet-black locks. Lithe and stylish, she was every bit the eccentric, style-obsessed diva you'd expect from a North Shore

Long Island professional with her pedigree. The only thing missing was Cruella's obsession with furs. Nor did she have any plans to skin puppies and was a card-carrying PETA supporter with two precious Cavalier King Charles Spaniels. The three were inseparable. Seeing me walk in, Cuddle and Smooch pounced. I pulled them in like a pair of Patrick Mahomes passes and toppled backwards onto the doc's sofa.

Doc Cooper settled into her egg chair and crossed her long legs. "Better than Valium those two, right?"

It wasn't the first time she'd seen me on an emergency basis. We had history, late night and early morning visits, squeezing me in between appointments even when it required a personal sacrifice. Tonight's appointment would make her late for dinner with colleagues. "Stuffy old farts," she called them. "They can do without me for a while."

She picked up her notebook and a pen. "I'm so sorry, Gwen. You're such a sweetheart. You don't deserve this, any of this. I don't know why bad things happen to good people."

I'd given her a broad strokes preamble over the phone—the initial disaster, the ensuing disaster, and the bombshell. She hadn't hesitated, didn't flinch. "I'm waiting for you," she said. "Come right over."

Dad dropped me off and was waiting outside in his SUV. Her office was on the ground level of her home in a residential section of Roslyn, fifteen minutes from the closest strip mall donut shop Dad could visit. He didn't complain—he never complained and told me he'd be outside waiting when I was done. I didn't want to impose, but I knew there was no way he'd leave me to fend for myself at a time like this, not now especially. I thanked him and strolled over the exquisitely cobbled walkway to the doc's side door, her office entrance. About an hour had passed since being leveled in Ohana's bunker after being told that Nas had dumped me for another woman. A New Jersey detective told Ohana that Nas was on his honeymoon and had only stayed at the New Jersey hotel one night before all hell broke loose. There were manhunts for the bride and a suspect caught on hotel video. An innocent man was dead.

"Are you sleeping?" she asked. It was always her first question. Insomnia was a gateway condition. It led to severe depression and any number of threatening psychological manifestations, all of them bleak.

"Yes. I can't tell you why, but I passed out last night *and* the night before. No meds." I added a shrug addendum, *Go figure.*

"*Phew.* That's fantastic." She noted my response and looked up, pensive. "Where should we begin?" She often pumped her foot when she needed to think. "You're not feeling guilty, are you? I hope not. I mean, you shouldn't, but it's not uncommon for victims to feel responsible in some way. If you are, you need to disabuse yourself of those thoughts. *Immediately.*"

"I'm not guilty. How am I to blame?"

"You're not. Not in any way." She made a notation. "Just checking boxes. So, this came as a complete and utter shock. You had no idea your fiancé was wavering? No idea he was hiding something?"

I had both hands going at the same time, petting Smooch and Cuddle. Smooch loved it when I rubbed his ear. Cuddle had more of a tummy fetish. "If he was vacillating, I didn't see it. I was there with bells on for our wedding, face painted, primped, and corseted."

The doc smiled sadly. "I'm sure you were a beautiful bride. You're *so* pretty, Gwen. A living doll." I'd lost track of her current hourly rate, but I expected a cleverer response for the money I suspect she was billing, something profound, some Freud-worthy epiphany shit, something capable of dispersing the cloud over my head, a silver bullet amulet.

"I don't understand how he could do it, Doc, lie to me and hide a serious relationship with another woman. I spoke to him that morning, and there wasn't a hint of hesitation in his voice. He wasn't saying goodbye. He seemed breathless with anticipation. How could he sound so sincere, so committed to us, and have another woman in his life just hours before I was supposed to walk down the aisle?"

"You said, 'Breathless with anticipation.' Could you have mistaken excitement for anxiety?"

I shook my head violently, and she responded with a hopeless shrug, no different than I'd gotten from anyone else. I guess I was expecting too much. She was a doctor but no more than flesh and blood. She wasn't omnipotent.

She didn't have all the answers. Armed with compassion, professional wisdom, and an array of wonders drugs, she was a potent healer—but was that enough?

"I'm so happy you're sleeping," she said.

What? Where did that come from? It seemed Doc Cooper didn't know what to say.

"Before we explore how you're feeling, let's talk about this, how do I say it? I don't know this situation in New Jersey. I'm trying to get my arms around what you told me. The woman they say your fiancé was with has disappeared? And a man was murdered? Honey, this is bizarre, and my gut tells me that there's far more here than meets the eye, something miles out of the ordinary. This man you were going to marry. I feel strange saying this, but he may not be who you think he is. Maybe what happened..." She paused and searched my expression. "Maybe, Gwen, it was for the best. Maybe you got out just in time."

Going back to the moment just before I realized Nas wasn't going to show, you could've come to me with concrete evidence that he was a serial killer, and I'd have refuted it, dismissed it out of hand. But now, hearing the words coming from Doc Cooper's mouth, I wanted to embrace it. I wanted to believe that only a madman could've done what Nas had done, that he was a confidence man extraordinaire and had honed his skills on other unsuspecting women, practicing betrayal, before I ever met him. I needed it to feel good about myself.

But deep down, I didn't believe it. Not because the evidence wasn't there but because, in my heart, I was sure of who he was. "That's one theory."

"That's right. It's just a theory. I bring it up so that you understand that these are not ordinary circumstances.

She's writing in her book again. Is it something professional, or is she doodling erotic art? Guess I'll never know.

"How are your meds working?" she asked. "Do I need to tweak anything?"

The sleep question was a component of her opening salvo. The meds question was part of her retreat. She was running out of time, winding down. Those stuffy old farts would only wait for her so long.

"They're okay, I guess. I don't feel like I'm too far up or too far down. I don't want to hurt myself. I'm managing, just barely, but I am managing. And like I said, I've been sleeping."

Her cheekbones submitted. She wasn't being polite or courteous. To my practiced eye, the smile came from the heart. She put down her writing materials and joined me on the couch. Cozying up, she joined me in petting the fur babies. "In other words, Gwen, you're working this out all on your own. You're standing on your own two feet."

Chapter Thirty-Two

Gwen Winter

The visit with Doc Cooper left me hungry for more facts about Nas and his mystery bride. Who was she? And, more importantly, why were they together? Without condemning myself for being naïve, I struggled to understand how Nas had balanced two relationships at the same time.

And if *I* didn't know about her, did she know about me? Was she a homewrecker, a woman who went after men in committed relationships? Or was it Nas who'd strayed? What did he see in her that made her a better match than me? I wasn't kidding myself. I knew this sort of thing happened. Eyes wandered. Couples grew disillusioned and fell out of love all the time. But in the days leading up to our marriage…? I had grown more perplexed than angry. How could he do it? How could anyone? With all the chaos in the world, I felt Nas was the one solid thing I could cling to. But rocks fall, I guess. Mountains slide, and lives get trampled.

The ride home from my session took us past one of our favorite diners, the landmark eatery was chrome and glass on the outside, hundreds of menu options on the inside, and a staff that knew and took great care of us. The Greek salad was enormous, a trough of vegetables and marinated chicken topped with an avalanche of feta cheese. It was so good, four out of five visits good, but I wasn't in the mood for it. I was suddenly ravenous, pit-of-the-stomach starving, and didn't think I'd find the kind of comfort food I needed at the diner.

Ten minutes off the beaten path was a Denny's and the Grand Sandwich, a grilled gastronomic time bomb I suddenly had to have. No problem talking Dad into the decadent sandwich. He was the one who introduced me to the epicurean monster in the first place. It was the closest thing to one of Mom's comfort meals on the planet, as satisfying as an all-you-can-eat pasta buffet.

Forty minutes later, I was challenging Dad for the last of the pancake puppies.

His smile was a combination of surprise and pride. "I've never seen you eat like this before. I guess your old man's genes finally kicked in."

It wasn't his genes. It was emotional hunger, but I didn't want to discuss stress eating with him. All the same, I nodded. "Guess so."

"Well, it does me good to see you enjoy your food. I guess Dr. Cooper was helpful?"

Nodding again. "Right now, I'm more curious than hurt. It's a mystery I can't deal with. Why can't I know what happened? I'm over being the victim. I just want to know why?"

"Sounds like you've made progress." He outmaneuvered me and speared the last deep-fried pancake balls. "Have I taught you nothing?" he said with raised cheekbones. "Never let your guard down." He winked at me as he stuffed it into his mouth.

God rest his soul, after he'd overeaten, my grandad often laughingly confessed that he was "Full up to his neck." I couldn't eat another bite and finally understood what he meant as I gulped coffee from a stained mug, thinking, like Drano, it would clear the clog. "Actually, Dad, you've taught me lots."

He playfully recoiled in shock. "This is too much for me to bear. You're beginning to scare me."

Hold on to your hat, Father. "I have to confront Nas. At the crack of dawn tomorrow, I'm going to drive out to New Jersey and pin him down. Gumshoe Dan knows where he is, right?"

"Now wait, let's think this through. Are you sure this is the best way to proceed?"

"Dad, for me, it's the only way. I can't deal with the secrets and bullshit anymore. I'm just so fucking tired of not knowing what happened." I sucked in as much air as my stuffed belly would allow. "It's the only way I can put Nas behind me. Now, does Ohana know where he is or not?"

He pushed his plate away before looking me in the eye. "If he doesn't, I think he can find out, but knowing where Nas is and seeing him are two different things."

"*Why?*"

"Well, for one thing, the police may not cooperate. It's a homicide investigation, and they may take a hard line. In their eyes, you're an outsider, a disgruntled ex-girlfriend." His gaze swept off to the side. "Nas may not agree to see you. You can't compel him to take a meeting."

"I don't know. I think the police might be very interested in what I have to say. Who knows more about Nas than—?" The words caught in my throat. When push came to shove, I obviously didn't know Nas at all. I thought I had, but now I knew better. I slammed the table with the heel of my hand. "You let me worry about the police. They'll either take an interest in me or they won't. As for Nas, get me in the room with the son of a bitch, and I'll get him to talk. I guarantee it."

Chapter Thirty-Three

Gwen Winter

Back in the truck, Dad was quiet, un-Hank-like in a way I couldn't quite get my arms around. He was always and had always been the bull in a china shop kind of guy. Shoot-from-the-hip-Hank had always been as patient as a provoked wolverine. Seeing him so contemplative worried me. Was there something he wasn't telling me, something he was worried I wouldn't be able to handle? The session I'd spent with him, and Ohana had been torturous but not terribly long in duration. Details came quickly after the initial slow blow. The Band-Aid ripped off, the balance of the story unraveled at blinding speed. Were they trying to spare me additional agony, or were they sparing themselves? Did they think I couldn't handle it, or could they not bear to watch?

"What's going on?" I asked. "You haven't said a word since we left Denny's."

He took his eyes off the road just long enough to make eye contact. "Just thinking is all."

"Care to fill me in?"

He inhaled, then blew a snort through his nostrils. "It's such a mess, Gwen. I just don't know what you're going to hear when you corner Nas. I figure the less I say, the better. I'm just trying to lower your expectations," he said with a hangdog face Ross Geller would've been proud of.

"I get it. Look, Dad, I completely understand if you don't want to be there. I can drive out to New Jersey on my own—all I need is an address."

"No. There's no way I'm not going. Get that into your head."

Turning to the side, I noticed the moon was full and particularly bright. I wasn't much for astronomy but I remembered something called a supermoon from a high school science class. It was the moon that made Lon Chaney sprout werewolf whiskers faster than a chia pet on fertilizer. "Just offering you a way out. This is my fight."

"And mine. And Mom's." He turned the wheel, pulled into a church parking lot, and threw the gear selector into Park. "We're all in this with you, Gwen." Unbuckling his seatbelt, he pulled me into his arms. "Don't you *ever* forget that." Not a bad hugger in his own right, Dad squeezed the living daylights out of me.

"Enough! Enough!" I pushed him away with a palm to the forehead. "You're like a boa constrictor."

He smiled. "Message received." Pulling out of the driveway, he took a wrong turn down a dimly lit residential street. "Shit. My eyes aren't what they used to be. Especially at night. I guess I'll have to turn around."

"No, keep going. You're not the only one capable of making a wrong turn, Magoo. If you stay on this until the end, you take a left, and it goes right by Alana's house. I presume you can take it from there?" I punched him on the arm, and he cut his eyes at me, smiling.

"I hope you're right, kid. Gas is going through the roof."

"I guess you'll just have to trust me." The road wound in and out, leaving doubt that my directions were accurate. "See where you are?"

"Yes, smartass, I see. Alana's place is just a few blocks up on the right." He turned the wheel and headed off.

Alana's place was in an older section of town. The lots were bigger, and the trees taller and more mature, with fifty-foot oaks and pines bathing the street in shadows. Up ahead, a car was running. The taillights on the Volvo convertible were distinctive: a pair of illuminated red eyebrows.

"I think that's Alana and Jack, Dad."

"Oh yeah?" He inched closer to the windshield, straining his eyes. "The girls should be in bed by now." He glanced over at the clock. "What are they doing outside?"

"Beats me."

Dad rolled down the windows as we approached. The mystery ended at once, Jack and Alana were going at each other, screaming in the middle of the street. I couldn't make out what they were saying, but I'd never before heard that level of volume and hostility coming from their mouths.

Dad tooted the horn, drawing a pair of angry glances.

I heard Jack shout, "Really, now *they're* here too? Fuck this!" He yanked on the Volvo's door and jumped in. Tires screeched as he pulled into the street and rocketed away.

"What the hell?" Dad said as he pulled to a stop in front of Alana and jumped out. "Sweetheart, what's going on?"

A Nile of tears ran down Alana's cheeks. I couldn't remember the last time I'd seen her that way. Maybe never. My unflappable sister had always been in control, cool, calm, and poised when around Jack, with the girls, with everyone. Seeing her broken down like that scared me to my core. I knew something terrible had happened, something with the devastating force to uncouple the heavens from Atlas's grip.

I wrapped my arms around her and could feel her quake. My big sister felt so small in my arms, fragile, compromised, raw. "What happened?" A handful of fresh tissues dissolved when they touched her face.

Dad was next to her. In his eyes, I could see that he was flustered. He was only used to one hysterical daughter, one hot mess.

Now, there were two.

It wasn't that he couldn't handle two emotional daughters. It was that one was Alana, the strong one, the one who had it all handled.

My mind leapt to that first meeting with Ohana. Looking out the window of his office at the ferry parking field and seeing Jack in the car with metamorphosed Imani Davis and the way she looked at him. The way he looked back at her. There wasn't a doubt in my mind as to what happened, as to why my precious sister was decomposing before my eyes. "I'm so sorry, Alana. He slept with someone, didn't he?" *Fucking men.* Was there a single one of them out there worth a damn?

She was completely still for moments, the quiet before the storm. I could sense that she was trembling within, about to explode. I tried squeezing her tighter, as if my puny arms could cap the lava-filled volcano that was about to erupt.

"*No,*" she wailed, long and wretched. "It was me."

Chapter Thirty-Four

Nasir Zia

Not every spring day is beautiful. Not every morning is sunlit, beckoning with the promise of a new day and all that life has to offer. Some days are simply bleak. Foreboding. They beg you to linger in bed, to pull the covers up, and wait out the storm. A Nor'easter had torn through the tristate with high winds and drenching rain. Rolling slowly, the heavy Crown Vic sedan snapped branches beneath its tires. No longer constant, heavy rain suddenly blasted the vehicle just when it seemed it had stopped for good.

Scoldari needed two hands to push the driver's door open against the buffeting winds. Nas waited for instruction in the passenger seat. Turning back toward him, Scoldari said, "Wait here. Understood?"

Nas nodded, signaling capitulation more than understanding. He'd assumed those specific instructions would be forthcoming. He'd gotten the talk on the ride out from the hotel. "Don't forget you're a civilian," Scoldari said. "Do as you're told. This case is a big pain in my ass already."

Pulling the hood of a rain slicker over his head, Scoldari stepped out and made his way toward a highway car parked on the shoulder with the beacon flashing.

Nas watched Scoldari approach the highway car. A State Trooper got out wearing a black poncho—all but the brim of the trooper's hat was covered by a vinyl hat protector. Through the rain-swept windshield, the trooper appeared as wide as he was tall. Nas watched the two men converse. It was only a moment or two before the trooper pointed at a set of muddy tire tracks cut in the grass, then through a clearing into the woods.

Nas saw Scoldari nod, and the two men followed the trail into the woods. He felt tension seeping into his bones as they disappeared from sight.

Days had flown by, and there was still no trace of Bahija or Uncle Huzi. Nas feared they were both gone for good. He knew neither could return home, not after what they'd done, not after blatantly forsaking Islamic law. They would be shunned and stripped of any standing in their community. Ostracism in the Muslim community was nothing to be taken lightly. If they'd colluded together and taken the time to plan their coup, they had certainly weighed the risks beforehand and understood the consequences their actions would bring.

There was one possibility he and Scoldari hadn't discussed: that Bahija was not a willing participant in her uncle's scheme and that she was also a victim. If a mullah had learned that he had ordained an unclean marriage, Nas might reason that he might take extreme measures to undo such a travesty. The seasoned detective seemed convinced that the two were working together. At least, that's how Nas saw it. Scoldari may have still been considering other possibilities, but he never talked about them.

The windows had become opaque with condensation, and the air heavy with humidity. The key was still in the ignition. Nas turned it to the Accessories position and cracked the windows, just enough to permit air flow but not enough to let rain enter the car.

Windows breached, the cabin filled with the random symphony of rain pummeling leaves and dripping onto the ground, splosh-splash notes that made up nature's composition. Water running through small rivulets, rushed and gurgled. The melody was hypnotic. Nas felt his eyelids growing heavy and was oblivious to the sound of foot slaps over soggy leaves and mud.

Scoldari tapped on the glass.

Glancing up, Nas was startled by the detective's somber demeanor.

"Get out," Scoldari said, wagging his finger as he turned away.

Nas flipped up the lapel of his jacket, but it did little to fend off the rain. He followed closely behind Scoldari as he threaded his way through the trees to a clearing. A gray sedan sat off-kilter in a shallow ditch, its hood pitched lower than the back end.

Nas felt the hairs rise on the back of his neck as heavy droplets of rain rolled off tree limbs and plopped on the top of his head. Coupled with intense humidity, his breathing became labored. "What did you find?" he asked apprehensively.

Scoldari pushed forward a few strides in front of him and answered without taking his eyes off the path. "Not what we expected," he said, his tone weary from the strain of the investigation. The aging detective took his time negotiating the muddy slope into a gully. Once at the bottom, he offered Nas a hand. "Watch your step."

Nas made it down the embankment on his own, his right foot sinking inches deep in mud at the bottom. He felt moisture creep over the tops of his shoes, saturating his socks and feet. His nose wrinkled as he turned toward the two police officers.

The State Trooper stood behind the car, his expression flat as he waited for Nas and Scoldari to join him at the rear of the sedan.

Nas panicked when he saw the trooper reach down to open the trunk. "Oh no. Please." His eyes were beacons projecting terror. "Tell me it's not her, not Bahija."

The trooper lifted the trunk lid. In the shadowy recess lay a man with dark, shortly shorn hair. A white skull cap rested against the side of his face and had wicked blood from the trunk liner. Below the beard line, a raw, blood-stained void separated the top and bottom halves of his throat.

His eyes bulging from the sockets, Nas's hand went to his mouth. Scoldari placed a hand on his shoulder and wheeled him around so that he wouldn't vomit on the corpse. Bent over from the waist, he gagged in waves. Involuntary spasms pumped bile up to his throat, out his mouth, and onto the ground, where it mixed with rain and bathed his muddy shoes.

Scoldari glanced at the trooper and shook his head, then cast his gaze skyward, allowing a barrage of rain to assault his face as he waited for Nas to settle down. He was patient until he wasn't, glancing at Nas repeatedly, his expression becoming more impatient with every turn. He finally placed a hand on Nas's back. "Breathe, buddy—in and out, in and out. You can't unsee what you saw. So, get past it." He glanced at the trooper. "Poor SOB was supposed to be on his honeymoon."

Several minutes came and went before Nas was able to stand upright, coughing to clear the acid from his throat as freshly fallen rain mixed with cold sweat on his forehead and neck. "Who-who's that?" Nas asked, his face the color of freshly sprouted grass.

Scoldari closed his eyes and shook his head with disappointment. The trooper nodded and shut the lid.

Chapter Thirty-Five

Gwen Winter

Thinking back, I could count on the fingers of one hand the number of times I'd sailed unimpeded over the Cross Bronx Expressway into New Jersey. Pure and simple, it was a parking lot, a dirty, congested parking lot, filled with pissed-off drivers and aggravated passengers, all wishing their car had come equipped with a Star Trek transporter.

And with the current weather bordering on abominable, high winds and torrential rain rocked the car. Par for the course, there was no traffic headed in the other direction. Sitting motionless, cars flew by in the opposite lanes, hit pooled water, drenching our SUV with nonstop tsunamis. I imagine it was like being aboard the Andrea Gail with forty-foot waves ramming the deck as it attempted to make its way back to port.

Leather steering wheel in his grasp, I could see Dad's knuckles turning white, and him wondered if he was strong enough to rip it off the stalk. With the big vein on his temple throbbing, he seemed more than capable. How badly did he want it?

"You picked a great-fucking-day, princess," he said. "The Garden State should be a lush jungle after this monsoon."

"I waited two days already. And how many times did I tell you I'm more than capable of getting to New Jersey on my own? We didn't have to make it a family outing."

Three hours later. Three-fucking-hours of standing still, creeping, crawling, complaining, and swearing. Three hours discussing my dear sister Alana, whose crisis was now more urgent than mine. Her wedding ceremony was always in my mind, and her, the most beautiful bride. The handsomest groom. The perfect ceremony. With such beautiful memories, did she have to elbow her way into my pile of shit? Did she have to do it now? Upstage me now?

Her marriage was ethereal, otherworldly, and strong enough to overcome anything life could throw at it, but could it withstand this?

Imani Davis, the mousy tub of lard, was now a size 4, a newly reborn hottie with undulating waves of shimmering hair and a valley of cleavage. She must've been a homewrecker, a seductress, a debauchee but not in the way I had seen coming.

Not at all.

No way in hell.

The three of us were shaking our heads over the news and sick with worry over Alana's marriage, not because she had strayed and not because she'd cheated with a gal. It was because it was Alana, Alana who had gorgeous loving Jack, Alana with two adorable cherubs, Ms. Perfect, Ms. Capable of Doing No Wrong. She was the gold standard by which every married woman and Mom should be judged. At least in my mind.

Explain that one.

Alana wasn't talking.

Jack wasn't talking.

Mom, Dad, and I were doing all the talking.

Jack had packed his proverbial bag and was bunking in with his friend Jeff. Alana managed to take a last-minute weeks' vacation. As far as little Madi and Sofia knew, Daddy was out of town, traveling for work. How long they could keep the charade going was anyone's guess. Two days had passed since Dad and I had inadvertently stumbled upon the Alana and Jack's front lawn blowout. What timing, right? And to think we would've missed the whole thing if Dad hadn't taken a wrong turn on our way home from Denny's.

It was some mind-blowing shit.

I ached for Alana. I ached for Jack and the girls and wished for a miracle that would allow me to undo the damage. But that's not life. That's not real. Nas and I were real, a steaming hot pile of excrement.

I hated myself for it, but I had to admit that Alana's melee served as a well-needed distraction. It gave me something else to focus on. It showed me that no one is perfect. In this imperfect world of ours, no one is without *tsoris*, a Yiddish word that is often used in my home. Incredible stuff that Yiddish, the ninth-century Jews had somehow created a lexicon of words capable of conveying emotion better than any other language developed since the dawn of time. Trouble and suffering, tsoris. Nerves, shpilkes. Balls, chutzpah. I rest my case.

I rode shotgun. Mom had chosen the back seat so that she could break down and cry whenever she needed to. The lives of her girls were in shambles, and the one she never had to worry about, the Temple of Alana and Jack, was crumbling like San Francisco during the great earthquake of 1906. I heard her blow her nose, then twist the cap on a bottle of water.

"You okay back there, Mom?" I asked.

I heard her sniffle before whispering, "Uh-huh." Then came more tears. I could hear her pulling tissues out of a box. "Do you think they're in love?"

"Who's in love?" Dad snapped. "Alana and Jack? Of course, they're in love. What kind of question is that?"

Dad didn't get the tone of Mom's voice. She wasn't talking about man and wife. She was asking about Alana and her lover, asking with trepidation. Would Alana reunite with Jack if he'd take her back, or was there no turning back? A shattered family with two darling kids caught in the middle bandied back and forth between their loving father and their…Gasp! Oh my God. It was jarring to think that Alana might not come out of a divorce alone. There was the possibility of shared custody between Jack and a two-mommy household. Wow! I wondered if Mom and Dad were capable of considering the possibility. *Shit!* I thought, panic-stricken. *Don't even look like you're thinking about it.* Dad would bust a gut. And Mom…? There'd be more water inside the car than descending from the heavens.

Why had I let the two of them come along? Why didn't I insist on going solo? I was perfectly capable of confronting Nas on my own, wasn't I? I had every right to an explanation, every right to look Nas dead in the eye and say, "Dude, what the fuck?

But how could I have left Mom at home? Alana wasn't answering her calls. Mom was devastated.

We all were.

"Finally," Dad said as the first exit in New Jersey came into view. "I've got to piss like a racehorse."

We pulled into a service station just as the rain stopped. The sun popped out, the glorious sun. The only thing missing was a fucking rainbow.

Dad bolted from the car. I wouldn't be far behind him. Mom was probably desert dry from all the tears she had shed. The poor thing, she probably wished she'd had two sons instead of two infinitely more complex girls.

I unbuckled my seatbelt, turned around, and took her hands. "Are you going to be alright?"

She sniffled, then nodded, doing whatever she could to appear strong, but I knew she was dying on the inside.

"Alana and Jack can get past this. They're both very strong," I said.

"Dear God, I hope so."

"Look at it this way," I said with a crafty smile. "At least we know Imani Davis didn't get Alana pregnant."

She laughed in spite of herself, laughed through her tears. "You're terrible, Gwen."

I saw Dad hurrying back to the car, checking his watch on the way. He was in the car, cranking the engine before I knew it. "No time for lunch. We're supposed to meet with this Detective Scoldari fella in ten minutes, and we're fifteen minutes away. If anyone has to tinkle, do it now while I gas up the truck."

Ohana had set the meeting with the detective handling the case, who wasn't going to put us in touch with Nas without meeting us first. Why? Maybe because it was his prerogative. Perhaps he thought we had information that might be useful. I didn't see how.

But I would.

Chapter Thirty-Six

Nasir Zia

Something was wrong with the police station air conditioning system. The air was humid and stale with the scent of machine oil. Scoldari presumed the compressor was shot, meaning a major repair was needed. Serious funds from the station's inadequate budget would need to be requisitioned. The prospect of a long, hot summer without air conditioning didn't help his demeanor, which was haggard, as if a crochet hook had been used to pull his nerve endings through the skin and set on fire like hair-thin firecracker fuses.

Having recently returned from the crime scene visit, the detective had been indoors, out of the rain, for more than an hour, but his suit was still damp. His wet shirt collar rasped against the skin on the back of his neck. He loosened his necktie and unbuttoned his collar before turning the handle and entering the interrogation room. This time, he didn't bring any food with him; no tea or sandwiches and seemed well past the imperative to be civil or care if his interviewee's stomach growled. Hunger was one of the few insidious tortures available in the detective's arsenal. He hadn't considered food and sleep deprivation tools in an interrogator's arsenal but wasn't above using those tactics if it would get meaningful results.

Entering the room, his expression broadcast every furious emotion he could display, every iota of irritation he was feeling. It caused Nas to recoil.

"Everything okay, Detective?" Nas asked, knowing damn well it was anything but; knowing a second murder had escalated the case from dire to an out-and-out disaster. He didn't know if Scoldari had handled a double homicide before, but if he did, he assumed those instances had been few.

"Hurray," Scoldari began as he dropped into the chair. "We've made the top one hundred, climbing the billboard charts with a bullet…knife. The FBI is on the way. The governor is chewing my ass like it's a Slim Jim. Bad news travels fast."

Nas felt himself shrinking in the chair, hoping to grow microscopic, invisible. "I'm sorry, but…"

"But what? You know nothing about it? That you're just an innocent bystander? Sorry, that shit doesn't fly anymore. I treated you like an honest-to-god human being. Extended every courtesy. And now a second man is dead. What the hell, Nasir? What are you hiding?"

The detective's intensity rattled Nas, and he began fidgeting in his chair as a shiver ran down his back. "What do you want me to say? I don't know that man. I never saw him before."

"That's irrelevant. I don't care who you've seen and not seen. Why are people dying, Nasir? There has to be a connection, and you're beginning to look like the fucking linchpin." Scoldari slid forward in his chair until his stomach pushed against the edge of the table. He leaned forward on his elbows, invading Nas's space. "Talk to me, man. Talk to me *now*. If you don't, *and* I connect you with this crime." His eyes widened. "Can you do serious jail time, Nasir? Are you prepared for that? Surprise visits in the men's shower? Having your face pushed into a fluids-saturated mattress while big hairy men pump you like a spare tire? That sound like fun?"

Nas fought the urge to gag, his hand flying to cover his mouth. The whites of his eyes spiderwebbed with red blood vessels. "I told you," he began, pleading, "I don't know anything."

"Everyone knows something—sometimes it's a lot more than they think. Maybe you don't realize how much you know. I'm betting there's something there, something that will help me with the case." He inched still closer. "So, try harder."

This is it, Nas vexed. *It'll all come out now.* His mind raced to come up with a reasonable lie, something he could sell. Wheels accustomed to turning smoothly went haywire and jammed. Slender springs snapped. His mind went blank.

Opening a folder, the temperature of Scoldari's gaze plummeted from cold to frigid.

"Osman Shehzad, thirty-one years old. Single. No children. Only child of Ali and Saba Shehzad." He closed the folder. "Dead man in a trunk, the trunk of the car Arshad Huzaifa drove across the GW. Any idea how Shehzad's body got there?"

"I'm very sorry," Nas began, a knot tightening in his throat. "I've never heard that name."

"A NYPD detective is helping me chase down leads—he just gave Shehzad's parents the bad news. They're *in-con-sol-a-ble*. That loosen your tongue any?"

Nas frowned, the corners of his mouth reached for his chin.

"Shehzad worships at the same mosque where Arshad Huzaifa, this Uncle Huzi, is so revered. I'm guessing they knew each other." He shrugged. "Ya think?"

Nas met Scoldari's gaze and saw the tortured look of a raving beast. "Very likely. I'm sure any worshiper would know his mullah."

"Especially since Shehzad apprenticed under him."

Nas felt a flash of relief in knowing Scoldari had locked onto a suspect. He waited, hoping Scoldari would open a door, a line of bullshit he could offer without divulging his dark secret.

Scoldari thumped the tabletop with his fingers. "I'm waiting?"

Nas rolled his neck. "I'm not sure what you expect me to say."

"All right, shitbird." Scoldari jerked back in his chair, stood, and put his foot on the seat. "Let me spell it out for you—your mullah did something wrong, something so fucking wrong it drove him to kill, something I think you're involved in. And your wife?" he sniggered. If you can call her that— being gone might mean being gone, or it might mean something completely different." The color drained from Nas's face. "Uncle Huzi might've pulled off a very rare feat, a mother fucking hat trick." He walked around the table and sat down on it, perched over Nas like a carrion-eating vulture. "You feeling the slightest little twinge of guilt? Responsibility? Or are you just stupid? Because if you're willfully withholding information in a homicide investigation, a *multiple* homicide investigation, well, sir, that's an indictable offense in this state. If I were you, I'd have my asshole laminated with Teflon because you're looking at long decades of sodomy."

An officer Nas had not seen before knocked on the door and came in. "You've got three unhappy civilians cooling their heels in reception." He checked his Timex. "A good half-hour now. They said they had an appointment. How long you gonna keep them waiting, Vito?"

Scoldari mulled the announcement, then shot Nas a heartless stare. It read *I don't care about you. Start talking, or I'll fuck you blind.* He stood and started toward the door.

The anonymous officer glanced at Nas. "The young man doesn't look too good. Should I call him a doc? Maybe order him something to eat?"

"Let him eat shit," Scoldari said and disappeared out the door.

Chapter Thirty-Seven

Gwen Winter

"It feels like a laundromat in here," I said after being shown to a conference room and waiting an additional fifteen minutes. "Haven't they heard of air conditioning on this side of the river?" There's a joke that's been floating around since forever, Why are New Yorkers depressed? Because the light at the end of the tunnel is New Jersey. New Yorkers had always looked down their noses at the Garden State and always would. The tepid air gave me ample reason to agree.

Mom knew enough to bring protein bars along for the trip. Twenty grams of protein was enough to keep the two ladies going, but Dad said that he was hungrier after scarfing it down than before. Hunger didn't bring out the best in him.

"Gwen, don't be such a drama queen," Dad said. "It's not that bad," then, in the same breath, added, "I'd kill for a cup of coffee." In sight of a coffee pot, he'd already be chewing at his leg to get to it like a wolf caught in a trap.

I heard a muted clang, then immediately felt cool, crisp air whooshing through the air vent, pushing stale, clammy air aside. "Hallelujah, it's a miracle."

"I'd rather be hot and well-fed," Dad said. "Where the hell is this detective anyway?"

"Right behind you, sir." A lean, older gent walked through the door. "I'm Detective Vito Scoldari. Sorry about the wait. Today has been a ballbuster of the first order. I'll bet you good people would like something to drink. Coffee? A soft drink? What'll it be?"

He grabbed the desk phone and placed our orders. Sitting down I could see that his hair was damp and there were water droplets on his neck. *I guess they ran out of paper towels in the men's room. At least there's a good chance his hands are clean.* He put down the receiver and was ready to do business.

"You folks get caught in the nor'easter coming out this way?"

"Three hours trapped in the car," Dad snapped, still angry, his temper no doubt exacerbated by hunger pangs.

At least you were in a nice dry car. I spent half the morning sloshing through the Jersey swamp. No picnic." He opened his notepad. "You came over the Cross-Bronx, I presume?"

Dad nodded.

"Big mistake. Go through Staten Island next time."

"What next time?" Dad asked.

"Figure of speech," Scoldari said. "It's longer, but you'll get across the Hudson in half the time. Traffic's not bad after the morning rush."

Dad should've said, "Thanks, I'll try to remember that." But the best he could manage was a quasi-neanderthal grunt and a hard stare in the direction of the open doorway as if he were trying to will someone to appear with his coffee.

"Let's get to it, Scoldari said, clicking his pen. "Nasir Zia, huh? Where the hell do we start?"

Where do we start? Where I need you to. "Where is he?" I said impatiently, entitled and frustrated. "He—"

"Whoa, whoa, whoa," Scoldari said. "Introductions first." He pointed at Dad. "Go." He went in order by descending age. Whether he did so out of respect or to piss me off, I wasn't sure. He jotted down our names, took addresses and phone numbers. "All right. I spoke with…" He flipped a page and found a notation. "Someone by the name of Daniel Ohana who claims to be a licensed PI out of New York. He said that Ms. Winter and Mr. Zia were engaged to be married and that Nasir—" Gritting his teeth, he completed the sentence, "left you at the altar." He sighed. "Sorry, dear. That stinks.

And you want to talk to him?" He squinted at me. "Are you sure? Do I need to check your purse for concealed weapons?"

My mother laid her hand on the table, something she did when she wanted to make a point. Or perhaps it was her way of making a personal connection. "Detective, my daughter is hoping for closure. She hasn't had contact with her fiancé since the morning of the wedding. You understand."

"Most certainly," Scoldari said. "Unfortunately, there's been a—"

I glared at him. "A murder? We know. Can't I talk to him for a few minutes? Is that too much to ask?"

"Believe me, I get it," Scoldari said, his eyes tall. "But there's protocol I have to follow in a case like this. I'd love nothing more than to sit you down in front of him and let the two of you go at it. Hell, I'd be happy to cuff him and let you wail away at him with brass knuckles. He's under the protective custody of the State of New Jersey. Whoever murdered the hotel manager… Well, how do I put this? He may have pushed the wrong guy off the balcony."

I sprang out of my chair. "Oh my God. What? You think?"

Dad saw me gasping, losing control. He stood and put his arms around me. "Detective, this is a theory, right? You don't know for sure."

"Sorry to get you worked up," Scoldari said. "Yes, it's a theory. And until this morning, that's all it was. But recent developments seem to support my belief."

"What is happening?" Mom said, her face growing pale. "What are you trying to tell us?"

The refreshments arrived. Sensing tension, the admin placed a tray on the table and backed out of the room without saying a word.

"First things first," I said. "Is Nas alright? Has he been hurt?"

"No. He's unharmed," Scoldari said. "I should've told you that up front."

Dad grabbed his coffee. Putting the cup to his lips, he scorched his mouth. "Shit, that's hot."

Scoldari hastily passed out the other drinks. "Everyone, take a deep breath." He didn't ask for silence, but the next sixty seconds were filled with it.

"Detective, we've already been through a lot," Mom said. "What happened this morning?"

Scoldari gritted his teeth. "A second homicide." Air whistled through his nostrils. "We think it's related."

"Related," I shrieked. "Related how?" I caught my parent's gazes. "How can you believe Nasir has anything to do with it?"

Scoldari pressed his lips together and cupped his chin in his hand. It looked as if he was weighing his words, going back and forth between what he could say and what he couldn't. "Ms. Winter, Gwen, am I correct in saying that you don't know anything about the woman your fiancé subsequently married?"

"*Nothing*. I don't know her—never met her—I don't even know her name. The first time I learned he married someone else was two days ago."

"Shit. I was hoping you could help me with her background. Her parents were supposed to meet with me voluntarily, but they didn't show up for their appointment."

"I'm at wit's end," I said. "I came out here to confront Nas. That's it. I don't care about her. Why do you?"

"Because I'm working a homicide case, Ms. Winter, and I believe that Nasir's marrying this woman is the reason two people are dead. Now, I've been questioning him for days, and I think he knows something he's not saying."

"You think he's holding back?" Dad asked, sounding suspicious of what he'd heard. "The three of us have known Nas for almost two years. He did a rotten, shitty thing to my daughter. I don't know why, but in my gut, I don't believe he's involved in two murders."

"I went so far as to threaten him with charges," Scoldari began, "pulled no punches, and his lips are shut tighter than a clam's ass. So, unless…" I could practically see a lightning bolt flash in the ether between his two ears. "Stay put," he said as he sprang to his feet. "I've got an idea."

Chapter Thirty-Eight

Gwen Winter

I wanted to go for Nas's throat.

Until I saw his eyes and love, adoration, and yearning, surrendering to shame as I walked through the door of the police station interrogation room. His head fell upon folded arms, and he began to cry.

Going against every thought I'd had in the past week, I wanted to go to him, wrap my arms around him, and wipe away his tears. I ached to absorb his suffering.

Then my head cleared.

He no longer belonged to me. He belonged to another, Bahija something or other, a Pakistani like him, a member of the same tribe. They prayed to the same god and would never be pulled apart by the inferno the Arabs and Israelis had ignited one hundred years ago, a firestorm that still raged with hate and consumed everyone in its path.

Still, I ached to heal him with all the love in my heart. I noticed the glass panel in the wall, the one-way mirror I'd only seen on TV cop shows—my parents and Scoldari were on the other side, looking in. It was a brainstorm that sent Scoldari flying from the conference room—he allowed me to see Nas, not to honor my request, but to see if I could get him to talk, to see if I could unlock the tawdry secrets the detective yearned to hear.

What my parents must be feeling, I thought. Watching me with Nas, their insides churning, their throats aching, dying inside. Their baby girl and the

Arab, how could it have happened? How had it gotten this far? A shattered wedding. Two people, dead. A litany of unanswered questions.

My heart was weeping—Dad had been right all along. It was never going to work. My engagement to Nas was a blueprint for disaster that I couldn't foresee.

Was Nas crying tears of sorrow, or was he crying because he'd been caught and now had to answer for what he'd done, for what he did to me? With his acts, like a sword, he ran me through, killed me, and fled without the dignity of a proper burial. And here I was, in the cold earth, like a haunted spirit unable to rest.

"Nas, look at me." I stayed on the far side of the table, well away from him. "Nas, please look at me."

His head remained buried in his arms. His crying grew louder, more desperate, the sounds of his tortured heart bombarding my senses. We'd been so much in love—how had we fallen so far, from moonlight strolls on the beach to a New Jersey-fucking police station?

"What happened? Nas, you owe me an answer. You left me at the fucking altar. So, pull yourself together and talk to me."

I imagined my parents on the other side of the glass, listening to our voices over a cheap speaker, on the edge of their seats, waiting for some closure and watching Nas whimper like a frightened dog.

Is this the man I was going to marry? I felt as if I didn't know him at all.

"I'm not leaving here until we talk," I said, staring down at the back of his head. *Be a man*, I thought, but didn't speak the words. It was too soon to emasculate him, but I'd do it if I needed to. It was there in the arsenal, waiting to be deployed. "Would you speak to me? Tell me something?"

I heard him sniffling. He raised his head—his eyes were red and watery, his nose wet. He looked pathetic and couldn't make eye contact. "Gwen, I'm-I'm so sorry."

You should be. "I don't want to hear how sorry you are. I want to know how you could pledge your love to me and then do what you did. How could you lie like that?"

As deeply as I was hurt, I didn't hate him, but I hated what he did. "Would you just talk to me?"

I could see my mother without seeing her, the look in her eyes, the strength and dignity she showed me the many times I was an emotional mess. I imagined that's how she looked at that very moment, to counsel me with her wisdom and fortify me with her heart. It took all I had to walk to the table and sit down opposite him, eye-to-eye. I reached out and took his hand. We'd never been on such unequal footing. It felt strange occupying such moral high ground. "Nas, where did *we* go wrong? What am I missing?"

He choked out a few words. "It wasn't you."

"What does that mean, that you take responsibility? That tells me nothing. You left me for someone else on the day we were supposed to get married. I need an explanation, and I'm not going anywhere until I get one."

He closed his eyes and shook his head. Opening them, he sighed, "I'm sorry."

"I need you to do better than that. When did you meet her, between our phone call in the morning and the time you were due for the ceremony? How long have you been seeing her behind my back? Do you know how badly you hurt me?"

The words "I'm sorry" formed on his lips, but he knew it was meaningless to speak them again. Of course, he was sorry. What warm-blooded creature wouldn't be?

"I know it's not easy, but I'm here, and I'm listening. Don't I deserve that much?"

"Yes."

"Well, I'm waiting."

"I-I didn't have a choice."

"You what? You didn't have a choice?" I shook my head in disbelief. "Was she pregnant? Did you get this woman pregnant?"

He held up a pair of trembling hands. "No, no, no, nothing like that."

Thank God. "Then what?"

"I had a gun to my head and I-I can't tell you any more than that."

I could see in his eyes that he was telling the truth. But what did he mean? "An arranged marriage? Is that what it was? Did Mohammad insist?" I had always known Mohammad Zia to be a warm and caring soul, but I knew he was also rigidly traditional. Did Mohammad have two faces? Had he been plotting to humiliate me all along? "Did your father make you do this?"

Nas stared at me, unable to speak. I could see that he was torn, that he wanted to explain, but couldn't.

"Where is your loyalty, to your father or to me? You promised you'd love me for all eternity. How many times did you say those words?" Tears ran from my eyes. "Is this how you keep your promises? Did you mean anything you told me?"

He reached out and took my hands once more. "Gwen, I want to tell you everything so badly. I want to—"

The door creaked behind me, then a man's booming voice shattered any hope of learning what had happened. "I'm Mr. Zia's attorney," the man said. "Nasir, don't say another word."

Chapter Thirty-Nine

Gwen Winter

And he didn't. Not a word. Not goodbye. Nothing.

Studying Nas's face as I was led out the door, I saw a pressure cooker after the steam valve was released. He was stunned to see a lawyer walk through the door, but looking into the attorney's eyes, he was relieved, like a child just rescued from certain peril, expressing unbounded gratitude for his hero.

I hated him for that, for using the damn suit to shun me. We waited around, hoping I'd get called back in to see Nas, but Scoldari convinced us it was pointless.

What now? I thought, *Back across the bridge, beaten and broken?* With no place to go, we found a gas station convenience store a short distance from the police station whose logo was a massive goose shitting on the name Wawa. We hunkered down, hoping that by some miracle, Nas would agree to meet with me again. Hours passed. Coffee and garbage convenience foods were consumed. Against better judgment, bathrooms were used. Several calls were placed to Scoldari, messages left. Three hours passed before we finally heard from him.

"There's no word," he said. "Nasir isn't talking to you or anyone else."

"That's what he said? He doesn't want to talk to me?" I asked.

"I'm afraid so, young lady."

"He said that or his lawyer?"

"What's going on?" Mom asked. "Put him on speaker."

I did as I was asked.

"They're one and the same as far as I'm concerned," Scoldari continued. "My advice: go home. Get a good night's sleep and plan your next move. I checked out this New York attorney of his, Miles Godfrey. He's a private practitioner, and he's no lightweight. You want to compel Nasir to meet with you, maybe think about getting representation of your own. Without it, you won't get to first base with this blowhard ambulance chaser. Worse, push too hard, and he'll hit you with a restraining order, and then you're truly fucked. You won't be able to come within a thousand feet of your ex."

"He could do that?" I asked.

I wasn't asking if Godfrey could do it. I was asking if Nas would, but Scoldari didn't pick up on the distinction. "I'm not saying he would, but he could. How badly do you want to hang onto this guy? He screwed you over. He's not cooperating. *And* he might end up doing time. Maybe you should consider moving on."

"Screw that! *You* move on." It was at times like these I missed old world phones so that I could've slammed the phone into the cradle. Best I could do was chip a nail hitting the End Call icon. Shit's just not the same.

Mom and Dad were standing next to me outside the store, breathing in fumes from the cars at the fuel pumps. "Do you fucking believe that?" I said. Anger and helplessness tore at me, competing for my attention. "What do I do?"

Mom squeezed my arm. Dad threw a fresh cup of coffee into the trash. Their reactions were diametrically opposite. The bottom line was that neither knew what to say.

I felt so weird, so totally uncomfortable in my own skin. Did I have a right to hear the truth, or didn't I? Nas wasn't mine anymore. That much was clear. And from what I understood, the new wife wasn't his either.

We were both alone.

I wondered how it would play out—if I'd have justice or walk away. I felt like a ball of twine, and everyone was pulling on a string. How much of me would be left before this was over?

"What do you think?" Mom asked. "This detective, he's not the kind of person you'd invite over for dinner, but…" It seemed as if she was afraid to finish what she was thinking. "Maybe he's right. The sooner you put all this behind you, the better." The peaking of her eyebrows finished the sentence. There was this patented way she cocked her brows. I wasn't sure if she was fully committed to the suggestion, but she put it out there.

"That's not what I want, Mom. I want—"

"You want what, more hurt, more to get over?" she asked. "Nas is a piece of garbage, and I can't bear to see him hurt you like this. Believe whatever explanation you need to so that you can live with what's happened and move on. You're a beautiful girl, Gwen, and there are a lot of fish in the sea, better men than Nas, smarter and most definitely better looking. Look at it objectively, sweetheart. What are you really giving up? Better it ends now. What if this happened years from now, and you had children? That would be so much worse. Make a clean break."

"Really?" I asked, disappointment registering as clearly as a shard of glass. "That's your advice?"

"You asked for my opinion, and I gave it. You can't be disappointed because you disagree."

Oh, no? Watch me. I turned to my father, who was still wiping coffee off his hand. I was surprised that he was so reserved that he hadn't blurted obscenities and punched out the store clerk. His silence spoke volumes, how heavily all this trouble weighed on him. Mom only sought to spare me pain, but that wasn't the way my father rolled. "Screw this guy," he said, "Screw him and the horse he rode in on. Trust me, this isn't Nas's doing. This is Mohammad, top to bottom. There's something going on here, and I won't be able to rest until I've figured it out." His eyes locked on mine. "What about you, Gwen? Can you wash your hands and walk away? You've been wronged, and you have every fucking right to find out what happened. Mohammad hired a lawyer, a fucking lawyer? They're a dime a dozen, even the hungriest sharks. That's what we'll do if need be. We've got moves we can make too. This attorney thinks he's got our backs against the wall? Bullshit." He perused the boulevard in both directions. "Let's find a quiet place where we can sit and have a discussion like human beings. I can't string my thoughts together standing out here in the middle of nowhere." I could see that he was boiling over, temper winning out over patience. "Come on," he said as he made a move toward the SUV. "Let's get the hell out of this roadside shit hole."

Chapter Forty

Nasir Zia

The interior of Godfrey's Mercedes was vault-silent until the bloated attorney switched on the radio that was preset to Bloomberg Radio. The top of his head glistened as if it had been buffed with carnauba wax but the hair covering his temples was rich sable brown. He didn't apologize as the reporter began spewing the day's market positions. It wasn't until he caught Nas's glare that he offered, "It was a little quiet in here. My broker rebalanced my portfolio. I was just checking to see if he earned his fees."

"I could've gotten back to the hotel on my own."

"No doubt," Godfrey said as he lowered the temperature on his seat cooler. He ran his fingers through his brown fur, then took both hands off the wheel to straighten his tie. "But we've still got lots of business to discuss."

"I don't see why. I don't know anything about these crimes."

"Yes," Godfrey said with verve, reacting to something he heard on the radio. "NASDAQ was up again. The son of a bitch was right."

"Did you hear me?" Nas asked. "I said—"

"Of course, I heard you, Nasir, but what you think of as knowing nothing might not make you as innocent as you believe. Attorneys like me exist for a very good reason. We protect the innocent." He cleared his throat. "At least that's what your father is concerned about."

"What are you talking about? I haven't told my father anything. How could he know about any of this?"

"We can discuss what your father knows and how he knows it when we get back to the hotel." Godfrey's eyes traveled to the dashboard clock. Away from his desk clock it was the equivalent of a taxi meter, calculating his billing at $350 per hour. He didn't often leave his Long Island office, but when he did, he made sure he was operating well into the black. "You seem like an intelligent young man, Nasir. Sometimes, the world as you see it gives a limited perspective. In the legal world, things are happening beyond the periphery that can have grave consequences. Suffice it to say that your father was prudent to retain me."

Godfrey's head rotated sharply to the left as they traveled past a stately catering hall with a substantial stone façade and congested valet station. The parking lot was filled with luxury automobiles. "I didn't remember that being where it was. Haven't eaten there in years, but, man, what a great all-you-can-eat seafood buffet. Unlimited lobster. Softshell crab when you hit it right. Scallops. Oysters."

Anger surfaced in Nas's voice. "Look, stop with the preaching and tell me why you are here."

"I told you, Nasir, because your father hired me." He blew out a sigh of frustration. "Should we stop for a cocktail or something? You seem a little wound up."

"No, I don't drink. What is this little road trip costing my father anyway?"

Godfrey cocked an outraged brow. "Exactly what it's worth, *Nasir*. You're not sitting in a police interrogation room anymore, are you? You should be thrilled that you're not being grilled by that decrepit Joisey guido or getting beaten to a bloody pulp by your ex. You seemed pretty damn relieved to see me walk through the door. Remember that, getting annihilated by the pretty little girl you left standing at the altar? *I'd* say I'm earning my keep. And don't you ever, ever challenge me on my fees. Is that clear?"

Nas seemed intimidated. "Yes." Pressing his lips shut, he closed his eyes, trying to blot out the world and all the stress that was coming at him. "My father told you all of that?"

"Don't be embarrassed. Being my client means never having to say you're sorry. Unless you lie to me, and then you'll be very, very sorry because I'm the only one standing between you and potentially serious criminal charges." Twilight had arrived. Lights on the buildings along the roadway shone brightly. "Doesn't look like such an awful shithole in the dark, does it? In broad daylight, though, the Garden State is a fucking eyesore."

The car rolled up the hotel's circular drive. Lampposts around the circular drive flickered simultaneously before fully illuminating. "This flea trap have a restaurant?"

Nas nodded. "A café."

"Good, here's the plan," Godfrey said. "Go upstairs and chill the fuck out. I'll meet you in the cafe in an hour. We'll put some food in our stomachs and talk shop. You good with that?"

Nas nodded, then opened the door and got out without saying another word.

* * *

Nas's skin was raw from a long, hot shower, his hair still damp. Sitting on the edge of the bed, bundled in a terry cloth robe, he shivered. It was as if he'd washed away the epidermis clear down to exposed nerve endings. He walked over to the thermostat and raised the temperature, not a degree or two, but five. He heard the heater fan click on. With the sun tucked away for the night, it would take time for the room to warm up. He quickly picked through his suitcase, selected his warmest long-sleeve pullover, and dressed. Checking the time, he still had twenty minutes left before he had to meet Godfrey in the café, twenty minutes without being harangued about his naiveté, twenty minutes without being told how badly he needed the preening lawyer's priceless services, twenty minutes of peace and quiet.

There was just the bed and a desk chair to rest on. He picked the bed. Fully dressed, he sidled up toward the headboard and layered pillows behind his back, which ached from sitting bent over in the interrogation room for so long. His neck was stiff and cracked when he turned his head.

Tragedies competed for his attention. He attempted to sort through his litany of troubles and prioritize the importance of each. Which could injure him the most, the woman he'd betrayed or the dead men, his conscience or the law, incarceration or a lifetime of mental anguish? Would his hell be a prison of the body or mind? Would it be forged of guilt and stronger than walls of concrete and bars of iron? He knew it was. He wanted to make an amends to the woman he loved but couldn't because he couldn't betray the secret he'd been entrusted with.

Godfrey was an overblown, self-serving shyster, a hired gun whose only allegiance was to money. Allegedly hired by his father, he presented himself as Nas's savior. *Why hasn't Dad called? Why didn't he tell me he'd hired a lawyer?* He wondered where his father had come across such a distasteful lout. Had he used Godfrey's services before? Never had he thought of his father in those terms. His father had always been the strong patriarch, the upholder of all that was proper. He found it inconceivable that the father he knew and revered had run afoul of the law and had needed the help of such a gangster, a man who bent the law to serve his purposes. "Unlimited lobster," he scoffed. *Is this the man I'm expected to trust? Dad, why haven't you called?*

And poor Gwen, he'd left her more broken than she was before, hanging by a thread, at wit's end, and still unable to learn the truth. *What will she do now? What* can *she do?* Bailing on his wedding had been terrible. He hadn't and couldn't have foreseen the ensuing catastrophic events. He hadn't expected one murder, let alone two, a criminal investigation, lawyers, and legal consequences. He wasn't prepared, wasn't equipped, and never would be. *Dad, why haven't you called?*

He heard hard rapping on the door, purposeful, knuckles-on-the-door knocking.

I've still got ten-minutes, Nas thought. "I'm coming." *Pushy bastard, he couldn't wait for me downstairs?* Slipping into his loafers, Nas trudged slowly to the door. It weighed tons in his hand as he twisted the handle and pulled it open.

"Nasir Zia," a uniformed cop said. "Please step into the hallway."

Scoldari was standing behind the officer. "What's going on?" Nas asked.

The cop ratcheted the first handcuff around his wrist. "Wait a minute. Detective, why are you—"

Scoldari moistened his lips. His gaze turned cold. "Nasir Zia, you're under arrest."

"Can you wait a minute?" Nas protested. "My—"

Scoldari silenced Nas with a raised hand and read him his rights. It wasn't until he was finished that he again made eye contact. "You were saying?"

Wrestling against the restraints, Nas glared at him. "What's this about?"

Scoldari sighed with genuine regret. "Accessory after the fact, Nasir. I told you."

"Told me what?"

"That you were playing with fire. I begged you to talk. I gave you every chance in the world to cooperate, but you shit on my advice, and now it's out of my hands. The DA feels he's got a case."

"But, my attorney, he's—"

"He's what?"

"He's waiting for me downstairs in the café."

"Godfrey's waiting downstairs?" Scoldari said with a surprised expression. "Well, thank God you told me." He tapped the uniform on the shoulder. "You heard him, right?"

"Sure did. Saved by the bell, huh, Vito?"

"Absolutely. That's some eleventh-hour shit right there," Scoldari said with a shit-eating grin. "Take him out the back."

Chapter Forty-One

Gwen Winter

Hank Winter was nobody's fool.

And neither was I.

At least that's the way I was beginning to feel, like I wasn't going to be taken advantage of again. I wouldn't be bullied. Not by Nas. Not by his overbearing lawyer. Not by anyone. Dad often tried to convince me that I had to talk the talk before I could walk the walk, that you had to get your head straight before you were capable of acting. Maybe that's what I was doing, convincing myself not to be a pushover, that I could be independent. Worth a shot, I figured.

Given adequate rest and the peace of mind to think clearly allowed us to formulate a plan. Not so much a plan but a list of actions we felt we were capable of carrying out. That and 30,000 frequent traveler points bought us a good night's sleep at an upscale-ish hotel with comfortable beds.

And knowing we had a course of action or at least a direction helped to push the tension aside. I'll be damned if I didn't get a reasonable night's sleep. Sure, I tossed. And turned. I woke up a few times but felt rested when morning light poked through the curtains.

Did it have to happen this way? Did I have to get knocked on my ass before I learned to stand on my two feet? Seemed it did. My emotions were no longer kryptonite. My feelings didn't amplify every little thing and make the insignificant seem insurmountable. Was it a permanent cure? Didn't know. Didn't care. The only thing that was important was that I felt whole in a way I was unaccustomed to and didn't need a man to make me feel that way. It was fucking inspiring.

Dad charged out of the bathroom, freshly showered and badly shaved. I expected better from a soldier who'd shaved out of a helmet with a muddle puddle for a mirror, but the overpriced disposable razor he bought in the lobby convenience shop hacked him up pretty good. We hadn't prepared to stay over, but where there's a will, as they say. He sat down and tugged on his shoes. "Dan should be here pretty soon *if* he doesn't hit a wall of traffic like we did yesterday."

"The sun is out, Hank," Mom said. "He should be able to sail right through."

"Yeah, right," he said. "Famous last words. "I'll leave you my truck. I'll go with Dan in his car."

"Are you sure this is a good idea?" Mom asked. "You're not the police, you know."

"Amen to that," he said, his brows rising perceptibly. "I promise we'll stay out of jail."

"I don't know, Hank. Are you sure you should be doing this?"

"Nothing ventured, nothing gained," he said as he handed me his car keys. "I don't think your mother is going to do too well with Jersey's jug handle left turns. I think it's best if you drive, Gwen."

Mom was a safe driver but easily flustered. She didn't protest. "I call shotgun," she said. "That's what shotgun means, right, sitting in the passenger seat?"

"Listen to you," Dad said as he stuffed his pocket with essentials, his wallet, phone, and pocketknife. He slipped a tactical pen into his shirt pocket. "You're a regular Bonnie Parker, dear. Your birthday's not far off—I'm thinking a Thompson submachine gun would suit you nicely."

The smartass comment warranted the finger, but Mom simply blushed. "Silly man," she said. "Don't get hurt."

"Hank Winter doesn't get hurt. He gives it." His phone buzzed. Pulling it from his pocket, he slid the patio door open and stepped outside for privacy.

"He'll be all right," I said, rubbing Mom's arm, reassuring her. "You know he can handle himself."

"I know he's a tough guy, but he's not a kid anymore." The corners of her mouth turned down, and her eyes became glassy. "I worry about him."

"That's your job, right, to worry about everyone?" I kissed her on the forehead. "Me, Dad, and—" Alana had been added to the mix of loved ones that kept Mom up late into the night. The girl who couldn't do any wrong had massively shit the bed. "Don't worry about Alana. She'll come out of this smelling like a rose. Maybe not a rose, but a tulip. Tulips are good, right? I mean, they don't make you retch like a pungent bouquet of lilies."

"I can't tell anyone but you, but I always worried something terrible would happen to your sister one day. I know it sounds ridiculous, but life has a way of balancing good and bad. And your sister—"

She didn't have to say anymore. Alana's life had been one glorious walk on the beach. Until now. There's an abyss waiting for everyone to fall into. We just can't see it until it's too late. God knows, I'd found mine. "Now, who's being silly?"

She shrugged and misted up. Clawing at Kleenex, she hustled toward the bathroom. "I don't want your father to see me like this. He's got enough on his plate."

The plate I had served my father was heaped with ignored warnings. "Don't get serious with Nas," he told me. "You're young. Explore your options." But would I listen? His being right meant I was wrong, wrong about Nas, wrong about my feelings, and naïve about the world we live in. It seemed I had to argue for argument's sake alone.

And now there was this, my vendetta. Scorned, I wouldn't walk away. Couldn't. I had to know what happened, even if it destroyed me and everyone I loved. Dad was about to go commando. Along with old intelligence buddy Dan Ohana, he was on his way to evaluate the area where Osman Shehzad had been found in the trunk of a car. Dad had no faith in the local police department to do a proper job. He and Ohana would look for clues New Jersey's finest had overlooked. He was convinced they had missed something important, something that would put them on the trail of the man the police suspected of murder and Nas's wife. Nas wouldn't talk to me and maybe never would. Perhaps his wife would be more forthcoming with information. Our guess was that she'd either run away or been abducted. We hoped trauma would shake the truth from her.

Dad stepped back inside. "Dan's ten minutes away. He stopped to fill his tank and pick up a case of water. I'm going to wait for him out front." He looked around. "Where's your mother?"

Mom stepped out of the bathroom, eyes clear, her makeup retouched. She threw her arms around him and gave him a kiss on the cheek. "No heroics, *right*? Remember, you promised me."

He shrugged. "We're going to traipse through the woods and have a look around. What could happen?"

Mom and I had a mission of our own. Hopefully, it would take her mind off everyone else. I wasn't counting on it. Worrying was what she did best.

Chapter Forty-Two

Nasir Zia

Nas heard Godfrey's booming voice through the bars in the lockup. The holding cells were located at the far end of the police station, but the baritone attorney's voice carried effortlessly down the long corridor. Were he a crooner, his voice could fill an auditorium without the need for a microphone. "I understand my client is here." Then came a pause. Nas pictured the desk officer handling Godfrey with seasoned indifference. "Show me to him *now.*" Godfrey's voice was authoritative. More, it was commanding. Nas was at home with computer codes and block server capabilities. He enjoyed working through a computer interface and shied away from face-to-face confrontations. Unlikable though he was, Nas took comfort in having such a blunt instrument advocating for him, running interference.

Nas was transferred to an interrogation room to meet with counsel, but the immediate slap of shoe leather against the linoleum floor didn't come until several minutes later. Nas presumed that the desk officer or Scoldari had thrown a hurdle in Godfrey's way to slow him down a step or two, enough to piss him off all the more, if for no other reason, because they could.

The chip on Godfrey's shoulder was impossible to miss—it was like Noah's Ark. The stout attorney forged through the door, scowling at the officer who closed the door on the way out, his aura fiery red hot.

"Pricks," Godfrey grumbled as he flicked dust off his lapel as if it were the irritation the police officers had soiled him with. "Fucking civil servants." Peasants. Plebes. A long list of expletives and insults ached to be catapulted past his lips like poison-tipped darts. He dropped his attaché case on the table, snapped the latches, and retrieved a legal pad without making eye contact with his client. He dropped into a chair on the opposite side of the table, his gaze cutting into Nas. "Not the scenario either of us had hoped for, is it? What the hell happened last night? Do you know how long I waited for you in that greasy spoon the hotel calls a café?"

Not long, I imagine, Nas thought. Everything about the man screamed impatience. *If he waited ten minutes, it was a lot.* Nas pictured Godfrey charging into the elevator, flying out on Nas's floor, and barreling down the hall toward his room, missing him and the police by scant moments. "They came to my room," Nas said.

Aghast, Godfrey fired back. "*And* you let them in?"

"I thought it was you and opened the door without checking."

Godfrey blasted air through his nostrils. "Well, did you make any attempt to tell them your attorney was there? That you had representation?"

"Yes," Nas said. *I'm not an idiot.* "They went out of their way to avoid you. They took me down the service elevator to the basement, and we left through the parking lot."

"Fuckers!" Godfrey pounded the table with a closed fist. "Showboating motherfuckers is what they are. And here we are, Saturday morning, with arraignment forty-eight hours away. They didn't have to do that," he huffed. "If we were in New York—" He became quiet. Rubbing his chin, he appeared to drift into thought. "It's New Jersey, and we're outsiders here. These underpaid Garden State barneys just live to stick it to New Yorkers. On my own turf, one call would've stopped the whole process."

Godfrey's bravado had become overwhelming. "And how would you have done that?" Nas asked dubiously.

"You don't have a record. Any ADA worth a shit would've agreed to voluntary surrender at 9:00 a.m. Monday morning at the steps of the courthouse. Now you're stuck here for the weekend, and there's not a thing I can do about it." Resting his forearms on the table, Godfrey leaned forward. "Are they feeding you at least?" Nas nodded. "I'll bet the toilet is a fucking pig sty."

"That's the least of my problems. Please, can you tell me why I was arrested? Detective Scoldari said something about being an accessory after the fact. What does that mean?"

"It means, *Nasir*, that you're knowingly withholding information that the police could use to apprehend an offender, one who presumably killed two people. It's serious. Adjudicated by an unsympathetic magistrate, you could be sentenced to several years in prison."

Nas recoiled in his chair. His face blanched. "You mean, if I'm found guilty?"

"Well, of course."

"But I don't know anything. I'm not withholding anything, nothing."

"Well, this greaseball detective believes you are. Worse still, he's convinced the district attorney that he's right." Godfrey pulled a pen from his lapel pocket and clicked it. Wetting the tip with his tongue, he wrote on the legal pad, then spoke with his eyes cast on the paper. "Your father didn't tell me much, only that you were traveling for your honeymoon and that the police were questioning you with regard to a homicide. I'm going to take a leap of faith and presume he didn't know very much or didn't feel certain of the details. If you want me to help you, you're going to have to tell me *everything*, every little detail. Let's take it from the—"

"Wait a minute," Nas barked. "How did he know?"

Godfrey looked up, flustered. "Complete sentences, please. How did he know what?"

"About the hotel manager falling from the balcony. I didn't tell him. I called him, but he said it was a bad time. He said he would call back, but he didn't."

Godfrey shook his head disappointedly. "You're not the only one with a telephone, Nasir. Scoldari asked your parents to come in for an interview. I'm sure that's how he heard."

Nas seemed perplexed. "I can't get my arms around this. My parents were *here?"*

"No, Nasir, you're not thinking. I'm here at your parents' behest. That's the way it works and your father was very shrewd to call me. Civilians don't perform well under these circumstances. He did the smart thing." He eyed Nas pointedly, his intent deadly serious. "Now it's your turn."

Chapter Forty-Three

Gwen Winter

The law offices of Fellini and Ross occupied swanky digs, an entire building of marble and glass with parking for at least a hundred cars. The large two-story building had an impressive lobby with a thirty-foot ceiling. I was surprised to see a concierge stationed at the front kiosk over the weekend. He checked us in and called for instructions. Mike Fellini was running late, but an associate brought us upstairs to the name partner's office, where we were allowed to wait.

His office was smartly designed and drew my immediate approval, so much so that I snapped a few pictures of it so that I had something to refer to the next time I was called upon to design a high-end office.

If I ever went back to work.

If a job was still waiting for me when the shit settled.

Fellini's desk was breathtaking, a slab of grade A Burma teak supported by what appeared to be solid titanium, twenty grand if it cost a nickel.

"It looks like Michael did very well for himself," Mom said. "I met him two or three times, but I never imagined this level of success. He was so humble."

A humble attorney, I mused. *That's something you don't see every day.* Dad, Ohana, and Mike Fellini had served together in army intelligence and had remained friends. So, when he got an urgent call from my old man, he hopped to it.

"Sorry I'm late," Fellini said as he breezed through the door. "We got stuck behind a foursome of slowpokes on the eleventh green." He strode up to Mom and hugged her. "Carol, you haven't aged a day."

"See honey," she began, turning her gaze to me. "I told you he was a good attorney."

"And this must be Gwen." He had a captivating smile, brown eyes, and dimples. Offering his hand, I noticed that Popeye-esque forearms extended beyond the short sleeve cuff of his golf shirt. He took a moment to study my face. "Lovely, like your mother. I wish we were meeting under better circumstances."

"Thank you for taking the time to see us," Mom said. "We know it's your day off."

Making his way around the desk, he waved his hand dismissively. "Hank and I have known each other for over thirty years, and this is the first time he's ever asked for a favor. Whatever I can do to help." Sitting down, he clicked a pen. "Ready. Now, Hank gave me the broad strokes, and, of course, I agreed to see you." He had a far-off look in his eyes as his head leaned to the side. "But I'm not sure what it is you need from me." He filled a glass with water. "Anything I can do, of course. Even if it's just a shoulder to lean on."

"Michael," Mom began, "you heard what my sweet daughter's fiancé did, yes?"

He nodded. "The guy's a louse. Given the chance, I'd kick his teeth in. But you've got Hank. You don't need me for that. From a legal standpoint, I'm not sure how I can help."

"Why?" Mom said, her temper surfacing abruptly. "Can you tell us why? He won't...he won't tell us a damn thing. Gwen would like to know. She'd like some closure."

His sympathetic eyes fell on me. "There are a lot of crazy, screwed-up people in this world, and I'm sorry you picked one of them to fall in love with, but you can't compel him to do anything. Unless, of course, you're prepared to file a civil suit. In that case, an apology or a detailed explanation could be tied into a settlement agreement. But you wouldn't do that here.

As I understand it, both you and your ex-fiancé are New York residents. You'd have to file in New York."

"Do people do that?" Mom asked.

"Carol, people do everything. You can't imagine some of the briefs I've filed. That said, I'm not encouraging you or even suggesting you pursue a legal remedy." He turned to me. "Time is on your side, Gwen. Maybe once the chips settle..."

"I don't want to be with him anymore."

"And I'm not suggesting that you do. All I'm saying is that guilt can be a powerful force. If it eats at him long enough, he may come forward on his own. Unburden himself."

"Mr. Fellini—"

"Call me Mike. Please."

"Mike, we got a courtesy call from the detective investigating the homicides." Hearing the word homicide, Fellini seemed to stiffen in his chair. Nas. Nasir, my ex, was arrested last night."

He rolled his neck. "Do you know what he was charged with?"

Mom quickly announced, "Accessory."

He gritted his teeth. "Accessory to murder? Before or after the fact?"

"After."

"That's a criminal offense. He may be looking at serious jail time if convicted."

I felt a knot tightening in my stomach. "How-how much time?"

Mike shrugged. "I don't know the facts, but he could be looking at ten years or more. It's impossible for me to say."

"But I know him. He wouldn't." My head and my heart dropped. I felt hollow inside, a shell emptied of flesh and blood.

Mike probably thought I was going to faint. I'm not sure he was wrong. He shot up and poured a glass of water for me while Mom rubbed the back of my neck. He waited patiently while I sipped the water. "Carol," he began, "Can I have a word with Gwen privately?" Mom nodded. "Great. We have a fully stocked kitchen. It encourages the associates to put in overtime. Help yourself to anything you like."

Mom kissed me on the head. "I was dying for a cup of coffee, anyway." Wink-wink. "I'll give you a few minutes together."

"Feeling well enough to talk, dear?"

I nodded because I felt I should. In truth, I wanted to lie down. I wanted the nightmare over. I wanted it behind me. Screw it, I wish it had never happened.

He sat down on the corner of the desk. "I sense that you still care for this guy. I'm not sure why, but I think I'm reading you pretty clearly. Why are you here, Gwen? Are you here for you, or are you here for him? Who is it you want me to help?"

I saw his lips moving, but his voice sounded as if it was coming from far away. My eyes filled with tears. "This is crippling me. It's crippling me and my parents." I felt my throat tighten. "What should I do, Mike? Can you tell me what I should do?"

His answer was quick and deliberate. No hesitation at all. "Walk away, Gwen. Turn your back on this turd and walk the hell away."

Chapter Forty-Four

Gwen Winter

The hotel pool looked inviting after we returned from Mike Fellini's office, but with the sun setting, it was much too cool to chance a swim. If the prospect of an ice bath wasn't enough of a deterrent, the squad of testosterone-charged teens tossing around a football and playing water grab-ass with their girlfriends most certainly sealed the deal.

With the sun dropping still lower in the sky, the breeze turned chilly. Sitting beyond the juveniles' splash zone, Mom and I pulled out sweaters and slipped them on.

"Better?" Mom asked.

I nodded after pulling the sweater sleeves over my bare arms, then sipped coffee from a cardboard cup. The coffee was no longer piping hot but still discharged enough heat to warm my hands. "My hands are always cold."

"Cold hands, warm heart," Mom said, dredging up the old proverb.

I've got no one to touch with these cold hands, no one to warm with my heart. What I had was an empty bed, a head filled with questions and conflicts raging like the war to end all wars. And a heart that felt as if it were filled with lead.

Mom reached into her bag and sneakily removed a small bottle of Jameson. Her eyes twinkled naughtily. "I think this coffee needs something, don't you?"

Grinning, she pried the lid of my cup and thrust it toward her. She topped off my cup, then hers. Mom toasted, "Over the lips, past the gums..."

"Watch out, brain cells, here it comes." Make me numb. Quiet my mind. I can only handle so much pain.

Our giggling drew the attention of the sophomoric pigskin cop-a-feel squad. One of the debutants was bobbing up and down in the water, intentionally revealing more and more of herself with every plunge. She wasn't the first woman to flash flesh to get attention, but the immature ploy was usually effective. Before our eyes, the developing down-and-out pattern migrated in her direction. The word *score* took on an entirely new meaning.

"What am I going to do?" I asked. The weight of my question hung in the air for what seemed an eternity. I could see Mom struggling to come up with a helpful response, but she was out. The tank was empty. She reached over, grabbed my hand, and rubbed in the kiss. A heart-warming smile was all she had left. Every encouragement and reassurance in her mother's love armory had been used and reused. She sighed.

I sighed.

Turn the page.

Our first full day in New Jersey, the first day of our self-appointed inquisition, hadn't turned out to be the auspicious event we had hoped for. Dad and Ohana had combed the Jersey swamp for hours with nothing to show for their efforts.

Upon returning to the hotel, Dad sadly admitted that New Jersey law enforcement seemed to have performed an adequate reconnaissance of the area where Osman Shezhad's body was found. Some of the telltale signs of a worked crime scene were evident. Police tape wrapped around tree trunks still delineated the crime scene search area. They saw where tire and footprint casts had been poured and found discarded evidence markers and plastic collection bags, nitrile gloves, soil collection tubes, and the whole forensic enchilada. Other than crime scene team rubbish, the area was clean and sterile, as in not a glimmer of hope.

Gritty and worn, they'd gone to their respective rooms to clean up and rest. I didn't expect to see them for a bit and was surprised to see Dad heading toward us with a bottle of beer in his hand.

"Couldn't sleep?" I asked.

"Couldn't even close my eyes. I'm too wired." He took a swig of beer and sat down side-saddle on Mom's lounge. "Come up with any brainstorms while I was gone?"

"Absolutely. Every mystery of the universe has been solved."

"Time travel?" he mused.

"Piece of cake."

"Black holes?"

"Debunked."

"Socks gone missing in the dryer?"

"Haven't cracked that one yet."

Dad wore a hapless expression. His shoulders settled. His arms elongated, the beer bottle dangled from his fingertips. "I'm disappointed. I thought we'd find *something*."

"You tried, honey," Mom said, rubbing his shoulder. "Tomorrow's another day. We should think about getting dinner. Will Dan be joining us?"

"You'd let him eat alone?" Dad said. "With all he's doing for us?"

"You're paying him for his time, aren't you?" I asked. "I mean, he's not working for free."

"Expenses only," Dad said. "His time, talent, and support, that's all on the arm."

"Maybe he's not so bad after all."

"Don't be so quick to judge, Gwen. He's done me a lot of favors over the years. And back when we served together…" Looking remorseful, Dad glanced at the darkening sky. "Lots of water under the bridge."

"Your father said Dan jumped at the chance to help us," Mom said. "He's been a good friend to your father. The least we can do is buy him a meal."

I nodded, acquiescing. "Vacation pay hit my checking account today. I'm buying."

Dad toasted with his beer. "Sure, be a big shot." He and Mom had plunked down a healthy piece of change for the wedding photographer, the flowers, and the limo. All gone flushed down the toilet, and he hadn't bitched about it once. Calling me a big shot was as close to bellyaching as he would come.

"Whatever he likes," I said. "He didn't have to do all this work for us. I'll bet he called in a lot of favors, tracking down Nas the way he did and running out here on short notice."

"That's right, Dad concurred. "He went above and beyond, and he won't rest until—"

"Hey, wait a minute." An idea was still forming. I had no idea if my idea was even remotely doable, but the possibility boosted my spirit. My heart lightened, and my spirit climbed. "Where's the car that man was found in?"

Dad shook his head. "No, that won't happen. I appreciate your moxie, Gwen, but that vehicle is in police custody, being processed. We won't be able to get anywhere near it."

"What Hank said is true," Ohana said as he approached. He was just a few strides away. "And it's Saturday evening. I'm afraid—"

"I thought you knew people," I said, sassing him. "Where's all that influence I keep hearing about? Come on, pull some strings, Dan." I challenged him with a pair of wide eyes.

He shook his head, then shrugged. It appeared that he was out of options when his eyes flashed. He grabbed his phone and strode off a short distance for some privacy.

"Who's he calling, do you think?"

"I don't know, Gwen," Dad said, "but whatever idea popped into his head was put there by you."

Chapter Forty-Five

Gwen Winter

There was no time for a proper sit-down dinner. We chowed down on drive-through tacos and fountain sodas during a thirty-minute drive to the state's regional crime lab. Four adults had been fed for less than thirty-five dollars. Although I'd gotten away cheap, I couldn't shake a nagging feeling that the Winters had sunken to a new all-time low, a clandestine rendezvous with one of Ohana's cronies for a sneak peek at evidence we had no right to see.

The 411 on Alex Kale was that he wasn't a dirty cop, but he wasn't exactly squeaky clean. With a son in Princeton, he wasn't above doing an occasional innocuous favor so long as it wouldn't come back to bite him in the ass. Ohana didn't know Kale directly, but a go-between vouched for him. Hard, untraceable cash was going to be exchanged, and no one got hurt. The transaction had the telltale earmarks of a deal about to go wrong. And the thought that something might be fucking exhilarating, like James Bond spying on Goldfinger's smelting plant in the Swiss countryside, belly flat on the ground as a Rolls Royce was melted into a pool of molten gold.

No bulletproof Aston Martin was involved in our covert operation, just Dad's three-row SUV filled with grease-impregnated fast food paper wrappers and giant soda cups, emptied of soda but still full of ice.

No one was getting close to the car Osman Shehzad's body had been recovered from. It was still being processed by crime lab technicians, and

Kale couldn't take a chance on a bunch of amateurs contaminating evidence. And maybe that wasn't important. Shehzad's personal effects had already been forensically examined, cataloged, and moved to the evidence room.

"We'll have to move quickly once we get inside," Ohana said as we pulled into the parking lot of a Greek diner, The Palace, as in the Palace of Bad Taste. It looked like almost every diner I'd ever seen, with the same bawdy chrome and glass exterior. Neon accent lighting blared into the night and onto a landscaped island in the center of the parking lot with a water feature and a sign that advertised the name of the landscaper who likely designed and installed the attraction, gratis.

Mom was the last one to finish her meal, savoring her $2.99 finger food as if it were a crêpe suzette and experiencing nirvana from franchise garbage that had been extruded through a sausage grinder. Dad had always been the pessimist, while Mom was the one who'd excavate a mound of horse shit, hoping against hope to unearth a pony. "Why is he meeting us here?" she asked.

"We're just a few miles from the crime lab," Ohana replied as he handed out latex gloves. "He said he'd have all the items laid out on a table in a private party room."

"Wouldn't it be simpler if we just met him at the lab?"

"Yes, Carol, it would be simpler," Dad said, "but there'd be a record of us coming and going, camera footage, and so on. No one can know about this. No one. We're not to speak of it to anyone. Not even Alana or Jack. Understood?"

That last bite, the bit of information, did her in. Mom withdrew the last bite of her taco just as it was about to enter her mouth. "I understand, Hank." The face she made, you could almost see her stomach souring as she tossed the scrap into a paper bag. "This is what happens when you're starving—you'll eat anything. Hank, do you happen to have a roll of Tums in the car?"

"Always," Dad said, grinning as he popped the center console hatch and handed her the antacid.

"And please," Ohana began, "No friendly conversation with anyone in the restaurant. We go straight to the back room without attracting any attention to ourselves. Avoid eye contact. It's best if no one in the restaurant remembers us."

"Is he talking to *me*?" Mom asked.

"No one's picking on you, Carol," Dad said. "Dan's simply setting the ground rules."

"But I'm the one he's worried about, right? Me, the yenta. Dan figures I'll stop to get a recipe for baklava."

"Enough, Mom," I said. This isn't about you. This cop is taking a real chance helping us like this." I took her hand. "No one wants to be doing this cloak and dagger crap, but…" I kissed her hand. "Fifteen minutes, and it'll all be over."

She blew me a kiss. "I've got a better idea. I'll wait here. I can use the time to clear my head and you can tell me all about it on the drive back to the hotel."

"Are you sure?" I asked. "We're all in this together."

"Yes. This kind of thing is not for me."

"What are you talking about?" Dad said. "You're the sudoku champion of Suffolk County. We need you on this."

"I'm sure the three of you can handle it," she said.

Ohana tapped his watch.

"Shall we?" Dad said. "Officer Kale has to get the evidence back and locked up before the shift change at midnight."

* * *

It was a feeding frenzy the likes of which I'd never seen, far busier than any diner I'd encountered, even on the busiest Saturday evening when sirloin steak appeared on the Specials menu. Every table in the main dining room was in use. The noise generated by flatware clattering against ceramic plates was deafening, like the mess hall on an aircraft carrier, or so I imagined.

It was hard to believe, but the diner was even brighter on the inside than it appeared from the parking lot. The radiation emitted from the recessed lighting fixtures was so intense it felt as if they'd been fitted with heat lamps. And the massive chrome-plated chandeliers seemed large enough to transmit satellite data. *That's probably how they manage to feed one hundred patrons simultaneously and still keep the food hot.*

I'd found that many Greek diners were family-run businesses. I took for granted that the Palace was no exception to that rule and that the woman behind the counter was a member of the tribe. She pointed out the direction of the private room and quickly snatched the bill and credit card from a patron standing next to Dan.

Dan waved for us to follow, and we made our way across the dining room, zigzagging through tables and doing our best not to attract attention from a member of the ravenous crowd. The door of the private room opened, and a gent, who I assumed was Kale, rushed us inside. The shades inside the small room were drawn.

"You're Ohana?" he asked.

"Kale, thanks for the assist."

"The name is Mud, as far as you're concerned." Kale watched as Dad and I entered the room and didn't look happy. "This isn't supposed to be a stockholder's meeting. I thought you were coming alone."

Ohana glanced at the table where Shehzad's personal effects were laid out. "Is that all of it?"

"Just the documents," Kale said. "I assume you're cool with that?"

Dad nodded.

"Meaning what?" I asked.

"Ordinary items have been omitted," Ohana said. "A tire iron is just a tire iron. A pack of gum is just a pack of gum—there's no need to review that kind of stuff. We're not reviewing those items for prints and so on."

Ohana handed Kale an envelope that went immediately into his breast pocket, unchecked. "Make it quick. You've got gloves?" he asked just as we were pulling them out of our pockets. "Be gentle with this shit. I don't need anyone asking questions."

"Got it," Dad said as we moved to the table. The items were batched, and Kale told us they should remain that way: wallet items with wallet items, the contents from the glove box to stay unto itself, and so on.

Dad picked up a pile of service receipts. He flipped through them, then pointed to something on one of them. "Shehzad has the car serviced at a gas station on Austin Street. That's not far from the mosque where Huzaifa worships."

"What is a Masjid?" I asked after unfolding what looked like a receipt for a charitable contribution.

"An Islamic community center," Ohana said. "A mosque."

"Shehzad donated one hundred dollars to the Masjid Tristate Association." I looked up from the receipt. "I wonder if Huzaifa's mosque is part of this organization."

"Good chance," Dad said. "There's not a doubt in my mind that's how Huzaifa and Shehzad knew each other," "Shehzad must've discovered something important, something outrageous."

"And Huzaifa killed him for it," I said. "And somehow, the man I was supposed to marry is involved in all of this."

Dad had always been belligerent toward Muslims. I wasn't sure if his animosity stemmed from his years in the military, the way he was brought up, or if something else had served as a catalyst for his preconceptions. His proclivity toward prejudging Arabs had always been there. It was most of the reason I ignored him when he warned me not to get close to Nas. "They keep secrets," he'd said. "They hide the truth." And the most terrible of all, "You'll never really know who he is."

I never believed him, not a word of it. I rejected his warnings out of hand because of the way I knew he thought, the way his brain was wired. But now it seemed, looking the other way and hearing only what I wanted to hear… It was all on me.

Even so, Dad was with me through the thick and the nauseatingly thin. There'd been lots of issues in my adult life, a lot of worry and aggravation. It never wore him down. He put his arm around me as he studied the document I'd been reading. Seeing everything I'd seen, he found something more. He pointed at the signature on the bottom of the receipt.

"Can you make this out?" he asked. "It looks like—"

The first name was a blur, a wavy line without discernible characteristics. It took a moment to decipher the chicken scratch surname, but I decoded it one letter at a time. I gasped, then locked eyes with Dad—I was certain he'd read it the same way. "Oh my God." The last name of the signature was Huzaifa.

Chapter Forty-Six

Nasir Zia

Nas didn't need to wake up when Sunday morning rolled around. He'd been awake most of the night and was still awake when sunrise arrived at the police station lockup. He expected another day of solitude and boredom, a day of pacing the cell, sitting and standing repeatedly. The only interruptions he anticipated were the deliveries of his meal trays, three quick visits over and done without fanfare.

Solitude provided a fertile environment for him to contemplate the worst likely outcome imaginable, years without freedom and living in constant terror. If and when he was finally released, what then? A life wasted, hopes and dreams up in smoke. And the greatest regret of all, losing Gwen. He knew she'd land on her feet with a great guy, not the one who robbed her of what should've been the happiest day of her life. She deserved so much more and prayed she'd find happiness.

The officer who peeked in on him during his rounds didn't engage in conversation and barely came near the cell. The expression the officer bore was one of disgust, as if he were spying on vultures as they picked out the eyes of a dead animal.

"You don't know me," Nas hollered. "Don't look at me like that."

The officer turned without acknowledging Nas and moved off. Nas didn't expect to see him or anyone else for another hour. Without his watch, he found it hard to judge the time, but he was sure far less than an hour had passed when he heard footsteps growing closer. *Anything to break up the monotony*, he thought. Any and all were welcome, even the cop who looked at him as if he were dirt.

Scoldari hustled through the doorway with a ring of keys in his hand.

Nas's eyes swelled. "You're letting me out?"

"It's not what you think."

"But you're—"

"Yes, I'm unlocking the cell," Scoldari said. "There was a sighting, a young woman that matches the description you gave us of Bahija Abidi. We've got eyes on her at a mosque the next town over."

"That's great news," Nas said, articulating his first positive words in days.

"Maybe," Scoldari said cautiously. "If it's her. I've learned not to count my chickens before they hatch. We've contacted Bahija's parents but it'll take too long for them to get here. I need you to make positive identification."

"But you arrested me. I'm allowed to leave?"

"In cuffs and under my supervision? Yes. You haven't been arraigned yet. So, don't bust my balls here, Nasir. Your liberty is at my discretion. How you behave and your cooperation today might motivate a judge to be lenient on setting bail when you're arraigned tomorrow."

Nas seemed shaken, eager to help but confused by what was being asked of him. "But my attorney said that—"

"Yeah, yeah, yeah. Look, I'm in a hurry. Whether you're granted bail or not isn't up to me. All I'm saying is that you being a shithead won't work to your benefit. Put your hands through the opening." Both hands extending out the pass-through, Scoldari ratcheted handcuffs over Nas's wrists. "Step back," he said as he unlocked the cell. "Do exactly as I say." He took Nas by the arm and led him out the door.

* * *

The same uniformed cop who arrested Nas at the hotel was waiting for them in a police car outside the station house with the engine running. Scoldari closed the door after guiding Nas through the rear door. The wheels spun the moment Scoldari's door slammed shut. Rocketing out of the parking lot, it was a short distance to the highway entrance. It wasn't until they went under an overpass that Nas noticed the strobe of roof rack lights flashing on the inner walls of the concrete abutment. He glanced at the speedometer, eighty and climbing.

"You say she was spotted at the mosque?" Nas asked.

"Yup," Scoldari said. "You heard right."

"But most Muslims visit the mosque on Friday. It doesn't make sense that she would go today."

"Makes all the sense in the world, kid. Why go when everyone else goes? There's a greater chance of being recognized."

"Ahh. I see." Nas settled back in his seat as the police car sped past all the vehicles in the right lane. *I hope it's her*, he thought. So many questions. No answers. Recovering Bahija might fill in some of the blanks. He hoped it would. At the very least, he'd know she was safe.

The driver hit the yelp just long enough to clear the lane in front of him. Passing a car that was slow to move over, Scoldari noticed the driver, a white-haired man driving a gold Buick Century, squinting, his face pressed close to the steering wheel. "God love 'em," he said. "That'll be me in a few years."

"Who are you kidding, Vito," the uniformed cop said. "That's you now."

Scoldari flipped him the bird, then abruptly tapped the windshield. "This exit," he said.

"But."

"No buts. Get off here. It'll let us off right behind the mosque. Kill the strobe and siren. I'm too old to chase a twenty-five-year-old runner."

The driver snorted and pulled off at the exit. Rights and lefts, Scoldari called out directions.

Nas could see the mosque come into view. It was a large building constructed of white stone with tall pillars and a domed roof. It was far grander than any mosque Nas had visited in New York.

"Vampire central," the cop said under his breath.

"What is that supposed to mean?" Nas said, his voice sharp.

"Whatever you think you heard, you didn't hear," Scoldari said. "Got that?"
"We'll park just out of sight of the front entrance. Let us know if you see her. We've got binoculars if you need them."

"I can see the vampires just fine," Nas snapped.

Scoldari looked over his shoulder. "Don't mind him, Nasir. He's got a weird sense of humor."

"He's a bigot. He's everything that's wrong with—"

"Hey! "Eyes on the prize." Scoldari pointed to the entrance. "This isn't a field trip."

Activity in and out of the mosque moved at a leisurely pace, with worshipers leaving every now and then. Nas watched intently. He saw no one with even a slight resemblance to his wife. *Then again,* he wondered, *will I know her on sight?* He'd seen so little of her, not even a full twenty-four hours of direct contact. *And after this, I'll probably never see her again.* Most of the worshipers were men. An occasional female exited the building. None gave him pause to consider if they were Bahija. She was very tall for a Pakistani woman. *She'll stand out,* he thought.

He was right.

She flew down the stairs and hit the parking lot before Nas was able to register that it was her. "I see her," he said, pointing to the tall woman moving swiftly through rows of parked cars.

"Gun it," Scoldari said. The police unit lurched forward. Lights and sirens wailing, it pulled into the north entrance. Panicked by the siren, Bahija froze in place. A man resting against the fender of a car near the exit spotted the police car.

Bahija turned to the man parked near the exit with panic etched into her face as the police cruiser jerked to stop in front of her. Her eyes were pinned on him as he got into his car and rolled unassumingly out of the parking lot.

Moments later, she was in the back of the police cruiser, sitting next to her husband.

Chapter Forty-Seven

Gwen Winter

"They look like the Keystone Cops," Dad said as we watched Scoldari and a uniformed cop take a tall Arab girl into custody, unaware that we were in the parking lot, watching them. And watching another man, watching them.

Ohana sniggered. "The left foot doesn't know what the right is doing."

"Can the two of you please just *stop*? Nas was in that police car," I said as tears rushed forward, competing against a flood of angst to see who would drown me first. They were together, Nas and his wife, reunited in the back of a squad car. Not the most romantic circumstances. Even so, she was with him.

And I wasn't.

She was his wife.

And I wasn't.

She was tall and raven-haired. Tall and gorgeous. I sniffled as I clawed at a packet of tissues.

She was Muslim.

And I wasn't.

"What's wrong?" Dad asked. "What did I say?"

"You're both brainless," Mom said, "both of you. Can't you see how your daughter is feeling? What she saw?"

Dad's expression was vacant for moments until the revelation finally hit him. I guess he was now picturing Nas and Bahija together in the back of the car, just as I had, minutes earlier. "Oh, sweetheart, I'm sorry," he said. "I didn't realize."

Ohana opened the door and got out without providing an explanation or comment. He didn't have to. He was an outsider and didn't belong with us at that moment. At least he understood his place.

"Did you see her? She's *beautiful*," I said. I wailed. I moaned.

"Oh, come on," Dad began, "She's all right. She no stark-raving—"

"Don't even bother," Mom said, raising her voice and her hand simultaneously. "We all saw her."

She was tall and lithe, almost regal in the way she carried herself. I dreaded my dad's next comment and prayed it would never come, a patronizing comment akin to beauty being skin deep, that it's what's on the inside that matters most. It was a brand of compassion I didn't care for, words too painful to endure. The meager bit of self-esteem I'd managed to cultivate had been a long time coming. At its best, it was never rock-solid. I was never truly self-assured, not even when Nas was in my life, not even with the security of his love.

Or the illusion of it.

Seeing the woman he'd chosen over me, any shred of confidence I'd hung onto was gone, obliterated, reduced to a wind-swept pile of ash.

And Nas was gone.

With her.

And she was gorgeous, drop-dead *fucking* gorgeous.

The bitch!

And Dad, bless his heart, persisted. "I know you're not interested in my opinion, but Nas being with this woman has nothing to do with her appearance. This is about one thing and one thing only." He challenged us with a sharp glare. "You know what I mean." He turned back toward the front seat. "There, I've said my piece."

I believed he meant what he said, and I wanted to take stock in each and every word, maybe too much. Maybe Nas's marriage to Bahija had not been precipitated by her Covergirl looks, but it certainly hadn't hurt her chances.

She was stunning and didn't need an arranged marriage contract in order to secure a husband.

But she got one, didn't she?

Standing outside the SUV, Ohana tapped on the passenger side window. Drawing Dad's attention, he tapped the crystal on his watch.

Ohana opened the door and looked in. "Hank, are we doing this or not?"

The signature on the charitable receipt we'd come across did not belong to Arshad Huzaifa, the mullah who'd blessed Nas's wedding to Bahija. It belonged to his brother, Ghazanfer Huzaifa, the Imam, the proverbial big cheese at the mosque standing before us. We'd made an appointment to speak with him. Under false pretenses, we'd managed to secure a brief audience in order to ferret out his brother's whereabouts. It seemed the police hadn't yet thought to question him. Perhaps, as Dad had quipped, they were like the bumbling Keystone Cops incapable of connecting dots.

I could see that Ohana had become impatient. Examining our faces, it appeared he was taking the temperature of the room to ascertain which way we were leaning. "He booked the hotels and the car rental for Nasir and his wife. The credit card trail showed us that. There's no telling how he's involved," he said. "We have to take this guy."

"*Take* him?" I said, "We're not *taking* anyone."

Ohana turned from me to Dad. "Brother, am I doing this alone?"

"What the hell is going on here? Dad, what's this all about?" Two scorching seconds ticked by. "*Dad?*"

"Sorry, Dan." He blew a deep and troubled sigh. "I'm out."

"Fine," Ohana huffed. He was about to slam the door.

"Wait!" Dad said, extending an open hand.

Ohana sneered at him, seething, shaking his head with contempt.

Dad's expression said, "You know what I'm talking about." He thrust his hand toward Ohana, insisting that he hand something over.

What the hell? I thought. What's this all about?

Dan stealthily slid an automatic from his waistband and placed it in my father's hand.

I gasped.

Slamming the door, Ohana stormed off.

"A gun?" Mom bellowed. "Hank, are you out of your mind? What's this all about?"

My father couldn't look me in the eye. He didn't have to. Ohana's help hadn't come free—it came at an extraordinary cost. Whatever was on Ohana's actual agenda, whatever Dad had agreed to help him with, had nothing to do with me. My father had deceived me and the price for his betrayal would cost him my love.

Chapter Forty-Eight

Nasir Zia

Nas understood the setup. He'd been played before.

Bahija was in the interrogation room with him, sitting across the table.

"You're a one-trick pony, Detective," he bellowed, making certain to be heard in the adjacent room, the room behind the mirror. He glanced toward the one-way mirror, cutting his eyes at the spot where he assumed Scoldari was standing, watching, listening, spying. "You can't get blood from a stone."

His head swiveled back toward Bahija. "The detective thinks he's clever. Putting us in the room together—he didn't do that for us. Reuniting a man and his wife means nothing to him. All he cares about is—"

She reached out and touched his cuffed hand. Her back to the one-way mirror, she winked at Nas. "I already told the detective I don't know anything about the two murders he's investigating."

Nas pressed his eyes shut. "This is such a nightmare. I don't know how it happened."

She continued to stroke the back of his hand. "You look tired, Nasir. Strained. Are they treating you okay?"

"You mean other than arresting me for no reason? Threatening me with years of imprisonment?" He wanted to ask her what had happened, the why and how of her disappearance. He was dying to know.

Not here, he thought. *Not with Scoldari eavesdropping on our every word.*

Though he could choose not to speak, he had no dominion over his eyes. "What happened?" They implored. "Where did you go?"

Her return glance offered little in the way of an explanation, nothing more than sympathy and the enigma she wouldn't speak about. She winked again, her code saying, "Play along."

The slightest nod communicated his thoughts. *I understand. Our secret is safe. My shame will stay hidden. Let's cherish this time together, short though it will be.*

Scoldari entered the room, his head down, his gaze scorching the linoleum. "The two of you look like you're waiting for the firing squad. You should be crying buckets. Where's the love? The emotion?"

Nas offered a blunt *fuck you* with his gaze. His eyes were cold, calloused. Something about him had changed in the short time he'd been imprisoned.

Looking around, Scoldari pulled over a chair and sat down. "I see what's going on here, the intimate little code you think the old codger won't pick up on." He eyed one, then the other, examining each for a chink in the armor, a sign they were weakening. "So, let me tell you how it goes. Your clever little repartee won't keep either of you out of jail." He allowed his comment to soak in before turning to Bahija. "Your husband has been arrested. The same thing could happen to you. There are two stiffs lying in the morgue. The killer is at large, and I think both of you know who it is. If the DA feels you're withholding evidence, well, as they say, 'That'll be all she wrote.' It'll be mystery meat and coarse toilet paper until you're eligible for Social Security. And you, honey, with that figure…" He eyed Bahija with wolfish glee. "You'll have a lot of company in the shower, more than you bargained for."

"That's enough," Nas screamed. "Stop terrorizing us."

"Wow," Scoldari said. "Look at you, Nasir, you've become quite the hardened criminal. That *was* fast. Did you channel Al Capone in your sleep? You fashion a shiv out of your toothbrush?"

"Leave us alone," Nas demanded. "Your little game isn't working on us."

"Oh, *I'm* sorry. Did you think this was a game? Do you think this is one of those escape rooms you hipster A-holes think are so cool? Well, it's not and you're both in a lot of serious-fucking-trouble. You may not like me or the way I do my job, but I'm on the right side of the law." It looked as if he was sucking at a crumb lodged between his teeth. "You know what? Forget it. It's not up to me anymore. The DA can have at you." He shook his head disappointedly. "You're both children, spoiled, entitled children. You think the world owes you everything, your lattes, your iPhones, and your destination-fucking-weddings. Well, you know what? The world doesn't owe you shit, and that's exactly what you're gonna get, shit. Once you're in the system, it's game over. Your life is ruined… *forever*." He rose from his chair. "Now, I'm going into the break room for a cup of brewed bowel movement we at the station house call coffee. I'll stop back after I'm done, and if you've changed your tune, that'll be just fine. If not, I'll phone the DA and see if he wants me to put the two of you in adjoining cells."

Chapter Forty-Nine

Gwen Winter

I slammed the door of the SUV and stepped back so that my parents could pull out of the hotel parking lot. Mom was behind the wheel. I knew she wouldn't be able to leave without saying goodbye one more time, without questioning my decision again. She lowered the window.

"Gwen, honey, are you sure about this? We don't mind staying."

"I don't want you here." I scowled at my father. His head was turned, and he didn't see me, didn't feel the heat of my stare. I don't want him here. "And you make sure that commando clown, Ohana stays the hell away from me."

Mom leaned out of the window, whispering to exclude my father from what she had to say. "I can send your father home on his own if you want me to stay, Gwen. Would you like that?"

I shook my head. "I have to handle this myself.

"But how will you get around?"

"I rented a car. It's already here in the hotel parking lot." Mom's was such an elemental question, but for a loving mother, it was indicative of everything she worried about. How will I get around? What will I eat? Will I get enough rest?

"I think Alana needs you right now, more than me," I said. "I was telling the truth and lying at the same time. I was giving her something else to focus on, something not quite so nefarious as my mess. Alana's situation was equally horrendous, but perhaps it was something Mom was better

217

equipped to deal with. "Look—" The words didn't come easily. "Right now, Dad and I need some distance apart." He looked over at me but then turned away—shame didn't suit him well. My life had devolved in such a short time. Not being able to respect my father was in a way worse than having Nas walk out on me. There wasn't a man in my life I could look up to or count on. And it hurt; it hurt worse than knowing I was destined to be alone. I stepped back once more. "I'll be in touch."

There were tears in Mom's eyes as she reached out and pulled me against the door, hugging me. "I love you, my girl. You know how much I love you, don't you?"

I nodded before kissing her on the cheek, then pulled away and watched the SUV move off.

I was slowly gathering steam as I turned and walked toward my rental car. Fellini had called, not because he had to or because he was obligated to but because he wanted to. He wanted to help and told me he'd continue to provide assistance wherever he could. He had numerous contacts in the New Jersey court system that he was willing to prevail upon and told me to call on him if I needed anything. He told me that Nas was about to be arraigned. There was still enough time for me to get to the courthouse if I wanted to. The question was, did I want to? Did I care to? Was there anything left between us or was it over? He hadn't been man enough to give me an explanation, not so much as a hint as to why he betrayed me. It was something I could never forgive and would certainly never forget. It was salt in a raw wound, a wound I wasn't sure I'd recover from. His explanation wouldn't heal me, but it might've eased some of my suffering. He knew it would ease the pain and still said nothing. He cried like a baby and watched me bleed. He watched me fucking bleed.

I was still unsure if I was going to see Nas arraigned in court, but I wanted to park the rental close to the entrance in case I decided to go at the last minute. I'd just thrown the gear shift into Park when I saw her. Her, she who'd bested me. She who'd so thoroughly enchanted Nas, rendering him content to leave me for dead.

Fellini told me that the DA hadn't yet charged her, but I never thought she'd be here, right under my nose. For all I knew, we were in adjoining rooms at the hotel.

Through the glass façade, I watched her cross the lobby with her long, purposeful strides, the ends of her head scarf sailing in the air behind her. With her oversized sunglasses in place, she was elegant, a Middle Eastern Audrey Hepburn.

Did she have to have it all: looks, long legs, and my groom? Why couldn't she have a nose like a ship's rudder and the knuckle-dragging posture of a sloth? Why couldn't she be vile with hair like barbed wire? Why couldn't she be an ogre? Why couldn't she? Why couldn't she? Why couldn't she?

Why couldn't I get over it?

She was still in the lobby checking her phone when a car with an Uber symbol on the windshield pulled up. Was she going to see Nas at his arraignment? Was she going there to support him? Was she going to support her man?

They say you always want what you can't have. I didn't make a conscious decision to follow her, but my hand moved to the gear selector, and I shifted into Reverse. I was out of the parking spot with the rental facing the exit when Bahija got into the Uber, and it rolled past me.

I took my foot off the brake and stepped on the gas.

Chapter Fifty

Gwen Winter

I wasn't at all familiar with New Jersey roads, but I figured I had sufficient know-how to follow a lime green Mazda with a chrome Jesus fish plastered to the rear hatch. Hidden behind dark sunglasses, I felt invisible and found the free-wheeling sense of daring-do invigorating. Where was she going? Would I be spotted? Why did I care? I had as much right to attend the arraignment as anyone else.

If not more.

My rental car wasn't equipped with GPS. The names of the roads meant nothing to me. For all I knew, we could've already left the state. My phone rang. Glancing at it, Ohana's name was displayed on the screen.

"The balls on this guy," I said out loud. "As if I might ever take your call, you conniving piece of shit." What kind of deal did you pressure my dad into? Ohana leveraged me, and he leveraged my dad. *What's his game?*

Under an overpass, then from the left lane to the center to the right. I saw the lane signal flash and the Uber took the exit onto I-280. He was slow on the ramp but took off after hitting the expressway. I accelerated to match his speed and fell in behind a Corvette about five car lengths back. The Vette's roofline was nice and low, affording me an unobstructed view of the vile-green Mazda.

My cell phone rang again. Again Ohana on the display. I double-clicked the side button, rejecting the call, and tossed the phone onto the passenger seat. "Leave me *alone*." Whatever he wanted, whatever he had to say, I wasn't interested. He'd infected my relationship with my father, the man I loved most in this world, and for that, he was dead to me, fucking dead.

Garden State Parkway. Toll Road. I saw the Uber heading toward it. "Not good. Not good at all." I didn't have an E-ZPass, which meant I'd have to stop at a toll booth and pay a toll or grab one of those annoying toll cards or something. The Uber would sail through, and I wouldn't. "Shit, I'll lose them. I'll fucking lose them." "Now what?" *Why am I talking to myself?* "Oh, thank God." Spying a short lane, I accelerated around the Vette and ahead of the Mazda to pull up to an unoccupied toll booth. I paid the toll and was off. I actually had to lay back and let the Mazda pass me, then the Vette. I once again fell back in behind the sports car as we fed onto the Garden State.

The phone rang again, but I let it go. It finally stopped but then started again immediately after. It rang and rang and rang again. *Insistent bastard, isn't he?*

And then it dawned on me that I assumed the courthouse was nearby and that we'd driven too far. *Where's this bitch heading anyway? If she's not going to Nas, then where?*

I heard the text tone notification coming from my phone. Reaching over, I saw that it was Ohana. The message read in all caps: STOP! DON'T FOLLOW!

"*What*? How does he know? I felt my pulse pounding in my ears as I looked around for Ohana's car but didn't see it. I felt my face grow flush as a new notification popped up. It was the same as the last. The Mazda was accelerating. I had to pull around the Corvette to stay close, accidentally cutting off a BMW. The driver flipped me off, then pulled up just feet off my rear bumper, flashing the brights. By the time I got out of the way, it was too late. I was on the exit ramp behind the Mazda, entering Newark International Airport.

She's running, damnit. What the hell?

The text tone sounded again. The Screen flashed, DANGER!

I felt my chest tighten. "Fuck, fuck, fuck, fuck, fuck." *What's going on?* What do I do now?" I was tense, no, frightened, bordering on terrified. The

Uber slid into the lane for Terminal B, International Departures. "Fuck, fuck, fuck." A second DANGER! Text flashed.

Carrying nothing but a large shoulder bag, Bahija was out of the car the moment it pulled up in front of the terminal. The Uber took off immediately, and I slipped into the spot it had vacated. I could see her inside, the tall brunette striding through the terminal toward the check-in counter.

"What do I do? What the hell do I do?" I wasn't thinking. Couldn't. My autopilot kicked in, and I bolted from the car toward the terminal."

"Hey," an airport security officer yelled at me. "You can't leave that there."

I was gasping for air, my heart hammering like a pneumatic air gun. "I'll just be a minute."

"Lady, you can't leave your car there."

"It's a fucking rental, and I fucking can." Leaving him speechless, I rushed into the terminal.

A good twenty feet ahead of me, Bahija was at the counter fishing in her bag. The phone rang again. The million years I said needed to elapse before I would answer one of Ohana's calls passed in the span between two consecutive heartbeats. "Dan, what the hell is going on?"

"Get out of there," He blurted. "Get out now!"

"But why?" I heard people screaming. The phone fell from my hand. Before my eyes, a swarm of police officers descended on Bahija, engulfing her and wrestling her to the floor. Bystanders screamed. Others rushed to duck behind anything that could shield them.

"She's got a bomb," someone yelled. "Run. She's got a bomb."

And then the whole place went fucking insane.

Chapter Fifty-One

Gwen Winter

The siege at the airport was over as suddenly as it began. Within minutes, most of the commotion had subsided, and travelers were once again going about their business, checking in, going through security, and hurrying here and there. It was as if Bahija Abidi was never there. I wondered where she had planned to go, to her ancestral home or to seek refuge in a place where she couldn't be found. I knew nothing about asylum for those fleeing the United States, but I felt certain her attempt to escape had been well thought out. She was running. Hence, she'd done something she knew was wrong, something not easily smoothed over.

Less than a handful of cops were still mulling about the concourse, mostly talking amongst themselves, saying whatever law enforcement people say after an arrest takes place. "Great takedown, Moe. Well-executed, Sarah. Went off like clockwork, didn't it, Erin?" The few remaining cops dispersed as well, leaving me wondering what to do next. Was there still time to attend Nas's arraignment? His exotic Barbie Doll was on her way to the hoosegow and wouldn't be in court to support him in his time of need. Would it matter to him if I were there? Would he care? I had to believe my presence would mean something to him. Would he be touched by my loyalty, or would it sting to know he'd lost a gem of a gal?

"Hey, lady, would you move your damn car?" It was the security officer I'd brushed off minutes earlier. "You've got exactly two minutes to get your car the hell out of here before I call for a tow." He checked his watch. "Starting right *now*."

Shit. I'd completely forgotten the car—with all that was going on, it wasn't even a thought in my mind. "Sorry," I said as I walked past him toward the exit.

"Don't ever pull a stunt like that again."

Or what? *I said I was sorry.* What could he do to me that hadn't already been done? Yell? Scream? Issue a summons? The kind of incidents that had sent me into hysterics in the past were now no more than water off a duck's back. Putting it into perspective, trivial things like traffic citations and irate traffic flunkies were bullshit and powerless to affect me the way they used to. What doesn't kill you, right? What I'd endured had transformed me and made me darn close to bulletproof.

Waiting outside, leaning against the fender of the rental was the pistol-toting asshole himself, Dan Ohana. I shot him a stink eye and tried to maneuver around him to get into the car.

"We need to talk," he said.

He wants to talk to me? Not in a million—who was I kidding? The last time I uttered that hollow threat I was able to abide by it a grand total of five minutes. And now there was the Bahija thing. If Ohana had been following me, was he doing so in the course of following her? Was I just in the way? I had to believe so. *Find out what the shithead knows*, I thought. *Use him the way he used you, the way he used Dad.* "There a Starbucks around here?"

He didn't answer my question but started toward the passenger door. "My car's in the short-term lot. You drive."

Giving me orders? He's got balls. Ohana was no longer the grandfatherly gent I'd met in his Long Island office, the one who'd been so concerned about my well-being. The new Ohana was all business, a purposeful machine without an ounce of warmth. Seeing him clearly, this was who the man was all along: a soldier, a calculating and manipulative intelligence officer. Helping me was only part of the plan so long as it served his purpose.

"Just drive," he said as he buckled his seatbelt. "I don't know New Jersey any better than you do. There's got to be a place where we can grab a cup of coffee nearby."

"Sure. I'll just drive around aimlessly." I pulled out my phone and got directions to a nearby diner. "This'll do," I said and started the car.

"I'm sorry about—"

"Sorry about what, using us? Handling us like an asset you were managing? Yeah, I'm sure you're good and goddamn sorry."

"I know you're hurt, Gwen, but your needs and mine were in alignment."

"Is that so? Just what exactly are your needs?"

Ohana looked downright uncomfortable. It wasn't the seating, it was being questioned that rubbed him the wrong way. He bore a hardened expression that said, "You don't have the right to ask."

Mine said, "I'm not backing down." Long moments ticked by. I guess my countenance won out over his.

"You do understand that we were soldiers, your father and me, and that once an intelligence officer, always an intelligence officer. It's practically in our DNA."

"You don't have to lay it on so heavy. I get the whole code of honor thing. Just tell me why you needed a gun yesterday?"

"Because I knew that animal in the mosque wouldn't tell me what I wanted to know unless he was staring down the barrel of my sidearm. That's why. Your dad and me, we know these people. You never saw a school bus explode before your eyes, tiny bodies on fire, flying through the air like charred ragdolls. It takes a certain kind of animal to do something like that, and Ghazanfar Huzaifa is one of them. I've seen the carnage these people are capable of, and it's not an image I can forget."

"You know this how?"

"It's what I do, Gwen, what I've always done. You think I'm some five-and-dime private detective tracking down runaway millennials? Seriously? I'm Israeli. We used to hunt Nazis. Now, we hunt terrorists, any group that threatens the existence of Israel or the Jewish way of life. You understand now? This man I saw yesterday funnels cash to terrorist organizations. And his brother, who no doubt murdered two men, has his hands in the same dirty stash of money. But without a gun to his head." His head dropped, his face awash with disappointment. "My only choice was to pass the information to the authorities. He's in custody now, and it was his credit card transaction that enabled the police to arrest Bahija Abidi before she could flee the country."

I absorbed his words without reaction and without surprise. Though my first impulse was to challenge him, I knew in my heart it was true. The image of burning children flooded my head, and I knew in my heart the pain my father felt every time he heard of a terrorist attack. And by extension, any time he saw me with Nas. It explained a lot about who he was and why he reacted to Arabs the way he did. The acts of terrorism Ohana spoke about were revolting. Like most, I'd only learned of them from the news. But being on the scene and seeing that carnage with your own eyes, I couldn't imagine experiencing such devastation, let alone processing it. My father and Ohana had lived through the searing trauma of terrorism, and this is how they dealt with it. Not just at the moments these unspeakable tragedies took place but every day for the rest of their lives. I didn't need coffee any longer. I needed a stiff drink.

"Did Ghazanfar give up his brother's location?" I asked.

Ohana shook his head. "No, that's why it was so important for us to grab Bahija before she got away. Ghazanfar Huzaifa is a hardened jihadi. He'd die before ratting out his brother or any of his radical cohorts. Bahija, on the other hand, might."

"Not quite as tough, huh?"

"No, Gwen, not even close."

Chapter Fifty-Two

Gwen Winter

Working behind the scenes, Fellini was able to find out that a judge had ruled there was sufficient cause to send Nas's case to trial and that bail had been set at $150,000, an amount Nas was unable to cover. He'd been transferred to the county correctional facility while Godfrey worked on arranging bail. Both Fellini and I presumed that Godfrey had contacted Mohammad to make bail arrangements and that a man of Mohammad's means would have no problem coming up with the money. Checking the time, I saw that it was almost four in the afternoon. Fellini had mentioned that county correctional accepted bail until 3:00 p.m. and not a second after, which meant that Nas, the man I had placed on a pedestal, was about to spend his first night in the big house.

As much as I hated what he did to me, I didn't hate *him* and didn't want to see him embroiled in such a sordid affair. I really knew nothing about prison except for what I'd watched in the movies and read in books. I didn't have a true picture of what occurred once you were inside. I didn't know if the clichés were true. But in my heart, I dreaded what might happen to him. I feared for his well-being and his life. I wanted him punished for what he'd done to me, but not like this, not prison, locked up with hardened criminals, with men who placed no value on human life. Why had he been so secretive? Why hadn't he told Scoldari everything he'd been asked? Did he have nothing to tell him, or was the truth so ghastly he'd forego his liberty to hide it?

"Any chance you can get me in to see her?" I'd asked just before getting off the phone with Fellini.

"Way too soon for that," he'd said. Bahija wasn't speaking with anyone but her attorney, not even her parents. "There's something seriously strange about this woman," he'd emphasized. "I don't know what she's involved in, but I can't wait to get to the root of it because my gut tells me something stinks to high heaven."

And by extension, so did Nas, my Nas, the man I thought could do no wrong. Had all gone to plan we'd still be lying on the beach. I should be sipping an intoxicating potion while sand sifted between my toes.

Instead of this.

Holed up in a New Jersey hotel, a prisoner to my mind, running scenarios about what my ex-fiancé was hiding from me, and now the world. Surely, the prospect of years in jail would compel him to tell the truth.

It had to.

Didn't it?

Soft rapping on the door, so soft I could barely discern it above the din of the TV that was on purely to fill the silence. It had to be Ohana. Yet another explanation for what he did. Yet another crumb of evidence to tantalize me with.

But I was so damn tired.

The knock on the door continued, growing slightly louder, then came a voice devoid of Ohana's Israeli accent. It took a moment to place it. Transported out of bed, I tiptoed toward the door, neither committing nor cowering, eager for an additional sample.

"Gwen?"

A man's voice, but it wasn't a lot to go on. I needed more.

"Gwen, are you in there?"

I unlatched the chain and twisted the handle. "Jack?" Gasping, I yanked open the door as I jumped into his arms. Tears ran down my cheeks as I buried my head on his shoulder. He was the only one left, the only man in my life yet to be tarnished by shame. "What are you doing here?" I asked with a you're-too-good-to-be-true crescendo in my voice. He was the last person I expected to see but the first one I would've wished for. In my darkest hour, Sir Jack of Perfection had come to my rescue armed not with a sword but a six-pack.

His smile was weak and yet overpowering. "I thought maybe you could use a drink."

Jack and I bandied our catastrophic stories back and forth, mine, then his. We cried, then laughed. Jack was mine, but only for the night.

And I was his.

Our agonies became remedies. We soothed each other's wounds with words. Whoever said, "Misery loves company," really knew their shit.

But in the end, there was only the uncertainty of my future without Nas and his with or without Alana.

"I don't know how to forgive her," he said, as his shoulders slumped. It had been a while since I'd seen him without Madi in one arm and Sophia in the other, his two beautiful girls. He always carried them up the front steps and through the front door before releasing them to run into the waiting arms of their grandparents. "I don't know if I can."

Seeing Jack so sad and broken, it wasn't in me to go on and on about Nas, about the absurdity of a relationship that should never have been. "We're not talking about love, Jack. You can't really think Alana is in love with Imani. It's just—"

"Poor judgment? A fling?" He shrugged. "I don't think it's love. I don't want to believe that, but I really don't know what it is. How can I accept that Alana would risk so much for a little thrill-seeking?"

"Do you have any idea how long it's been going on?"

"No. Your sister's not talking. Either she won't, or she can't."

"I think she's still in shock. I don't think she ever saw this coming. I tried to talk to her, but every time I opened my mouth—"

"She shut you down?"

"Yes."

"All I could ascertain was that she's overwhelmed with guilt."

My fiancé and my sister, the two people closest to me in the world, were unable to explain their actions. I felt for Jack, not only because he'd been hurt and betrayed, but because he was going through the same searing hell I was.

"What do I do, Gwen? I'm lost. I'm just fucking lost." I saw such loneliness in his eyes, such agony and vulnerability. They said *I'll see your own hellish nightmare and raise you one of my own.* Two beautiful daughters as well as a wife, who up until days ago, had been his soulmate, the relationship he valued above all others. His dilemma was so much worse than mine, his hurt so much deeper, fathoms deeper.

And look who he comes to for advice?

"Look at me, Jack."

He looked into my eyes, not knowing what I was getting at.

"Do you see me, Jack?"

"Of course. But what?"

"And I see you. We're both still here."

"What does that even mean, Gwen? I feel like I want to—"

"Like you want to die? That's how I felt, but I don't feel that way anymore. You won't die. You can't. You and Alana will find a way to work this out. Because you'll fight for it. I know you will."

I threw my arms around him and could feel all of his strength surrendering to my embrace. "When did you become the strong one?" he asked.

I'm not. I'm simply doing what everyone did for me. I'm telling you what you need to hear. What happens after this? "Damned if I know."

Chapter Fifty-Three

Gwen Winter

The secret me was a lousy vamp, a man-seducing trollop, a home wrecker.

I slept with Jack.

Perhaps only in my dreams, but the passion was as intense as if his flesh were pressed against mine. I felt every caress and every kiss. I stirred, I writhed, and in the end, I awoke a hot, sweaty mess. Heart pounding, chest heaving, the sheets and the blanket were twisted into knots. The pillows were on the floor.

I had long fancied him with me, and now we were finally together. I was one with the man I would never and could never have. I didn't feel shame when I looked in the mirror the next morning—I embraced the lust that had ravaged me, and it left me feeling empowered. And a small part of me, the tiniest ember, felt as if it could've happened last night before I told him to leave, if I led Jack that way, if I was an awful and selfish bitch.

But I wasn't.

I couldn't.

Never.

Jack's place was with Alana and the girls, and I'd do everything in my power to encourage him to give her another chance. "Go home," I said. "Fight. Battle. Tear each other to shreds. But in the end, reach out and find each other again. Make it work."

Mike Fellini was on the phone within moments of me stepping out of the shower. It seemed loyalty meant more to him than money. He'd made himself my self-appointed advocate. I had no doubt his resolve was born out of his devotion to my father, and I had no doubt Fellini was sharing all the same information with him, which was okay with me. I didn't want my parents in the dark. I wanted them to know it all and it was fine for them to be kept informed as long as I wasn't the one passing along the information, as long as I wasn't the one reporting back to high command.

"Bahija is being arraigned in federal court this morning, and I can tell you without equivocation that she won't be granted bail. Her passport's been revoked. Homeland Security and the FBI were both in on her arrest at the airport. In addition to accessory charges for two murders under investigation, she's looking at a lifetime sentence on two separate terrorism charges, harboring terrorists and providing material support to a terrorist organization. I hope she's got one hell of a good lawyer."

No shit! That'll teach her to horn in on someone else's man, my man. Making light of Bahija's problems made me smile. Reveling over her comeuppance gave me a sense of victory. But I still knew nothing about why she and Nas were together. I didn't want to believe that Nas had been involved in such horrendous activities. Then again, what did I know? All of it might've been true. Nas had spent the night in jail. I imagined him lying awake, fearing what awful deeds might befall him before morning.

And I spent the night with Jack. Cheating on Nas, if only in my dreams—somehow, it helped even the score.

Fellini was inquiring to see if Nas would allow me to visit him in prison. As for confronting Bahija and trying to wrangle some manner of explanation out of her, Fellini made it clear that it was not going to happen, not now and possibly not ever. "She's radioactive," he began, "suspected of crimes against the state. That's very serious shit."

All I could do was sit around and hope that Nas would say yes, that I could visit him in prison, and that maybe he'd say something, anything. Maybe the night behind bars had changed his perspective. Maybe he'd be willing to tell me what I ached to hear. And more importantly, perhaps he'd cooperate with the authorities. Maybe he could tell them something that would move them to dismiss the charges. Maybe. I hoped so. I didn't want to see him lost in the penal system. Even with what he did, he didn't deserve that.

So, now what?

Go for a swim?

Mani-pedi?

Brunch for one?

None of the options excited me.

I heard the phone ringing from the bathroom where I'd left it.

Who's that? I wondered as I went off to retrieve it.

Mom? Fellini? Alana? Who else would be calling?

It was that strange 518 area code I'd seen days before. My new BFF was calling. Rosemarie, my new rock.

"Hey, babe," she said, her voice cheery and a song in her heart. She was one of the good ones. Bull in a china shop I'd been the day my life shattered, I was lucky to have collided with such a wonderful soul. "You over that turd yet? Sexy mama, are you putting yourself out there again?"

"In your dreams."

And last night in mine.

"Get back on the bicycle, babe."

She didn't know what had transpired since meeting me at the mental hospital. She had no idea what I'd lived through, was living through. "Not quite yet. Are you checking up on me?"

"I *am.* Hope that's all right. We're sisters, right?"

"Absolutely. How's upstate life?"

"Interesting. That's the other half of the reason I'm calling."

Do tell. "I'm listening, Rosemarie. What's going on?"

"I just got a call from someone on the nursing staff at the Mental Health Clinic at Mather Hospital. That's not far from you, right?"

Mather Hospital wasn't far from my parent's home on Long Island. "About a half-hour away." I was getting super curious. "Why?"

"A staff psychiatrist was questioning Jana Zia's medications and dosages. Apparently, this doc felt she was being overmedicated."

Rosemarie's statement answered questions and raised others. I now knew where Jana had been transferred to and why. Following my visit to the upstate hospital, Mohammad probably wanted to move her somewhere closer to home, somewhere he could keep a sharper eye on her. The overmedication part was curious. "What came of it?"

"I tried transferring the call to Doc Bellows, but he barked at me and said he'd have to return the call at another time."

"Gee, very professional."

"Yeah, the doc doesn't like to be challenged. If I know him, it'll be a while before he calls back. He gets resentful like that. Anyway, I was sure you'd want to know."

"I *so* appreciate this, Rosemarie. You have no idea."

"And you're welcome. All kidding aside, are you feeling any better?"

"Yes," I replied truthfully. Nas was a puzzle I wanted to solve, but no longer felt would kill me. Learning his secret was now intense curiosity more than dire need. "You know, one day at a time, right?"

"Exactly, darlin.'" She abruptly went quiet. "Ahh, shit, that yappy little dog, Bellows, is marching down the hall, shooting me daggers. Sucks to be the messenger. I've got to go." She disconnected.

Now what?

It didn't take a moment for me to arrive at an answer, pack up, fire up the rental, and pray it didn't take an eternity to get back over the Cross-Bronx Expressway.

Chapter Fifty-Four

Gwen Winter

I heard Scoldari, that infuriating, old-school cop, talking in my ear. His advice had somehow embedded itself in my brain. He'd told my father that taking the Cross-Bronx Expressway was always a big mistake and that he'd have made better time taking the longer route through Staten Island. Thinking nothing could be as bad as the trip we'd made the other day, I rerouted the GPS on my phone. The drive seemed to take forever, but I still managed to chop a full hour off our time from the other day. I guess the irritating old buzzard knew what he was talking about.

I arrived at Mather Hospital an hour too early for patient visiting hours. It gave me plenty of time to grab a snack and freshen up at a nearby pizza joint. The pizza was good, and the restroom was immaculate. All in all, I'd call that a win. The owner seemed to take a liking to me and brought me a complimentary glass of chianti, which was so very on-point, exactly what I needed. Recharged and much less travel-weary, I headed back to the mental facility.

Far more competent and level-headed than when I assaulted Rosemarie the day of my marital catastrophe, I asked to see Jana and answered yes when asked if I was family. I told the receiving nurse that I was her sister. And I almost was—I should've been if my world hadn't been turned upside down.

Then I sat down and waited. Whether Jana would see me or not was anyone's guess. I didn't have the fair-hearted Rosemarie to advocate for me, the bride in distress. Praying wasn't my thing but I implored in my own indelicate way, *Would someone please tell me something? Anything? For god's sake, how long do I have to be in the friggin' dark?*

As if by divine intervention, someone spoke. "Ms. Zia will see you now," the receiving nurse said, followed by the routine security preamble about not giving anything to the patient, limited physical contact, and not getting the patient worked up.

I'm good with the first two. As for number three, I'll try.

She pointed to a door. "I'll buzz you in."

Psychiatric wards were secure areas. Safety and security, that and don't let any looneys escape from the bin were among the staff's uppermost priorities. I'd been a psychiatric patient myself, not often, but there it was. I knew what it was like to sit on the other side of the table, to feel wretched and pathetic, to live for the few minutes when the family came to visit. Alas, I knew the drill all too well.

Jana was dressed in exactly the same outfit she was wearing when I saw her last, but she seemed different. Her posture was straighter, her expression more relaxed. She was by no means a ball of fire, not even close, but the dull shroud that had been hanging over her was gone. Her eyes seemed clear, more focused. I knew what she must've felt like before, that overmedicated feeling, as if you were trapped in a different world, out of touch from everyone else. She'd yet to utter a word but I somehow sensed that she'd left that person behind in the old upstate hospital.

"I knew you'd come," she said. "Can you tell me something about my brother?"

Her immediate concern for Nas told me I was right. Straightaway, I felt that she'd made a leap from when I'd seen her last. She wasn't self-absorbed with her own pathetic and retched situation, alone with a mind she couldn't trust. How could I answer her without sending her crashing back into the abyss? The truth about Nas, it was more than a loving sister could bear, even one in full command of her mental faculties. I didn't want to lie to her.

But I knew she couldn't handle the truth.

"He's on his honeymoon, Jana." I could see she was having trouble dealing with what she'd heard. "With his new wife, Bahija."

She reached out and took my hand. "What happened between you and Nasir? I thought—"

"It didn't work out," I said, pouting. "Nas is with someone else now."

"But I never met her. Nasir and I…I feel certain he would've introduced us. We shared so much, everything. He would never have chosen someone to marry without telling me, without bringing her to meet me." She shook her head, casting her worried aura this way and that. "Something must be wrong with him. And you, how could he not marry you? He—"

He loved me? I felt my throat tightening. "Things don't always work out the way we want them to. I wish they had, but they just didn't." There was no point pushing her further. It was clear she knew nothing about what was going on with her brother, why he'd married someone else. *Damn it! Nas's secret is still buried.* The pain I'd kept bottled up was beginning to rise up again.

She must've seen it in my eyes and tried to soothe me, rubbing her hands over mine. "I know he loves you, Gwen. He told me so."

Oh my God, that one really stung. Her words were meant to comfort me, but they had the opposite effect. Knowing he loves me, or loved me, and that we were going to be together was overwhelming. Unbearable. Soul-crushing. *Please help me. I don't want to cry in front of her.*

"I miss my brother. Do you think he will come to—"

Visit you soon? You can't ask me that. I don't know how to answer you. I closed my eyes.

And someone answered for me. "Such a silly question." I opened my eyes and saw Amira standing behind her daughter, stroking her long black hair. "Of course he will." Amira's eyes were red, glassy. The tears rushing forward were not her first. Like me, she was in agony. Was she devastated because she couldn't tell her daughter the truth? Or was it something else? She kissed Jana atop the head, then turned her gaze to me.

I felt a pang in my heart. There was more.

Chapter Fifty-Five

Gwen Winter

"I can't stay very long," Amira said as she got in and closed the passenger door of my rental car. We'd left the hospital together. A light drizzle had begun to fall, and we ran to my car, which was closer than hers.

"Don't tell me that. This is uncomfortable for you? Well, too bad. You owe me, Amira. You, Nas, and your husband. I want the truth, and I want it now. This mess is a lot worse than it appeared when I showed up at your house with my parents, and Mohammad promptly called me a whore."

Amira's eyes grew large. "Gwen, he did no such thing."

"Please, now you're covering for him too? What is with you people? Can't you ever admit the truth? Sharmoota, we heard him say that clear as day."

"Oh, Gwen, Mohammad wasn't saying that about you." She took a deep breath. "He was saying it to me. You have to understand how my husband was raised back in Pakistan. He's very traditional, and when Hank called him something nasty, a slur, as I remember… And when I rushed in and begged you to stay…" Her head fell. "In his eyes, I dishonored him. I betrayed him. My role as his wife is to stand by his side, no matter what—as I always have. And when I didn't, he called *me* a sharmoota, a whore. He may have never wanted his son to marry a Jew, but he would never call you that. Never."

I was shocked, unnerved. "Mohammad called you a whore? You, his wife? I can't believe that."

"I'm sorry to say it, but he did. I was looking straight at him when the venom dripped from his tongue. He would, and he did." She frowned. "You don't know what is expected of a Pakistani woman. You'll never know, and I'm glad you won't."

Part of me wanted to comfort her, ached to. I wanted to tell her I was sorry for what she must've endured, but it was time for me to be selfish. It was time for answers. "I've got nowhere to go, Amira. You're going to answer my questions until I'm satisfied and I finally understand what's happened to my life."

Her head reared back. I could see she was having trouble getting air, so I opened the windows an inch or two. "Better?"

She nodded. "Thank you." She took tissues from her purse and dabbed at her eyes. "Yes, Gwen, you have a right to know, but I really have to be somewhere before five o'clock."

"I don't care."

"No, Gwen, I think you do. I have to post bail for Nasir."

"You?" Her words didn't make sense. "Isn't that something Mohammad should do? Nas told me he oversees all the finances in your family."

"We have to put up a real property equity bond, and the house is in my name. It always has been. Mohammad's people told him it was the only way to insulate the house from potential lawsuits on his business."

"Lawsuits? Are you telling me you're broke?"

"I didn't say that. Protecting the house from possible legal action is a far cry from being broke. The house is in my name, the business in his. Does that make sense?"

"Nas always told me the two of you were very comfortable. I mean the house, the cars—you and Mohammad don't seem to want for anything."

"You're right. We don't. Mohammad is wealthy. He has all the money he will ever need."

"Then what's with the property bond? His son's in jail. Why doesn't he write a check?"

It seemed like a very simple question—I expected an equally simple answer. Why shouldn't I? Why shouldn't Muhammad post bail for Nas? He should've done so immediately and without reservation. But once again,

I was reminded how very naïve I was and how little I understood about human nature. "Because," she screamed, her hands shaking and her face turning red. Her chest began to heave. Despite the huge breaths, it seemed the air was not getting to her lungs. Turning to me, her face was awash in tears as she whimpered, "Nasir is not his son."

Chapter Fifty-Six

Gwen Winter

"Nas is not Mohammad's son?" I couldn't believe what I'd heard. I rejected it. Covering my ears, my heart pounded, and my throat turned to sand.

It's not possible.

Why didn't he tell me?

I couldn't get the thought out of my mind. Nothing about Nas was true, not who he was or who he loved. The more I looked, the less I wanted to see. How could I have ever fallen for him? Was he such an accomplished actor, or was I such a staggering fool? Dad's words blared like a siren in my head, "You'll never really know who he is."

I was in shock as I followed Amira to the bail bond office and sat patiently while she presented all the documents required to post a real estate bond secured by her home. I had to know it all, the rest of the sordid lies. With the working day almost over, I had no choice but to put my burning curiosity on hold until Amira could do what she had to.

The office was small, two side-by-side desks, wood paneling and steel door separating the front and back offices. The lock on the door buzzed, and a woman as wide as she was tall emerged. She pulled a folder from a filing cabinet, then returned to the seclusion of the inner sanctum.

"Deed," the bondsman said, all business as he extended his hand for the document. He was a good-looking guy; late twenties, maybe early thirties.

The plaque on his desk read Fred Munsey. The plaque on the adjoining desk had belonged to Walter Munsey. A framed photo on the unoccupied desk was inscribed, May He Rest in Peace. It seemed Amira was dealing with the new owner.

Amira thumbed through the documents she'd brought with her and handed one across the desk. "This is it, yes?"

Flipping through the deed, he reached the end and looked up. "You're Amira Zia?"

"Yes."

"I'll need two forms of photo ID," he said, "License and passport?"

What was the story with Nas? He never hinted at the fact that he was adopted—he hadn't dropped the subtlest clue. You'd think he'd want to tell his future wife something like that. You'd think he'd want her to know. *Could that be why he fled?* No. No way that was a big enough reason for him to do what he did. I mean, unless his bio dad was Adolf Hitler.

The submission of documents continued. Fred Munsey was an efficient machine, an automaton. One by one, he requested documents, then checked them off on the file cover sheet: a paid property tax bill, assessor's valuation of the home, mortgage satisfaction—I thought the requests would never end. Then came the signing of documents, an endless stream of paperwork, grants, permissions, and disclosures, all required Amira's John Hancock. Where was Mohammad while she was signing away her life? Okay, so the house wasn't in his name; she was still his wife, his life partner. Why wasn't he here with her, helping her and standing at her side as she had so often done for him? Where was the support she deserved?

What was I thinking? Of course, why wouldn't he be absent? Nas is not his son. He'd refused to fund Nas's bail and was hanging Nas out to dry, severing the poisoned limb. Nas's existence tainted Mohammad's reputation, and he refused to become collateral damage.

Amira and I agreed to sit down and have a quiet talk when she was done posting the bond. It was once again too late in the day for bail to be posted. Nas would have to spend another night in a prison cell.

Mohammad had always seemed so devoted to his family. Whether or not he was the true father, how could he abandon Nas in his hour of greatest need? Because he wasn't Nas's biological parent? *Oh come on, the two of them have been together since forever, literal decades.* Did that count for nothing? How could he not love Nas as his son?

God, I hope Nas is all right.

"I'll process and transmit all the documents," Munsey said. "With no issues, we should be okay on the bond by tomorrow morning. Let your attorney know where we stand so that he's ready to post bail at the correctional facility before 3:00 p.m. tomorrow afternoon."

"Do I have to come back?" Amira asked.

"No, ma'am, it's all electronic these days. What would we do without computers, right?"

Her head was hanging in shame as we left Munsey Bail Bonds. I could see her looking around, checking the faces of passersby to make sure she wasn't recognized leaving the bail bondsman's office. Reaching into her purse, she pulled out her phone. "I want to make sure I hear the phone if the bondsman calls." She raised the volume. "Where should we go?" she asked. "Some place quiet."

Thinking about restaurants in the area, I mentioned a local Mediterranean place because I was a sap and automatically prioritized her dietary needs over a place where I could get a swimming-in-grease cheeseburger, real comfort food to gorge on while my heart was being ripped out of my chest.

It wasn't a total loss—the restaurant had a bar. Amira didn't drink, but that wasn't going to stop me from imbibing. The thought of absorbing her family's devastating secrets required proper sedation, and no one was going to tell me how to self-medicate, not at a time like this. I was so tense I could barely breathe. Frequent, steady sips of a martini slowly helped in regulating my respiration.

Amira drank hot tea while she dipped pita wedges in a dish of baba ganoush. "This is delicious," she said, making small talk to avoid diving into her family's murky waters.

"I think it's time we talked, Amira. Really talked. Why did Nas—? Damn it, just tell me what happened."

Still stalling, she fussed with her tea, adding lemon and sugar. She eyed me suspiciously. Some things are better left unsaid."

"No. I have a right to know why Nas left me high and dry on my damn wedding day."

"Yes, I understand. It's just very difficult for me to talk about. I've never spoken to anyone outside the family about it." She looked into my eyes, imploring me to let her off the hook, but I wouldn't yield. "It puts great shame on my family."

That ship has sailed, sister. Nas screwed me over, and now he's behind bars. Shame? Get the fuck over it.

She dabbed at her tears. "I suppose I'll have to start at the beginning."

"Uh-huh, the beginning."

Her phone rang before she could begin. "Sorry," she said as she picked up the phone and answered the call. It took scant seconds for distress to register on her face. "Mohammad, you *bastard*," she said as she covered the phone. Pointing at my martini, she implored, "Please, Gwen, order me one of those."

Chapter Fifty-Seven

Mohammad Zia – 1995 – Pakistan

Tall, ornately decorated burlap sacks lined the front of Zia Masala, the spice market Chawish Zia had opened more than twenty years earlier. Mounds of spices, in hues of orange, yellow, and green, rose above the level of the open bags and imparted heavenly fragrances that were savored by all shopping in the market. Chawish stood behind the bags of spices, watching the market square with great anticipation. His son, Mohammad, was returning from Upper Punjabi after nearly a month of supervising the spice harvest. There was so much he needed to tell him, so much he'd been holding inside, awaiting Mohammad's return.

Under the best conditions, the trip from the spice fields in Faisalabad to the markets in Karachi took most of a day, but often longer. Mohammad had called before setting out at 5:00 a.m. that morning, but with the sun falling in the sky, Chawish was losing hope that he'd see his boy before the end of day and was wondering if the truck had broken down on the road. Worse, he worried about insurgents who stopped vehicles at gunpoint, demanding bribes and stole cargo. Mohammad was a capable young man and carried a rifle with him on his trips, but his willingness to use it had never been tested. Money and raw spices could be replaced, but the risk to his son's life made Chawish uneasy.

As the afternoon shadows grew, the brightly colored spices appeared to darken—the light orange colors looked brown and the reds, black. Another business day drawing to a close, Chawish gave his clerks the signal to secure the merchandise for the night. He was eager to get home and see if Mohammad had called from one of the villages along the way. The risk of Mohammad falling prey to bandits grew greatly with the coming of night. Chawish's stomach churned. He worried that he might have to go out after him.

He was ready to padlock the shop's front door when the sputtering of a diesel engine spun his head. Steam rose from the front grill as the truck lumbered toward him. The cost of the presumed truck repair mattered little. His son was home.

Clapping his hands to hasten his employees, he directed them to unload Mohammad's truck as quickly as possible. He embraced Mohammad the moment he jumped out of the cab. "Praise Allah, you look okay. What happened?"

"Radiator hose," Mohammad said.

"Where?"

"Near Sukkur. I was able to patch it with duct tape, but working in this heat, it took hours before the engine was cool enough for me to go near it."

"Ah, but you're here now—that's all that matters," Chawish said, sporting a warm smile. "I was worried that you encountered bandits. I hear they've gotten more brazen, demanding larger bribes and stealing cargo."

"Praise Allah, there were no outlaws today." Mohammad took notice of the employees unloading the sacks of spices. "Where is Little Princess?" he asked. "She always works until closing time."

Chawish's smile faded. "She's unwell, Mohammad."

"But I can't remember the last time she missed a day." Chawish didn't comment. "Nothing too serious, I hope." He was silent while waiting for his father to allay his concern. "You're uneasy, father. What's wrong?"

Reaching into his pocket, Chawish tossed the store keys to one of his workers. "Lock up when you're done and drop off my keys at the house on your way home."

Acknowledging his responsibility, the worker snatched the keys and nodded dutifully.

Chawish took Mohammad by the arm. "You must be exhausted. Come. I'll tell you everything after you've put some food in your belly."

"Father, can't you tell me now?"

"No," Chawish said as he hustled Mohammad down the street. "On this, I insist."

* * *

The Zia's lived well. Their home in the posh Clifton area was located on a tall bluff with a view of Baba Channel Harbor. The dining room was decorated in ivory and gold with a marble floor and a grand mahogany table. Facets on chandelier crystals twinkled overhead as the Zia's dined.

Mohammad was practically giddy as he consumed the feast that was laid out before him. "Everything is delicious, Ammi. I haven't had delicacies like this in so long. Thank you."

His mother leaned over and kissed her son on the head. "Your enjoyment is my reward."

"Your mother knows you eat like a peasant when you supervise work in the fields. She's been talking about what she was planning to prepare all week long. 'Bring home fresh garam masala,' she said. 'My spices have lost their fragrance.'"

"Well, they had," she said.

"When did this happen?" Chawish asked, teasing her. "All month long, they were fresh enough for you to serve to me. Now, all of a sudden, they have to be thrown away. It's a good thing you came home when you did, Mohammad or I'd still be eating tasteless meals even today." He toasted Mohammad with a glass of lassi. "A thousand blessings on your return, my son."

Discussions flowed easily while the family caught up on their time apart. The hour had grown late when Mohammad finally blew out a puff of air and pushed his plate away. "I can't eat another bite."

"You call that an appetite?" Chawish said. "I could eat twice that amount when I was your age. Your belly must've shrunken from eating peasant food while you were away."

That moment in every discussion when banter ebbs finally arrived. Mohammad took advantage of the lapse in conversation to restate his earlier question. "What's wrong with Little Princess?"

Chawish had just bitten into a piece of peshwari. He placed the rest of his bread on a dish and slowly chewed the bit that was in his mouth. "Lasna, the maid is gone?" he asked as he turned to his wife.

"Yes, my husband, long gone." She averted her eyes.

"Good," Chawish said. It took a moment before he continued. "Mohammad, Little Princess is with child."

Astonishment spread over Mohammad's face. "So soon? She just became engaged. Was she—"

"The poor girl," Chawish said. "Her engagement has been broken off, and I fear she has no future."

The immense weight of Chawish's implication settled over the room.

Mohammad gasped. Lines formed in his forehead you'd expect to see on a person of advanced years. "Who is responsible? Someone must come forward and restore her honor. She'll never be able to marry."

"She has three siblings," Lasna reminded him.

A woman suspected of immoral behavior would bring dishonor to her entire family. Her siblings would be ridiculed and may also find it impossible to enter into marriage. "Her family isn't planning to—?" Mohammad asked, his chest heaving, his lips pressed tightly together. After committing an illicit act and shaming her family, honor may be restored by publicly killing the woman who engaged in the forbidden act.

"No," Chawish said resolutely. He studied his son's face and allayed the boy's fears. "I have interceded. There will be no honor killing. Little Princess will not be put to death."

Mohammad clutched his heart. "Thank you, father. She's been with us so long—to see her put to death...I wouldn't be able to take it. She's like one of our own. Like family."

"Thank you, my son," Chawish said. "My heart swells with your compassion. Thank you for coming forward to marry this poor urchin girl. Your benevolent deed will restore honor to her and her family. Praise Allah, it will be so."

Mohammad's mouth fell open. "*What*? Me? Why me? Why not the bastard who dishonored her?" He waited for a response, but none was offered. "I don't understand, father. Why won't you answer me? Why must I be the one to make such a sacrifice? I have a girlfriend." He struggled to tell his parents that which he was unprepared to announce. "And I love her. I was planning to ask—"

He stopped at the sound of his mother crying.

"Amma," Mohammad implored. "Please stop. I don't like seeing you this way." But she was unable to stop. The flood of tears only grew heavier, her wailing louder. She sat with her head buried in folded arms, devastated. She lifted her head just once to scorch her husband with a fiery gaze.

Watching the moment unfold between his parents, the answer became clear to him. "*You*, Father?" he asked incredulously. "*You* did this?"

Chawish refused to look his son in the eye.

Chapter Fifty-Eight

Gwen Winter

Amira thanked the waitress and promptly sipped her second martini.

"I thought you didn't drink. I thought—"

"I know what you thought, that Muslims don't drink alcohol, that it's considered sinful. Well, I don't, not publicly, anyway. After what I just told you, I'm doing what I need to get through this. As you're learning, my husband is not an easy man to live with. Besides, what's one more secret?" she said flippantly. "Compared to everything I just learned?"

Amen to that. How could it be? The truth was so horribly difficult to accept—Amira was Little Princess. The name Amira was a direct translation from the Arabic language, and the part about her being little was certainly apt. The poor thing was entitled to an occasional buzz after all she'd just told me, that Chawish had raped her and that she would've been put to death if Mohammad hadn't agreed to the forced marriage that restored honor to her and her family. But Mohammad had insisted on a deal. He would marry Amira but only on his terms. He was permitted to move to America with Amira before she began to show, avoiding humiliation and embarrassment. Mohammad became the majority owner of Zia Masala and would run the company from New York, while Chawish remained in place in Pakistan to oversee supply and exportation.

The call Amira had taken before telling me about Mohammad's youth came from Fred Munsey, the bail bondsman. He told her there was next to no equity in their home. Mohammad had somehow taken a loan out in her name, pledging the property as collateral. The loan had only recently been taken out and had just been recorded with the county. Amira was devastated. Hence, the two martinis.

And perhaps more coming.

We were fortunate to have been shown to a secluded table at the rear of the restaurant. Even so, her sobbing drew a lot of attention.

"I never saw Mohammad this way. He's a real piece of shit," I said. It wasn't about the name-calling; it was a way of consoling her. Between the lines, I hoped she'd read, "It's not your fault. You tried. You did the best you could."

Fuck! What's Nas going to do now?

"Amira, do you have any other assets? A hundred and fifty thousand dollars is a lot of money, but in this day and age?" I implored her with my gaze, hoping for good news.

"Pennies, Gwen. I have a small savings account in my name with fifteen or twenty-thousand dollars. I honestly don't know. Mohammad set it up for emergencies, and I've rarely bothered to look at it. I've never needed to. Mohammad oversees all our finances and pays all the bills." She took a healthy swallow of her cocktail. "I've never said this before, but damn that son of a bitch."

I'd never heard her speak of anyone, let alone her husband, in anything less than complimentary terms. Then again, I'd never seen her this angry before. "Is there no one else you can ask for help, a wealthy relative? Anyone?"

I could see that she was deep in thought, trying to jam round pegs into square holes, forcing the pieces to fit. "I'm not sure, but possibly. Some of our extended family is quite well to do, but I don't know that they will go against Mohammad after learning that he refused to post bail for Nasir. They all owe him in one way or another. Biting the hand that feeds you...I don't know if any of them have the guts."

I put my hand on hers. "Maybe there's still hope. Once upon a time, he did the right thing by you."

"And he never let me forget it, abandoning the woman he loved, leaving his homeland, raising a bastard son. Not a day goes by that he doesn't throw it in my face." The martini glass empty, she signaled for one more.

"Amira, I think you've had enough."

"He hates me for it. He doesn't let anyone else see how he feels, but when we're alone."

"It's been decades—he's never been able to let it go? That's a hell of a lot of resentment. I mean, you raised a family together."

"*We*? He did nothing. He went to work, and I raised our children. He only saw them as an obligation, the boy Chawish fathered and the daughter who's spent her adult life in institutions. Don't you see, Gwen, I am the face of all his pain, the dishonored tart he had to rescue, and the children he doesn't love. Everything is on me."

Fuck

All the hand patting in the world wouldn't help. This poor woman had suffered for decades, and now her son was going to jail. Talking to Mohammad wouldn't do any good. This was his revenge, and he was savoring it like the sweetest nectar. He'd be rid of his father's child, once and for all. Nas's only chance was to tell the police everything he knew. Hold back nothing. I wondered if Nas understood how bleak his prospects actually were. Did he have any idea how much animosity festered in Mohammad's heart? How could he? If what Amira said was true, Mohammad had only directed his resentment at her.

Still, Nas is bright. He's intuitive. He must— A thought clubbed me over the head. I lost my breath and could feel my heart thudding in my chest. *It has to be. That's the only explanation.* Gasping, "Amira, does Nas know?"

"About not making bail?" She sobbed. "No, not yet."

"Not the bail, Amira. Does Nas know Mohammad's not his father?"

Chapter Fifty-Nine

Gwen Winter

Drunk and emotionally depleted, Amira was unable to drive home. I'd never seen her like that before, sloshed. Improper. I gave her a lift and said goodbye to her after making sure she was comfortable on the couch in her family room. Looking around her beautiful home reminded me of all the time I'd spent there and how well I'd been treated. I realized it was all a façade, a radiant palace disguising the misery that dwelled within.

In all the time I'd known Nas and his family, I never once saw what Mohammad was hiding, the ugliness he kept bottled up, that his son was poison to him. He resented the boy his father had sired and everything about him.

That's when it struck me: the reason Mohammad never opposed our marriage. He was cutting the cord, terminating the obligation he'd undertaken decades earlier. It didn't matter to him that Nas was marrying a Jew. The boy wasn't his. If anything, by allowing the marriage of Nas to a Jew, Mohammad was delivering one final blow to Chawish, the father who'd raped Amira and abandoned his unborn son. One final fuck you.

My hostility toward Nas was dissipating. I still didn't understand what had precipitated his running off and marrying Bahija, but I now pitied him for the lie he had endured. The truth was slowly being revealed. My hatred was now focused on Mohammad—everything I now knew about the man was toxic. From the moment I met Mohammad, right up through today, I was part of his lie, his Machiavellian scheme to shed the burden of a bastard son and thrust swords through the hearts of his father and wife.

Becoming aware of all the troubles around me, the lie the Zias lives, and the marital problems that had befallen Alana and Jack, well, it almost made me feel like the lucky one. I didn't have a threatened marriage with two beautiful little girls caught in the middle. I hadn't endured decades of emotional torment.

Funny how you can see things one way, then differently the next moment.

Me? I'm lucky? With what I've been through? If I'm lucky, everyone else is completely fucked.

I had to share what I'd learned. If Alana was up to it, strong enough, she was going to be the lucky recipient of what I'd discovered. Her shoulder had always been there for me, and my shoulder would be there for her.

She opened the door with a finger to her lips, instructing me to be quiet. "The girls just went down for the night."

Alana backed away from the door so that I could enter. She didn't look great, but shitty for Alana was more than acceptable for most mothers of two at the end of a long day. Entering the kitchen I noticed an open bottle of some sweet frou-frou rosé, a wine you can chug down all night long, the kind that goes down like iced tea.

"Is there enough for me?"

She opened the refrigerator. A shelf was filled with chilled frou-frou. "Knock yourself out." She abandoned me to fend for myself and trudged into the den. I could hear the news playing at a subdued volume on the TV. A crocheted throw was wrapped around her and her feet were up on an ottoman. She looked worn, had every right to feel that way.

She turned away from the TV when I sat down. "Watching the world go to shit makes me feel better about myself—at least I haven't killed anyone." Speaking into her rosé, she muttered, "Not in a physical sense." She clicked off the TV and turned to face me. "Who goes first? Do we talk about your fucked up situation or mine?"

Yours. Yours is simpler. No less terrible, but simpler. Yours doesn't have to solve the problem of two dead men, the possibility of terrorism, and a bastard son."

Alana fired her wine through her nostrils like a side-by-side shotgun, both barrels discharging at once. She gasped. "A bastard *what*?"

"Nas. Amira got knocked up by Mohammad's father. But where are my manners? We agreed you'd go first."

She flew off the sofa and landed at my side, practically on top of me. "*Ho-ly* shit. When did you find out?"

"Just now. Amira told me after three martinis."

"Wait, Amira *drinks*?"

I winked comically. "Just one of the Zia's many secrets. "To be fair, it took Mohammad's refusal to post bail for Nas to make her come unhinged. Oh, and he also mortgaged their home to the hilt."

She gulped the contents of her glass. "Son of a motherfucking bitch."

"All part of his grand scheme to cram decades of resentment up everyone's ass."

She siphoned the last few drops out of her wine glass. "Bitch, you left the bottle in the kitchen" She stomped off and returned with a full glass and an uncorked bottle, no corkscrew, but then, our frou-frou wine, like most inexpensive blush wines, come with twist-off caps. There wasn't enough wine in the bottle to abate the ocean of tears we poured out over our respective problems. Back and forth we went, hashing and rehashing, letting blood, praying for miracles.

Jack had called Alana. I didn't know if my clandestine tête-è-tête with him had provided the motivation for him to reach out to her. Alana didn't mention it, and I certainly wasn't going to tell her that her wounded husband had showed up at the door of my hotel room with a six-pack and a powerful need for soothing.

"So, how did it go? Does it sound like he might forgive you?"

Alana's glass was empty. She set it on the coffee table without refilling it. "He made me feel really shitty about myself."

"I think you had that coming."

"I know what I did was wrong." She looked me in the eye, confiding without looking for sympathy. "But, Gwen, I *really* enjoyed it."

I recoiled at her admission. "Really, you enjoy fucking? Whoever thought intercourse was pleasurable? What the hell are you telling me?"

"I'm telling you that I enjoyed having sex with Imani. There, I said it, and there's no taking it back. I did it with another woman, and I liked it."

"Katy Perry would be so proud." My crack earned me the finger. I can't say I didn't expect it.

She turned away from me, hiding the guilt she couldn't suppress. "I know you think I'm crazy, but working, parenting, every waking moment…I don't know how to say this."

I understood her. I couldn't believe it but was able to comprehend her marriage, her romantic life with gorgeous Jack, it had gone stale. "Alana, my big sister, and guiding light, are you telling me you enjoyed it, and it's over, or are you telling me you enjoyed it and you're giving up dick? There are two innocent little girls upstairs depending on you to do the right thing. Not to mention you're married to the hottest guy this side of Henry Cavill. Are you ready to call it quits on all of that, and accepting shared custody of the girls, fighting over assets, aggravation, embarrassment?"

She fell quiet.

"Alana, I don't know why you did it. With all the support you've given me over the years, I've come to think of you as more than human."

She threw her arms around my neck. "Are you saying I'm Supergirl?"

"Oh, *babe*, I'm going way beyond that. I'm saying this Imani chick is Lex Luther. What she's hiding in her box is kryptonite, and it will most definitely kill you."

Chapter Sixty

Gwen Winter

I crashed at Alana's after each of us had bared our souls. She was still on hiatus from work, but didn't want the girl's routine to change. I let her sleep in and set the clock to get Madi and Sophia up and ready for daycare. I found the car keys on hooks near the coat rack. Each of the car keys had their own hook. The Convertible hook was labeled FUN. The Minivan's, KTV, which I knew stood for Kid-Totting Vehicle.

Sharing the same zany air with those two little clowns was so much fun. Their spirit and the joy-charged aura they projected was positively energizing. Watching those two excited faces in the rearview mirror as we drove to daycare made my heart light up. So much love in those little hearts. They didn't know about betrayal and lies or uncertainty. All they knew was fun, having it and expecting it, wash-rinse-repeat. Thinking about Alana and me as young girls, I remembered that our relationship closely mirrored that of the two cherubs in the back of the minivan. Life was simple—hearts were pure. I didn't know if Alana and Jack would make it. She'd hurt him badly and didn't seem overly repentant over the jagged rift she'd caused. In my heart, I felt she'd come around. She'd given so much of herself to me over the years. The least I could do was support her in her time of need.

And give her nudges in the right direction. Her family was worth fighting for. Worth far more than a newly self-discovered gal pal.

No matter how much fun it was.

At least, that's the way I saw it.

I'd do everything I could, even if I was still dying on the inside. The man I'd loved but no longer wanted was sitting in a New Jersey prison cell, and the mystery that began the moment he left me high and dry remained unsolved. Layers of deception had been peeled away, but as yet, the answers I searched for remained beyond my reach and locked within a tomb guarded by Mohammad, the two-faced fuck, lord and master of all Zia secrets and lies.

The phone rang while I was sitting in front of the daycare center, collecting my thoughts. Mom was calling, no doubt checking in to see where I was and what was going on. Was I eating, sleeping, and in good spirits, all the worries that made my mother the loving noodge she was.

"Hello, sweetheart, it's your mother. How are you?"

Calls from her often began with her saying, "It's your mother." I mean, just in case her phone had been stolen and she was being impersonated by an internet stalker.

"Hello, *Mother*."

"Are you still in New Jersey? Any new leads in the case?"

"No, actually, I had a sleepover with my big sister."

Her voice filled with excitement. "That's so good to hear. Did you get her talking? Is she all right?"

"Talking, yes." TMI actually, lots of startling insights about her gender fluidity.

"Has she spoken with Jack? Any movement?"

"They spoke." I took a deep breath and gave her tough love. "They've got a long way to go, Mom. This isn't exactly an all-is-forgiven scenario. It's going to take time. Anyway, no, I haven't heard anything new from Fellini in the past twenty-four hours." I thought about how to broach the subject, how to tell them about Mohammad's shocking past. It wasn't exactly a phone conversation, but I hadn't yet reconciled with my father. Ohana, being a wacko shoot-'em-up mercenary, didn't give my dad Carte Blanche to strike a backroom deal with him. Besides, Hank had yet to apologize. Certainly, he owed me that.

"Gwendolyn—" she began. Prefacing a sentence with my full name was always a prelude to serious business. There was also that telltale hesitant tone in her voice.

Now what?

"As long as you're in the neighborhood, we were wondering if you might stop by. Your father doesn't want this thing between you to fester."

I wasn't sure how I felt about it, if I was ready to mend fences. He was a big boy, he didn't need to have my mother do his dirty work. Still, I understood more about why he did what he did. The soldier behind the man had seen a lot of painful shit with his two naked eyes. The little pep talk from Ohana gave me a fresh perspective on how my dad thought about things.

"I have a mandel bread in the oven and fresh coffee brewing. Any chance you might come by for a nibble? *Please.*"

That voice, that heart-warming sympathetic voice, the voice of the woman who'd given me life, how could I say no?

* * *

It was a short ride to Mom and Dad's, not a real long time to think, but I managed to figure out how I'd handle my old man. Walking through the door I gave him the death stare, setting him up for the kill, then played chicken, coming straight at him to see how he'd react. Would he flinch or pull me in for a hug? Our reunion went as expected.

"I don't want any bad blood between us," he said. "You've been through enough."

"No argument there." It was more in the silence than in the words that we found a way back to each other, in the warmth that pervades two people who truly love one another.

"I hope you can forgive me."

Mom had been standing next to him, her eyes sparkling as the magic spell took effect. She hugged me, then bolted for the kitchen. "The mandel bread, it'll burn."

I could tell that the oven had opened because the intoxicating bouquet of her sweet confection wafted through the air.

Comfort food and hugs, what could be better?

The sliced delicacy was set on the kitchen table, steam still rising from it. Coffee was poured. Dad scooped up the first two slices and placed them on my plate. He took them from the center of the loaf, where the dense bread was crammed with molten chocolate. He always served me and Mom before himself, but I could tell by his actions that he was still apologizing. It was time to put our hurt in the past. "I decided to go back to work on Monday. With Nas locked up and Bahija in federal custody, what can I really do?" Mandel bread is the Jewish equivalent of an immense warm chocolate chip cookie. I took a bite and savored the warm, gooey chocolatey goodness. Heaven, I decided, is what comes out of my mother's oven. I took a sip of coffee allowing the sweet and bitter to mix in my mouth. "Oh my God, *so* good, Mom. Amazing."

She smiled one of those your-words-touched-my-heart smiles. "You were saying about going back to work, Gwen?"

"I think it's time. I need routine in my life."

She sprang out of her chair and hugged me. "I'm so happy to hear that."

She meant it. After all the years of depression and the many times I'd succumbed to anxiety, allowing it to incapacitate me—standing strong was of greater importance than standing next to a groom. Seeing her reaction confirmed what I was feeling.

"So, after all these years, your sister decided she likes girls?" Dad asked. "I don't know about anyone else, but I'm surprised as hell."

"Why?" I teased. "You like girls."

"Yes, so?"

"Think about it, Dad, we're better. We're softer, prettier, and way more fun to be around."

"All true," he said, embarrassment knocking at the door. "But two women, there's a vital missing part."

"Easily purchased anywhere online," Mom blurted, shocking us. "You men, it's time you got over yourselves. A penis isn't the end all and be all of pleasure." She glared at him, lightheartedly trying to intimidate him to see if he would blink first. She lost. Clutching her chest, she roared with laughter. "Hank, the look on your face—I thought you were going to keel over."

He couldn't get over it and was still laughing over his wife's breakout stand-up routine when his phone rang. Glancing at the screen, his rosy cheeks blanched. He pushed back in his chair to get up and walk off when I stopped him.

"Anything to do with me?" I asked.

He nodded, then showed me his phone. It was Ohana.

"Put it on speaker, Dad."

The phone volume was high. We heard a mixture of voices and commotion, bleeding out the phone. "Hank," Ohana shouted, making sure he could be heard above the turmoil. His voice sounded robust. "We got him, Hank. We got him. The FBI took him down just minutes ago. Son of a bitch, we got him."

Ohana didn't have to reveal the name. We all understood that he was ecstatic over Huzaifa's capture, the man that had sanctioned Nas's marriage to Bahija.

"Bahija gave him up?" Dad asked.

"In a heartbeat," Ohana said. "Faced with life behind bars? I'd have bet the ranch if Vegas were taking bets. They just put him in the police van. He's done."

"Thank you so much, Dan. I—" Looking into my eyes, he told him, "*We* owe you so much. I'll be in touch." He disconnected. Reaching out, we held hands. Our heads and shoulders dropped as if a huge weight had been placed atop the three of us. And our eyes, crying with laughter minutes ago, now rained with tears of relief.

Chapter Sixty-One

Gwen Winter

Each day was an agonizing death, waiting for the phone to ring, begging for news about anything. There was too much going on after the capture—I was unable to return to work after the weekend came and went as I'd planned. Because I was too wired to think about anything but what Arshad Huzaifa's arrest might yield. Would his arrest lead me to what I wanted to know? Would I finally have closure? Whether or not he'd murdered those two men was important to me, and maybe it should've been uppermost on my list of concerns, but it wasn't. I mean, yes, I cared about those two slaughtered men getting justice, but not as much as the backstory I longed to hear about. What was the force that drove Arshad Huzaifa to take two lives and motivated him to go after Bahija? What could influence a pious man to do so much damage?

Arshad Huzaifa was arraigned in federal court and was being held without bail, charged with the murders of Ronit Latif and Osman Shehzad, not to mention a litany of terrorist-related charges. His capture made the headline of every major news service, from CNN to Fox, and every newspaper with even a modest circulation in the tristate area. If convicted, he'd never be a free man again. What could push someone to take such risks?

You messed up big time when you screwed up my life, Arshad, and payback is an annihilating bitch.

Mom, Dad, and I booked a small New Jersey house on airbnb.com, a place with quick access to the federal court building and the Department of Justice offices in Newark. Although we were living in the era of lightning-fast communication, I couldn't bear to be physically distant from where the answers might originate. Having iPhones in our hands was no substitute for being tangibly present when and if important news came forward or, God willing, the truth was revealed. We had to be part of the story as it unfolded, if only to hear the news with our own ears. If justice had a particular look, we needed to see it as it was served, raw and unfiltered.

The wait continued in our Airbnb. Each passing day felt like a year of agony with no news being released to the public and nothing proprietary leaked to us by our legal mole, Mike Fellini. Was the federal prosecutor still building his case? Had Huzaifa talked or turned to stone? Did they know anything at all? What the *fuck* was taking so long?

I knew Fellini was doing his best to ferret out even the smallest tidbit of information that might've become available, but details were few. The bits that sifted through were trivial, bordering on inconsequential. He checked in with us on a daily basis whether or not he'd heard any news. As of the last report, Arshad Huzaifa hadn't talked. Wouldn't talk. The son of a bitch was mute, except to communicate with his own attorney.

Misery might love company, but company deplores misery. We were all getting on each other's nerves. It was a small house, two bedrooms and just enough common area for us to trip over one another, one TV, and no streaming services. And listening to the news twenty-four/seven will make you put a gun to your head. Waiting for any relevant news while intra-day broadcasters covered high school Lacrosse matches had us all at wit's end. The monotony got so bad that we began taking turns covering the broadcasts, an hour or so of torture at a time, while the other two went out for a walk or escaped to the local Starbucks for a cobweb-clearing nitro brew.

Mom and I were hustling back with a giant iced coffee for Dad when he appeared at the front door, waving his arms like a lunatic, signaling for us to get back in the SUV. His face was flush, his eyes wide.

This is it, I thought, *a break in the case. The news I'd been dying to hear.* I unlocked the doors, and he practically ripped the door off the hinges getting in.

"Drive," he said.

I was behind the wheel. "What happened? Drive where?"

"To the damn courthouse. I just got off the phone with Fellini," he said as he checked his watch. "There's just time—the Attorney General called a press conference for three o'clock."

Fuck, fuck, fuck. Where do I go? Looking up the road, my mind went blank. I was so flustered I'd forgotten that we'd stored directions to the courthouse in the GPS.

"Hit the button," Dad shouted, "the damn button."

The button? Oh yeah, the button. My finger moved to the voice command button on the steering wheel.

"Navigate to court?" Dad bellowed from the backseat.

The woman living behind the dashboard had sharp ears. She said, "Destination set," then broadcast the required cover-your-ass safety instructions. I hit the gas so hard I burned rubber down the street. Under normal circumstances, my old man would've torn me a fresh one.

"Go, go, go," he said, fist-pumping as we tore asphalt. Turn after turn, the roads were clear in front of us. We'd driven the route a few times, had committed it to memory, and only hit the brakes when it was a matter of losing control. Then, onto the freeway for a quick one-exit sprint to the courthouse off-ramp. Up the entrance ramp, accelerating. Accelerating. Stop!

Me: "Shit!"

Dad: "Fuck!"

Mom: "Oh no."

I jammed on the brakes behind a wall of stopped cars. Each of us rubbed our abruptly-creased foreheads.

"Now what?" I asked, utterly frazzled as I recalled the frustration of sitting still on the Cross-Bronx Expressway weeks earlier. "New Jersey," I swore, "what a fucking joke."

My father stared at his watch, concentrating so hard it looked like he was trying to will the hands to turn backwards.

"I see lights flashing up ahead," Mom said. "That's not a good sign."

My heart sank. "We're not going to make it. All this time living in that Airbnb shithole so we could be here when news broke" I looked back at my dad with desperation in my eyes, but all he could offer was a hopeless shrug.

Tick—tick—tick. Motherfucker.

* * *

We pulled as close to the court building as possible and ran as if we were possessed, as if the last starship was departing from a planet that was about to be annihilated by the Death Star.

Approaching the courthouse steps, I could see the Attorney General making his way to the podium. "We made it," I shouted, running backward, relaying the good news to my parents, who were a few yards behind me. Hearing the AG's voice over the PA, helped me to find another gear. His voice became comprehensible as I drew closer.

"Thank you for coming," the AG said, a short man in a blue suit whose necktie was so long it covered his privates. "In the case of the United States vs. Arshad Huzaifa, District Court Judge Avril Lansing has found sufficient cause to proceed to trial."

A battalion of reporters was assembled at the base of the courthouse steps. They edged forward, ravenous beasts sensing succulent bloody prey.

"Working in conjunction with the state Attorney General my office will proceed to the discovery portion of the criminal process. I'll take a few questions."

Each reporter shouted louder than the next, vying for the attention of the Attorney General, each hoping to be called upon.

"Mr. Attorney General," the first reporter began, shouting to be heard over the clamor of fellow reporters. "Kyle Chan, ABC News. Arshad Huzaifa is a suspected terrorist. Should we be worried about a planned attack on our shores?"

"The Department of Homeland Security is ever vigilant in these matters, but we've learned nothing to indicate the accused was involved in the planning of an imminent attack. Next question." The AG selected the next reporter.

"Mindi Ryan, CNN. Mr. Attorney General, you've mentioned nothing about the case against Nasir Zia. Can you comment?"

I felt my heartbeat fade away, my body emptying of life force as I hung on what the AG might say.

"In the matter of the United States Vs. Nasir Zia—" He paused and looked up the steps to where two figures stood well behind the glass courthouse doors. He continued, "My office will not be moving forward with that investigation. *However*, whether or not the state prosecutor will follow suit has yet to be determined." He raised his hand, signaling that he'd had enough. "Thank you. No more questions."

What the hell? Facing my parents, I saw that they were as speechless as I was. How was Nas getting off the hook? I inched forward as the crowd of reporters dispersed, trying to see who the AG had turned to before announcing that he was dropping Nas's case. Whoever had been standing there was no longer visible, but I continued forward, hoping to catch a glimpse of whoever had been standing there.

Most of the reporters were on their way back to the parking lot, but I patiently stood my ground.

There was no sign of anyone behind the glass court building doors until there was.

I probably wouldn't have recognized the face behind the door at the distance I was standing had I not been familiar with the figure's particular facial features. My brain lent a hand, filling in that which I couldn't see, building a composite of a person I knew. Doing so, I understood why this person was here at this particular time. It was to rescue Nas from the clutches of evil.

Chapter Sixty-Two

Gwen Winter

I ran at breakneck speed, vaulting the immense checkerboard squares of gray and white stone that were laid out in the plaza in front of the Martin Luther King, Jr. Federal Courthouse and past the enormous, blindfolded bust of justice. There were about a half-dozen steps leading up to the area in front of the glass doors. I took them in three giant bounds.

"Gwen, where are you going?" Dad asked, calling after me. I didn't stop to reply. I knew he and Mom would follow me inside. Pushing through the glass door into the lobby, I saw two women being led through a doorway at the end of the hallway. The heavy door was about to swing shut when I called out, "Stop!" The door continued to close, the light from within growing narrower and narrower until it was little more than a crack, a sliver of light that was about to fade before my eyes. I called out in one last desperate attempt, "Please, *stop*."

The door closed.

And then it opened.

The door was so heavy the petite woman was barely able to push it open. Amira looked feeble as she squeezed through the opening into the corridor. She looked into my eyes, then lowered her head and didn't lift it again until I stood before her after racing the length of the corridor.

Her eyes were glassy, red, shame-ridden. Dark pouches sat below her eyes at the base of the orbits. It looked as if she hadn't slept in days. Her lovely olive skin looked unnaturally pallid. "Amira, what are you doing here?"

"Gwen," she began in a wretched voice, "I can only stay a minute."

"You helped? I know you did. You helped, Nas?" I knew that was the reason she was there, to help her son the only way she knew how.

"I couldn't stay silent any longer and allow my son…"

To rot in prison.

To bow to Mohammad's will.

Not any longer.

"The Attorney General said he's dropping the charges against Nas. What did you tell them?" I asked.

She could barely look me in the eye. "I told you why Mohammad resents us so much, but what I didn't say—" She broke off and buried her face in her open palms, weeping. She looked as if she was about to collapse. I put my arm behind her and rubbed her back. She shook her head, her lips pressed so tightly they grew pale. Tears dripped from her chin.

I expected something shocking, but what I didn't anticipate was that the words she was about to speak would have to travel from the depths of hell to reach her lips.

Chapter Sixty-Three

Gwen Winter

I'll never know if Amira would've told me the full details of Mohammad's scheme while we were standing together in the corridor of the federal courthouse because the Attorney General came out into the passageway and dragged her back into the sealed room. In my heart, I felt she would have seen her mission through if she'd had more time and the strength to go on. I wish I wouldn't have had to learn the terrible truth at the same time as the rest of the American public, via press releases and the media.

The friends, relatives, and invited guests who'd attended my wedding ceremony and witnessed me stood up at the altar had kept that shame to themselves. But now, with the media whores who were making bank off my story, I became the social media poster child for abused women the world over.

Chawish Zia's violation of Amira and the abuse of his only son were vile and reprehensible acts.

What Mohammad did to Bahija Abidi and his son, Nasir, was one thousand times worse. He expelled thirty years of festering animosity in one fell swoop.

When Faisal Abidi, a single father with a young daughter, came to Mohammad begging for his help to keep his drowning business afloat, he didn't realize that he was signing a pact with the devil, a devil that didn't care who got hurt as long as he was avenged. Over a span of many years, Mohammad invested his time and money, his business acumen, and connections to build Faisal's business, asking nothing in exchange except a modest return on his investment to be paid years and years hence and only when Faisal's business was healthy.

Mohammad waited patiently for his reward, not the interest on his investment and not the hundreds of times Faisal had thanked and blessed him over the years. What Mohammad wanted, what he had schemed for years to carry out, was an agreement with the forever-indebted Faisal, who owed Mohammad his life to agree to the forced marriage of Faisal's daughter Bahija to Nasir. It was a marker that Mohammad waited more than a decade to call in. He waited until scant days before Nas was scheduled to take my hand before taking Bahija's virginity, leaving her soiled, her and her father disgraced.

He'd done to Nasir exactly as Chawish had done to him, robbing him of his true love and sentencing him to live a lie.

The press reported that Amira Zia testified that she stood faithfully by her husband's side when they approached Arshad Huzaifa, a respected mullah, asking him to sanction the marriage of their son Nasir to Huzaifa's niece, Bahija Abidi. Failing to report Bahija's rape, their union seemed reasonable and appropriate. And with this swindle, Mohammad and Faisal made Huzaifa an unwitting accomplice in Mohammad's sinister plan. Huzaifa sanctioned the marriage as if both Bahija and Nasir were as pure as the driven snow.

Faisal Abidi turned a blind eye. By bartering his daughter, he fulfilled his obligation to the devil. And the treacherous plan might've worked out exactly as Mohammad had intended it to had he not underestimated Bahija, who left alone in her hotel bedroom on her wedding night found the strength to take matters into her own hands.

Chapter Sixty-Four

Mohammad Zia

Sitting comfortably in his first-class seat aboard an Emirates flight to Dubai, Mohammad Zia looked out the cabin window as the coastline bled into the aquamarine waters of the Persian Gulf.

The chocolate mango tart he'd enjoyed for dessert was still sweet on his tongue as the flight attendant came by to clear his dishes and flatware. "One last glass of white wine before we land?" the flight attendant asked. "I think there's one bottle left in the galley."

"Why not?" Mohammad said with a cavalier lilt in his voice as he turned back to the window. Watching the breakers caress the sandy beach, he'd abandoned all the cares and troubles he'd left behind, seven thousand miles back. He'd been back to his homeland of Pakistan on a regular basis as required to run his business, but he'd never been to Dubai, which had grown into a modern oasis abounding with cutting-edge architectural beauty and resorts nestled within man-made islands bulldozed into the shape of palm trees.

The flight attendant handed him a glass of Howard Park Allingham Chardonnay, perfectly chilled and filled to the rim. "I don't think we'll be getting any more of this," the flight attendant said. "2017 was an excellent vintage."

"That's a shame," he said, although he had no plans of ever returning to America. He toasted her and again returned to his splendid view. As the jet descended through tufts of dense nimbus clouds, he had a crisp picture of the beach and the towering skyscrapers that lay farther inland, just past exclusive beachfront properties. He could practically feel the sand under his feet as he padded along the beach at sunset.

The apartment he had purchased was strictly mid-tier cost-wise and nowhere near the expense of the upper-floor properties owned by the robber barons and captains of industry who resided above the clouds. Still, his business had always been based offshore, and thanks to the internet, it could be run from anywhere in the world. And now, living a mere two hours from the spice markets of Karachi, he expected the business to grow steadily.

Mohammad managed to drain his glass of chardonnay before the flight attendant collected it prior to landing. "I hope you enjoyed flying with us, Mr. Zia," she said. "It was a pleasure serving you." He lingered on the gentle sway of her hips as she moved off and belted in for landing. The taste of wine was new to him, as would be the next chapter of his life, living life on his own terms and not a player in the sham production his father had forced him into.

After the jet taxied to the terminal, Mohammad unbuckled his seatbelt and stretched. Reaching for the cabin ceiling, he heard his spine pop as his fingertips grazed the ceiling panel.

The passenger sitting behind Mohammad had been completely invisible to him during the entire eighteen-hour ride across the Atlantic, not speaking, barely moving, causing no disturbances whatsoever. Mohammad was surprised to hear such a robust voice.

"What a wonderful flight."

Mohammad turned around, smiling, intent on mirroring the gent's sentiment. His jaw dropped. "*Faisal?* But what are you doing—" Like tumblers in a safe, everything fell into place and he spontaneously understood, his scheme, the avarice, and cruelty, there was a price due for the suffering he'd caused.

Frantic, Mohammad turned away and unlatched the overhead compartment. Seizing his carry-on bag, he attempted to step into the aisle to get a jump on Faisal and the other first-class passengers getting off the plane, but the garotte Faisal had fashioned from nylon monofilament fishing line sewn into his suit was already twisted around Mohammad's neck, cutting off his air and voice. He struggled momentarily, but Fasil was a large and powerful man, and the garotte he'd braided over the course of the long flight was strong enough to hook a great white shark. Mohammad collapsed into his plush leather seat, never touching the sands of Dubai's majestic beaches.

Chapter Sixty-Five

Gwen Winter

On the morning following the state attorney's dismissal of the charges against him, Nasir Zia walked from the prison grounds to freedom. Mine was the only recognizable face he saw when the security gate opened on that miserable, overcast day.

I had to be the very last person Nas expected to see, but perhaps the one he'd hoped for the most.

After all he'd done.

After everything he'd put me through.

Part of me wondered why I'd come. Pressed for a valid reason, I didn't have one except that I wanted him to realize that I knew what happened and that I understood how they'd all lied to the mullah, Arshad Huzaifa, so that he'd agree to Nas's marriage to Bahija. Huzaifa's learning of the fraud ignited a fuse that could not be stamped out. Fearing disgrace, he set out to rescue Bahija from her unlawful marriage. And in his anger, pushed an innocent man to his death, a man he presumed was Nasir Zia, the intended groom who'd lied to him in the face of God.

Osman Shehzad was the voice on the other end of the line when Bahija called for help on her wedding night. Alone and miserable, fearing an eternity married to an utter stranger, she begged Shehzad, a cleric at the mosque where Arshad served as mullah, to reveal the fraud to the mosque elders and formally undo what had been illegally done, a request Shehzad agreed to but not before doing the honorable thing, revealing his intentions to Huzaifa, his mentor and the man who stood to lose the most, to lose everything he held dear.

Fearing humiliation and disgrace, Huzaifa begged Shehzad to stay quiet while he tried to undo the damage he'd unwittingly become party to.

Shehzad declined the mullah's request.

And in Huzaifa desperation, the two men fought.

A second innocent man was dead, deeds Huzaifa was solely responsible for, acts he alone would be held accountable.

Mohammad's evil, like a deadly virus, had infected everyone it touched, lives ruined, innocents murdered.

Where would it end?

Here.

It ends here.

With me.

I waited for Nas to traverse the parking lot until he was so close I had to raise an open hand and say, "Stop." Despondency dripped from his eyes. He knew his time with me was over.

That's as close as I'll allow you to get to me.

You'll never again know my touch or the love I once felt for you.

This is where it ends.

"It all came out," I said. "Your father's curse, the lie you and Amira protected, Bahija's rape…everyone knows. The world knows. How could you, Nas? How could you mislead me the way you did? This mockery wasn't even about me. Mohammad was taking revenge on his father and Amira."

I was no more than collateral damage, a fragment of charred rubble from the explosive charge Mohammad had set off.

"Did I mean nothing to you?"

I watched his eyes for a reaction, but he said nothing, his head hanging like a thrashed puppy.

This is where it ends.

"The worst part is that my father had been right all along. He warned me repeatedly. He said I would never really know who you are. And I refused to hear him because I thought our love—" I pulled in a deep breath and sighed. "What does it matter what I thought? Can you tell me, Nas? Can you tell me why you had to make my father right? You chose loyalty to Mohammad over your love for me. I thought we had a future together. I thought—"

In the intended marriage of Gwendolyn Winter to Nasir Zia, there were no winners, only carnage and mental scarring no length of time could ever erase.

Looking into his eyes for the last time, I felt only pity, pity for his blind loyalty to a father who never considered Nas his true son, pity over the disgrace that was now his life. And yet, one monumental question remained unanswered. "You couldn't tell me before our wedding day? Did you have to bludgeon me on the day we were to wed? When did you know? How long did you hide this scheme from me?"

His lips trembled, and his shoulders rose like a child caught in a terrible lie, but he said nothing, and, in that moment, the answer was clear. He hadn't had the guts. He hid it from me because he was a coward.

Pathetic, the thought churned in my gut. "This is where it ends, Nasir." *I wish you...* Searching my heart and mind, I couldn't think of anything I wanted to offer him.

Nothing. I wish you nothing.

I understood what had happened, the foul web of deceit I'd become entangled in, but I could never accept what he had done nor forgive his betrayal. I'd loved him once, but that love had been destroyed. Seeing him, thinking about him in any way, left me frigid.

The wind kicked up, blowing cool air into my face. *This is over,* I thought and unexpectedly remembered how I felt on the morning we were to be wed, as if life held endless possibilities, as if tomorrow and each day after would be better than the last. It was on me to make sure that happened.

I turned my head and walked away.

Acknowledgements

The production of a quality novel is a massive undertaking requiring the inspired touch of many talented people. First and foremost I would like to recognize the assistance I receive from my wife, Isabella, the unsung hero of my work who quietly reads late into the night to make sure that each and every one of my books is the best it can be. At a time when good people can be particularly hard to find, this author has struck gold with Shawn Reilly Simmons and the fabulous team at Level Best Books. I'm so very happy to be aboard. Many thanks to Lynn Chandler Willis and Karen Fritz for their assistance and inspiration in the shaping and polishing of this book.

About the Author

Lawrence Kelter hails from New York but now calls North Carolina his home. He is the bestselling author of more than thirty mystery and thriller novels including the Stephanie Chalice Mystery series that has topped bestseller lists in the US, UK, and Australia. In 2017, he penned *Back to Brooklyn*, the studio-authorized sequel to the cult comedy classic *My Cousin Vinny*. Early in his writing career, he received direction from literary icon, Nelson DeMille, who edited portions of his early work. Well before he said, "Lawrence Kelter is an exciting new novelist, who reminds me of an early Robert Ludlum," he said, "Kid, your work needs editing, but that's a hell of a lot better than not having talent. Keep it up!"

SOCIAL MEDIA HANDLES:
  Facebook: https://www.facebook.com/larrykelter
  Twitter: https://twitter.com/larrykelter
  Instagram: https://www.instagram.com/lawrencekelterwriter/

AUTHOR WEBSITE:
  http://www.lawrencekelter.com